Author's Note

This content notification may contain spoilers.

This romance follows a grave-digging serial killer who stalks a depressed crematory operator. As such, this story contains the death industry, mental illness, suicide (ideation, attempts, and flashbacks to a secondary character's completion), forced incest *without* permission, necrophilia, abusive caregivers (with extensive flashbacks), blackmail, and murder. Furthermore, the couple indulges in dark games with and *without* permission. These scenes include fear, spit, blood, water, other copious secretions, asphyxiation, and weapons.

It should also be noted that the serial killer sees all people as less than human, including the heroine. At times, he also tries to force himself on other female victims; however, he abandons this goal. There is *no* cheating.

For exact details on the content, please visit the author's website.

This is a *dark* romance. Reader discretion is advised.

Grave Love

Chapter 1

Blaze

The whisper of a moan escapes down the corridor, sneaking toward me like a spider hiding in the cracks of a wall. I step forward, then ease the door shut behind me, my boots inaudible against the tile. Moonlight creeps in through the curtained windows, illuminating the caskets like they're trophies on display. Gilded urns. White flowers. Clean tile. As if this is a luxury store, and not a mortuary.

Another primal moan. It's mournful, in a way. The base of my neck tingles. It's a feminine moan, one that indicates pleasure. I raise my brow, keeping my ear aimed toward the sound, itching for more of it. She—whoever this stranger is—must have a key to the funeral home like I do. A coworker of mine, perhaps.

And she's getting off.

This time, the sound is deeper, demanding more. I step in time with her cries. As I draw closer to her, my fingers skim against the wall, and I pretend like I'm touching her bare skin.

The storage room's entrance is open. I stop. One of the refrigeration units is ajar, exposing a naked corpse. A woman. Mid-twenties. Its eyes vacant.

Earlier today, this same body was wearing black pants and a stained white shirt. The difference sticks with me; I don't give a shit about a corpse's modesty, but the fact that the body is now naked intrigues me.

Must have to do with our little trespasser.

I glance around. This whole situation has distracted me. Supposedly, the owner leaves the funeral home unguarded after hours, which would have given me a prime opportunity to dispose of bodies here. But that noise—that sorrowful, pleasure-filled noise—grows louder, chaotic in its lack of structure. The compulsion builds in me, parting my lips. The need to know. The impulse to hunt.

Who is she?

Why is she here?

The door of the crematory is left open, the sporadic groans of the conveyor belt adding to the orchestra of desire. The scent of musk and ash fills the air. A body twists on the conveyor belt, writhing like a demon conquering a body, dominating its final host. A canvas bag covers the face, and black hair streams out from under the edges of the haphazard mask. The buttons on the black pants of the twitching body are undone, a hand inside, between the legs. The white shirt crumpled over the stomach, blood dotting the fabric like a constellation of violence.

This woman stole the clothes from the corpse back in the refrigeration unit.

Her breathing grows frantic. Her writhing unpredictable. She's a woman *possessed*. I gleam at her with sudden focus, my pulse increasing. The need for proximity. The desire to know more. I can't see much of her body; the clothing covers it. Blood swells in my bulge anyway. My hand clutches my length, urging my natural response to cool. This arousal is not about the physical attraction—I can't even see her face—it's about her *helplessness*. She doesn't know I'm standing right above her.

I finger the switchblade in my pocket, licking my lips as the blade clicks open. She practically screams in lust this time, so unaware of the knife. Her body bucks, her back arching, the shirt stretched across her frame. My bulge twitches, and I lean down, holding the knife an inch above her neck, so close it's practically breathing on her skin. All it would take is a slice across her throat, and she'd be humiliated in her final moments, left pleasureless and alone. Anyone who found her would think that it was a political statement—finding a disheveled corpse with bodily secretions strewn across a funeral home—but I would know the truth.

She did this to herself.

The stranger jerks in bliss, reaching that ultimate peak, and I pull back instinctively. I angle my head to the side, my tongue skating over my teeth. She's not my *usual* type. Skin tinted with golden-yellow hues. Black hair. Not pale like me. Not blond like them.

I'm not one to jump to conclusions, but I know a good opportunity when I see one. For fuck's sake, she's lying on the conveyor belt leading to the crematory.

She could be practice for me.

She reaches up, a flash of a tattoo on the top of her hand. A rope, maybe? I can't quite see. Frantically, she pinches the canvas bag over her nose as the other hand vigorously circles her sensitive flesh. Going for multiple, I suppose. In this position, her hands stay in place long enough to give me a clear view.

A noose on one hand. On the other hand, a gun. As if she's carving her own desires into her flesh.

Finally, a sigh expels from her chest. Another peak reached. Her body deflates like a balloon, then she lies still, her uneven breaths filling the empty space. Exhaustion. Sleep overwhelming her.

Killing her would be *something*. Perhaps it's the change I need.

Even so, it's not what I *want* right now.

I make my exit.

The next morning, I clock in before the funeral director arrives. I scan the area, searching for evidence of my fellow trespasser. The doors of the storage units are closed now; the metal gurney is folded against the wall of the crematory. No evidence of a break-in or of any uninvited presence. The black-haired woman has practice at this herself.

How long has she been breaking into the mortuary to masturbate?

Once I have my sunscreen and black clothing protecting my

skin, I get to work, using the excavator to hull out another beachside grave. It's a big machine; the arm scoops down into the earth, then pulls out as much as it can into the bucket. In the distance, a tourist walks across the white sand, glimpsing up at the gravestone-littered hill, then walks quicker across the beach, as if the dead will sense his presence marking the sand. As if the rotting meat buried in this hill will rise from the ground to cast their revenge.

The dead don't give a shit.

A flash of black hair crosses over the windows of the mortuary, leaving the break room. I quickly power off the machine and remove my gloves, then head inside. The scent of burnt coffee fills the air. I leave the break room and turn toward the crematory.

I see her.

Black hair cascades over her shoulders, stringy and thick with natural oils, framing her face like the strands of Spanish moss gripping the branches of a tree. Her cheeks full. Round face. Pink lips pursed in pensiveness as she studies the dials of the retort. Hands fidgeting in front of her. Those two tattoos—a noose and a gun—like beacons of certainty. The little masturbatory trespasser. Her dull brown eyes focus on the numbers in front of her like she's done this a million times before, the same thing day in, day out.

I wait for a few minutes, my nose finally growing numb to the acrid stench in the air, curiously entertained by the woman in front of me working her magic. She mumbles to herself, perhaps speaking to the cooking body. My gaze sears into her, encouraging her to look at me. To confirm my suspicions.

She never once looks up. So focused on her own little world.

Physically, she's different from the others. Perhaps somewhat behaviorally too.

That doesn't make her special.

What interests me is that instinctual emptiness inside of her—her *lack*. It calls to me. I recognize that absence in myself. It's lust, in a way. A need. Sailing through life as if nothing else exists besides desire. Pleasure. And pain.

Her eyes flick over the door frame briefly, immediately returning to her work. Assuming I'm another mourning customer.

I knock on the director's office door. The redhead flashes a soft smile. She opens her mouth ready to regurgitate her standard response.

I stop her. "Who's the crematory operator?"

"Oh, Ren?" she asks, tucking a strand of hair behind her ear. "Ren's a good girl. Been here for years, actually. Always does her work. Here on time. Never asks questions if I need her to stay late. Hasn't even asked for a raise, actually. Oh! By the way—" The funeral director takes off her glasses, giving more thought to our conversation *now* that it's on her terms. "How are you liking it here?"

I didn't come to Last Spring Mortuary for manufactured pleasantries, nor for the discount on my own prepaid plot. I don't need the comfort of knowing my corpse will enjoy a seaside view of the sunset. I get sunburned easily, and the thought of my meat roasting in the sun annoys me.

In this industry, there's typically a high turnover rate until you find someone solid. Someone like Ren. The groundskeeper before me lasted a month, and the employee before that? Even quicker to flee. In the death industry, they're always desperate for more bodies, living and dead.

Finally, the director learned to advertise the job for what it is: gravedigging. I jumped at the chance.

Without answering the director's question, I shift the conversation back to my interests: "Would Ren be willing to teach me the ropes?"

The ropes. Like that deathly tattoo.

The funeral director laughs. "Have you cut the grass yet? I've got a showing today, and I—"

"Ren," I repeat. "Does she *like* it here?"

The director pauses, finding a respectful way to explain her hesitation. Half-hearted amusement tugs at my mouth. The phone rings, and the director holds up her hand.

"Just a second," she whispers. She answers the phone, her voice both solemn and friendly as the caller wails on the other end. She gives her full attention to the potential customer, thwarting my attempt to gather more information on Ren.

Not that I give a shit. All I care about is keeping my record clean until I find my new rhythm. A craving like mine doesn't go away overnight. Going on seven months of being this wholesome, *clean* person in this tourist-filled town, the desire *aches* inside of me. The itch to do more. To gut a woman until a scream shudders out of her body. It gnaws on my bones until they're chewed up glass.

It's only getting worse.

I rake leaves. Reposition a headstone. Pull weeds around the mausoleum. Hours pass.

I watch the windows, waiting until the funeral director is in the showroom with a new client, then I slip inside of her office and take a quick picture on my phone of Ren's driver's license. You never know what you might need when it comes to these things.

That night, I park across the street from the mortuary. Ren exits her car, her black hair swishing as she draws toward the funeral home. She checks both ways before reaching the entrance, cautious of being caught, and yet there's a fluidity to her movements that indicates a definite pattern.

She grabs her key. Twists the lock. Opens the door and disappears inside.

A smirk paints my lips. I don't care what she does in her free time. It is amusing, though.

The masturbator of all things dead and dying.

The lights in Last Spring stay dark. Eventually, I glance down at my phone. I've been sitting in the Margarita Shack's parking lot for over an hour. I should leave. I should try to think of my other victims. To remember why I came to this vapid town in the first place.

I can't get caught here. If I want to keep my plan, I need to be careful.

The image of Ren lying on that conveyor belt, a bag covering her head, fills my groin with blood, that pressure surging through my body.

Somehow, those goals seem irrelevant right now.

After some time, Ren leaves, hastily driving away. Another ten minutes go by, then I flick through my phone's gallery to find her address. I drive to her home.

The house is lush with blue, purple, and pink tulips decorating the front yard, a stone path lining the grass. Two cars sit in the driveway, one that I recognize as Ren's, and another environmentally-friendly option. A boyfriend's car, perhaps? Or a roommate? A family member?

I hop the fence. Faint snores greet me through an open window. An invitation. Bending over the frame, I see her sleeping form on the bed against the opposite wall. I climb silently inside, my heart pumping in my ears. I don't know how many people live here, and if I screw this up, it might be my last time hunting prey.

Oil and smoke permeate the air. Ren's legs spread across the small twin mattress. Black hair sprouts from between her legs like spindling vines, her musk thick with come from her nightly ritual.

Stringy black hair covers her face, hiding her expression. My fingers twitch, itching to rip those strands from her scalp.

A pill bottle catches my eye. I pick it up from the nightstand, scanning the label. A prescription for Xanax. I skim for the patient's name. *Donna Richmond*. Ren's last name is Kono, though a different last name doesn't mean anything. Is Richmond her mother? A grandmother, perhaps? Does Donna—whoever she is—even use the Xanax, or is this secretly *Ren's* medication?

A screw-capped wine bottle, half-empty, sits next to the prescription. Red, like blood.

A pile of laundry lies on the floor. I pull out her underwear—a stretchy mix of nylon and polyester, seamless, dampness lining the crotch. I bring it to my nose and inhale deeply, the blood rushing from my head to my bulge.

She smells like death. Faintly sour. A sweetness locked inside of the harshest scents. The musk is heady, like the foam on top of a beer, dripping with shame and desire. The violence to cut through her grows inside of me.

I move forward, then slide open the top drawer of her nightstand. A rope tied in a hangman's knot, like her tattoo, is crumpled inside. No gun though.

Her hands are stuffed under her pillow, tucked underneath the weight of her head. A bluish-green bruise circles her neck. Visible. Fading fast.

She *is* fucked up.

Like me.

An idea burns inside of me. I've used a woman while she's dying before, but I've never once used a dying woman that *enjoyed* the torture of her inevitable death. When I close my eyes, I picture the fear in my first, the second, the third—how tight they squeezed around me, fighting for another breath. How the will to survive *always* overpowered their anger for me.

I thought choosing victims that looked alike would help; that satisfaction never returned though. It was only the first that meant something to me. The only kill that got me high.

Ren is different though. She may be the exact thing I need.

I stare down at her, rubbing my palm over my straining erection. She whimpers, then gives a subtle snore, and my head rushes, being filled with air. She might've taken a benzodiazepine and consumed the wine. It might've been her goal to die *tonight*. An overdose may take longer, but still, it's simpler than a noose.

The idea sparks me. How ironic would it be to use the blackmail of her after-hours activities to force her into an arrangement where we both get what we want? She could teach me to work the retorts, and I could give her that deadly rush. I could even kill her exactly how she wants.

She doesn't look like the others, but looks aren't enough. I need some way to confirm that she'll scratch that itch. I won't chase a false high again.

Which means I need to know Ren. To learn her. To consume her every moment.

The little corpse wants a taste of death?

I'll force-feed her it.

Chapter 2

Ren

"Is this a circus act?" the client asks.

I gaze down at the body on the stainless steel table. A sheet is pulled up to the clavicle. Tinted red cheeks. The unnaturally curved eyelids, like his wife is simply asleep. It reminds me of my mother. The image I have of her has changed over the years. I was too young to understand, so my brain fills in the missing pieces. I imagine her asleep, hanging in the balance, like a pendulum about to draw forth again. A mirror image of me.

Two hours. That's all that's left in my shift.

"I'm sorry, sir," I say quietly. The words come out stiff, inappropriate, as if I'm over in Rosemary Beach, apologizing for serving a one-percenter the wrong kind of fork with their salad. I just cleaned his wife's naked body, stapled her mouth shut, filled her with chemical fluids, and used enough makeup to give her the appearance of life. 'Sorry' is a little understated.

I glance at the clock on the wall again. It hasn't moved.

"That's not good enough," he says, his words sharp. "I should've gone to the city. The funeral home over there has been around longer. They know how to treat the dead with some goddamned dignity. But *she* wanted to be buried here, and I—"

The anger quivers, dissolving into sorrow. He slams his fist into the wall, the thud of his punch startling both of us. He's grasping at rage. It's easier than the alternative.

He holds his head against the wall.

"I'll get the director," I say.

He swats a hand in my direction, his eyes closed. "Don't bother. Let's just get on with it."

I leave the room anyway; the director will find him soon. Technically, I have my embalming license, but our embalmer is out, and I have to fill in. I prefer the crematory. Once they're in the retort, you click a few buttons, wait for their bodies to cook in the oven, and grind up whatever bones are left. It's safer. Less to screw up. An automatic habit. Like everything else in my life.

I head to the break room. Yesterday's coffee is still in the pot—the director must've forgotten to toss it out again—and so I dump it myself. Start a new pot. Several spoonfuls of generic grounds. The machine whirs, and black liquid drips from the spout. I breathe out, exhaling as slow as I can, trying not to let any of that madness escape.

But I'm mad. *Infuriated.* Angry at my boss for forcing me to take over embalming, angry at that client for unloading his frustration on me like I'm responsible for his wife's death, angry at the fucking world. Angry at *myself.* So angry I want to scream.

I think about it again. For the second time today.

What if I never woke up?

The tears form, burning my eyes. I blink and quickly wipe them away, careful not to let anyone see. I'm not suicidal. *I'm not.* And though I haven't been to therapy since I was a child, I know I won't kill myself. It's not like me. There's too much effort, and I just want to stop thinking for once.

Instead, I think about it every day.

The pain builds behind my temples, my throat aching. The blood vessels in my face and neck constrict, seizing my chest, my world spiraling out of control.

You're fine, Ren, I say to myself. *Nothing is wrong. You are the definition of one of those millennial snowflakes that can't tell the difference between depression and a minor irritation. The kind the media always makes fun of. You're crying for nothing, and yet you can't stop thinking about killing yourself.*

You're pathetic. You're like a bored housewife, making up issues just to see your husband react. To pretend like he cares about you. Except you're not even married. You haven't dated in years. You're worthless. Who would date you?

My shoulders squeeze. Everything wells up. I swallow it down. Down. Until it gets stuck deep inside of me. Until I can't dig it up anymore.

A throat clears. In the doorway, Denise, the funeral director and owner of Last Spring Mortuary, stands with a hand on her hip. A sympathetic expression pulls at her lips, her brows angled down, like she's been there too.

I see through it. It's the same smile she gives to every mourner that walks through the entrance—a practiced mask meant to entice even the saddest souls to upgrade their loved one's final arrangements.

"The coffee is done," she says. "I heard it beep a while ago. Thanks for making a new pot."

I blink rapidly at the machine. She's right; the pot is full. I pour a mug, narrowing my eyes at the liquid. There's barely any steam. How long have I been standing here?

I put the mug in the microwave.

"You doing okay?" Denise finally asks.

"I'm fine," I say. It's the same response I give to everyone. It doesn't matter what you say, because no one—not even me—gives a shit either way.

The microwave beeps. I remove the mug, clutching the warmth in my palms.

"Don't let him upset you," she says.

I raise a brow.

"Mr. Johns?" she clarifies.

"Oh. The husband," I say. Also known as the embalming client that I pissed off earlier. I could tell Denise that he was just the tip of the iceberg today, but I don't. It wouldn't matter anyway.

"He was always going to lash out," she says. "Doesn't matter how beautiful his late wife looks in this state. *I* could've screwed it up for him, you know?"

I roll my eyes. It's funny, in a way. It's not like this was my first embalming. I've been working here for years, and I can't even get *this* job right.

Ugliness creeps inside of me, digging through my skin, begging to come out like insects crawling up to the surface. I'm a waste of air.

"Anyway," Denise says, then holds up a folded piece of paper. "One of tomorrow's services asked for a special arrangement. Can you take this to Blaze? I have to go back to the showroom. I've got a couple waiting for me."

My jaw hangs open. That name is familiar. I can't quite grasp it. "Blaze?"

She angles her head to the side. "The groundskeeper?"

"Groundskeeper?"

She sighs slightly, then forces a smile. "The new gravedigger? He digs the graves and mows the lawn? He's out in the cemetery right now."

My body heat rises. I try to focus on the information. A man is working here, and I don't even know what he looks like.

"How long?" I ask.

"How long, what?"

"How long has he been working here?"

"A few weeks now."

My neck pinches. "You—"

I don't finish. What would I say? *You said you didn't like working with men in this industry. You said a lot of things, and one by one, they turn out to be lies.*

"What?" Denise asks.

My eyes fall to the floor. I stare at the scuff marks on my black flats.

"I didn't know you hired a man," I say quietly.

"Don't think about him," she says. "Just give him the order, and you won't have to say anything to him. Focus on you, okay? It's not a big deal. He won't bite."

Bite. Hah. As if *that's* why I don't want to talk to him.

Denise wants me to do this. I don't have a choice. It's always the same with her: *One day at a time. Take life as it is. Control what you can control.* The same sayings we've all heard a thousand times before.

"Have you considered taking that job at your grandmother's school?" she asks, breaking the silence. "I'd hate for you to leave, but maybe that's what's best for you right now. A change, you know?"

I glare at her. Did my grandmother tell her about that?

I don't want to know.

I snatch the order from her hands, then grab a bag of chips from the fridge. The same bag that's been in there for months now.

"I'm going on lunch," I say.

I exit out the back, with the chips and my coffee. I set my lunch down, then quickly walk across the lawn to where the excavator is parked. There are no signs of the groundskeeper. On the front seat, I lift a bottle of water, placing the order underneath it.

I return to the back patio. A high garden smothered in white flowers separates the mortuary building from the cemetery. The flowers act as a subtle barrier so that death is more palatable for the living, for people who aren't around it constantly like we are. No one *wants* to notice the other dead lying around their loved ones. No one wants to remember that we all end up the same. And why would they?

I lean on the wall, a spot right across from the lilies and daffodils. Past the flowers and a few gravestones away, a preacher raises his arms in the air. His audience bobs their heads solemnly. I don't know which is more irritating—a celebration of a deceased's life or the mourning of their death—but I know no one really wants to confront death. Not a husband of a late wife. Not a mother of a child. Not a daughter of a mother.

Unless you're like me.

The mourners take turns shoveling clumps of dirt into that large, rectangular cavern. I imagine taking that person's place, locked inside of that wooden prison, listening to the soft thud of dirt like rain sprinkling on a tin roof. Death seems peaceful like that. The end of it all. An endless sleep that you'll never wake up from. An eternity where you don't have to confront your failure every day.

Maybe that's why my mother isn't here. I try to picture what she must've looked like when she died. Instead, images of myself fill my mind: a gunshot wound in the side of my head, red droplets painting the wall like splatter art, my body the final canvas to display my inner thoughts.

I rub the tattoo on the top of my hand. A rope and a gun. I should've carved them myself. A knife wound. Scarification. Something like that. But I'm a coward when it comes to so many things. It's why I'm still here.

A shadow passes across my peripheral. Behind the funeral service, a tall man with wide shoulders trudges across the lawn. He pulls the order from under his water bottle, reads it, then scans the area for whomever left it. His light eyes meet mine. His teeth gleam with sharpness, like the jowls of a hyena. Pale skin. Blond—almost white—hair. Gaunt cheeks, the curves of his skull angular, like the pieces of a modern puzzle.

He lifts the order, nodding to me, acknowledging that he knows it's from me. A shudder crashes through me. He raises his free hand, offering it to me. As if introducing himself. As if asking me if I need *his* help crossing over to the other side.

The dread turns into fear. I incinerate it, replacing it with annoyance. I cross my arms, determined to keep my place and not be frightened by an intruder. Before I can stop myself, I scratch the back of my neck, trying to get rid of these emotions. It doesn't work.

Then I march over to the director's office, then bang on the door, each pound echoing through the building. A few clients in the lobby scowl in my direction. I ignore them.

"Weren't you off like an hour ago?" Denise asks. She tilts her head; I grit my teeth. I still have an hour left in my shift. She likes to pretend sometimes, taking pity on me so I can go home and get out of her hair sooner. Sometimes, I take her up on it, because I have no will to argue.

Today, it's not like that.

"You need to take the embalming off of my paycheck," I say,

as if that explains why I'm here. It's not. I'm pissed that she hired *that man*, but I know she won't do anything about it.

This—paying for that client's embalming—is the *only* thing I may be able to control right now, and damn it, I want some strength for once.

"Oh, stop thinking about that," Denise says. "Get some rest. Looks like you need it."

I hate her sympathy. Hate everything about her sometimes, even though she's never done anything wrong. She's never hurt me. Never made me feel like I don't belong here. Just like Mr. Johns took out his anger on me, it's easier to hate Denise than it is to search inside of myself and acknowledge why she seems to look down on me.

"Are you okay?" she asks.

Denise's careful eyes meet mine, and I'm suddenly aware of how much time has passed. Slipping off like that keeps happening to me more and more lately. I can't remember where I've gone or what I'm doing until someone else points it out to me.

"Yes," I say.

Eventually, I do leave. Sitting in my car, I rest my head on the steering wheel.

I should go home.

The thought of potentially seeing my grandmother eats away at me though. We don't talk to each other anymore; we simply exist in the same house. Sometimes, I can't even deal with that.

I'm weak.

The tears sting in my eyes, my throat tight. I just want it to end. To go to sleep and not wake up. To never have to think about these stupid little things that make me want to jump off a bridge. To stop trying so hard when I'll never measure up anyway. To find comfort in knowing that I won't have to deal with anything anymore.

My nose stuffs up. I can barely breathe. It's irritating. These thoughts and emotions are like drowning in the ocean's rip tide when you *know* how to swim. You should be able to handle this, to find the shoreline safely. Instead, you're drifting off, only able to float for so much longer. It's another reason why I'm a mess.

Then do something about it, a voice growls inside of me.

I inhale deeply, centering myself. The world tilts like a kaleidoscope, shifting over and over again. I drive anyway. Around the golf carts on Front Beach Road. Down Richard Jackson Boulevard, past the off-beach hotels and medical offices. The drive-thru line of a coffee shop chain spills onto the street, filled with doctors, patients, and tourists. I stop at the intersection next to it, my eyes fixating on a sign next to the drive-thru.

Eternal Hope Medical Spa.

Hope. It's a strange concept.

I overheard a client once say that Eternal Hope Medical Spa offered medically assisted suicides. She thought that's what happened to her husband. She couldn't explain his death any further than that.

The idea has its appeal.

But a medically induced death would give a doctor full power over me. And for once in my sorry life, *I* want to control, even if it's only over how I leave this world.

Or maybe that's the excuse a coward uses to explain why they're stuck hiding underground. I don't know.

Maybe I want to feel something.

Maybe I want to sleep.

But right now, I don't want to wake up.

Chapter 3

Blaze

It's almost as if she's taken by mental consumption, wasting away each day. Each night. Each pill. Each gulp of wine. Each *breath*. While she doesn't go to the funeral home to indulge in self-care every night, she *needs* the pills to sleep. The assistance of their calming warmth. Their sweet embrace.

I could tease Ren with my knowledge of her secret craving, but I don't approach her. Not yet. I need to learn everything about her so that I can extract exactly what I want from her body.

So I hunt. Like I did to steal from my mother's *special* friends. The same way I hunted my second and my third. When you learn someone, *truly* learn them, you begin to know every place they feel safe. Where they store their money. Where they go when they need something. Who they run to for help.

With Ren, it's exceptionally easy to blend in. Stupidly, in fact. She's practically *inviting* me. Even after she finally saw me outside and was clearly disturbed by my presence, she's found a way to pretend I don't exist. I'm always just outside of the line of sight. She refuses to see me holding the knife at the edge of her periphery, too busy with her own morbid thoughts.

She reminds me of my first. So caught up in her own fucked up little world that she can barely recognize the decay around her.

Usually, you expect those chaotic, disturbed souls to not give a shit about the people around them. They find the nearest person, give that person their wrath, and then they do the bare minimum to survive.

Ren is like that in *some* ways. She functions, then fills her nights with chaos and error. She's unpredictable in her masturbatory ways. Her desire to *get* caught. But then, there's her difference: it's as if she's taking out those aggressions on herself.

In the first week, I copy her work schedule and read over her driving record: two old tickets for running red lights. Another sign of her recklessness.

During the second week, I research the grandmother: Donna Richmond. Private elementary school owner and principal. Mother of a dead daughter. Caretaker to her only granddaughter: little Ren.

A quick internet search gives me a picture of Ren, her yellow-haired grandmother, and the dean of a university in Tallahassee, the details of Ren's acceptance into the doctorate program in the caption underneath. The article boasts that it's an honor to have the granddaughter of such an esteemed educator, and as such, the grandmother and dean beam with pride. Ren's expression is void though. Smiling but empty.

The university's website shows no official record of Ren's graduation.

When I'm sure I know Ren's patterns like the flakes of dry skin on my arm, I wait until Ren leaves for the mortuary. I sneak in through her bedroom window, my boots thudding on the carpeted floor. A nearly empty wine bottle stands erect on the nightstand, the last thing Ren sees when she falls asleep. A new pill bottle next to it.

I lie on the mattress, staring up at the ceiling like Ren waiting for sleep. It's endless stucco, like the imprints of raindrops on a sandy white beach. I try to imagine Ren's thoughts. Get inside her head. What she must think when she lies here at night, sober and alone. Dreaming of something else. Dying by the hands of another. The saccharine ecstasy of death.

A snore like a groaning bear shakes through the walls, then falls silent. The grandmother.

I sniff the sheets, sucking in Ren's mildly sweet, ashy scent. Like an orange cake, the edges burnt, left in the oven until it's too dry to eat. I unzip my pants, then grip my dry cock, the friction of my rough palm tantalizing. Soon, I'll use it to keep her obedient, but for now, I stare at the ceiling, jerking off to what she sees, to what she must *feel*—

The hum of a car approaches; she's back sooner than usual tonight. The hairs on the back of my neck rise, the anticipation like magnetic balls bouncing off of my skin.

I slide into the hallway. Avoid the bathroom. Open the closet door. Find enough space between the washer and dryer to stay out of sight and watch her.

If Ren goes anywhere, she'll probably use the toilet before going to bed. Hiding this close to the bathroom, I'm practically begging her to find me.

Her shadow hovers. Stops near the slats. She studies the laundry closet, peering into the darkness. Perhaps she can sense my presence here.

I dare you, little corpse.

Her hushed footsteps angle toward the bedroom. The door clicks shut behind her. I can imagine it now; she thinks she's imagined it all. Not even a potential intruder can bother Ren from her vacant existence.

Once I'm sure she's asleep, I gently open Ren's bedroom door. The window casts light onto the desk in the corner, illuminating a handwritten note.

I added a late fee, it reads. *You should put the tuition payments on auto-draft, like I told you last time. PLEASE DO THE LAUNDRY. THANK YOU.*

An envelope labeled *Mrs. Richmond* sits next to the note, full of cash.

Tuition payments. A late fee. Ren must be paying back her grandmother for the doctorate program. The choice of words —*please* and *thank you*—is amusing, like the grandmother thinks she can dispel any hard feelings by spitting out those polite platitudes.

A loud snort erupts through the walls, like a guard dog startling itself awake. The grandmother again.

I push open Ren's bedroom door, drawing forward slightly, then I creep toward that noise like a rat in the sewers. The carpet shifts from matted fibers to soft, long threads. My mind wanders: did Ren refuse to get her carpet replaced, or did the grandmother deny Ren of that comfort, not wanting to give her granddaughter any more than she already had?

I turn the doorknob, timing it with the next snore. Then, at the next grumble, I click open my switchblade.

The grandmother lies on her back, her cheeks fluttering with each breath. A silk nightgown covering her body. It's funny; Ren sleeps naked, as if she wants to be seen. Donna Richmond is the opposite of her granddaughter.

My knees skim the mattress, the memory foam soundlessly curving to my form. The grandmother's nostrils flare, deep in a comfortable sleep.

It would be so easy to kill her right now.

I put the knife right above her neck like I did with Ren the first time I stood over her lying on the conveyor belt.

The grandmother bears down on Ren like a finger squishing an ant. It's not exactly like my past, but it's familiar enough, and that hatred grows inside of me.

Killing the grandmother *might* give me the satisfaction I crave. The thought is enticing.

She looks like an older version of the others. Her yellow-blond hair has white roots, and I'm done with blonds. Besides, killing the grandmother will only force Ren to creep deeper inside of herself, burrowing until there's nothing left. I can't let that happen. Not yet. Not until I know exactly how to bring Ren's desire out into the open. I have to kill Ren *first*.

Ren is too interesting to waste. I'll make my connection with her, then kill *her*, and if I'm not satisfied, there's always her grandmother.

The old bitch sighs, then flips over in bed. She groans, stirring awake. The laundry closet in the hallway calls to me. I open it and fold myself inside.

I can clean up a mess if I have to, but I'd rather take my time with Ren.

A few seconds later, the grandmother shuffles out of the bedroom, pausing right outside of the closet. Her silk nightgown flashes through the slats, bright like a lighthouse, warning others of what waits in the distance.

The grandmother sniffs in my direction. A grimace pulls at her lips, broken up by the slats in the door. Sensing my presence, just like her granddaughter.

Come closer, you fucking cunt.

She turns toward the bathroom, and I smile. No mess for me to clean up tonight. I can imagine the grandmother's next note: *Do the laundry. PLEASE. The whole house smells, Ren. THANK YOU.*

She urinates, the stream loud through the closed door. Then she sits for a while. Minutes pass. Eventually, the bitch shuffles back to her bedroom. A loud snore rattles through the walls.

I return to Ren's bedroom.

This time, Ren is lying on her stomach, her face toward the open window. Black strings of hair still cover her eyes. I tease my bulge through my pants. I'm already hard and greedy for her, but I don't take it out. Not yet. I'm saving it for her warmth.

Instead, I take the knife and pull a lock of her hair. The knife cuts easily, slicing it off like scissors to paper. Knowing her, she won't notice.

I stow the hair in my pocket.

I lift the pill bottle from the nightstand. *Donna Richmond. Alprazolam. When taking this medication do not drink alcoholic beverages. Taking more than recommended may cause serious breathing problems and death.*

Ren steals her grandmother's pills. Uses them to sleep rather than suffer her nightly thoughts. I've known people like that. They can't stand to confront themselves or the world around them. Their fists fly. Their legs spread. They find the people they hate the most, and they use *them* to satisfy their own urges. Violence. Lust. Intoxication. Anything to forget the way they hate themselves.

Ren is like that too, though she *relishes* in that self-hatred. She barely lives day-to-day, and still, she craves violence. She even inflicts it on her own body.

It would take one extra pill, and she could end her life.

I dump the contents into my palm, the white pills piling up like fungus sprouting across the top of damp soil. I shove them in my pocket. Ren won't be ending her own life. She needs help from someone else.

If anyone kills her, it's going to be me.

Chapter 4

Ren

More nights. More days. More mindless shifts. Like always, I head home.

The driveway is empty, and I sigh in relief. My grandmother —a woman I've called Mrs. Richmond since I can remember— owns a private elementary school, the only one on the beach. Her entire life is dedicated to helping children get what they deserve, and when she's not managing the business side of the school, she's meeting with teachers and parents over dinner and planning the next semester.

As long as it means I don't have to see her yet.

I slip inside the house. Electricity strums through me, anticipating that sweet sleep. I shuffle toward my bedroom on autopilot. I pick up the pill bottle. It's light.

I shake the bottle, searching for a rattle. It's silent.

My legs bounce as I race to the bathroom. The medicine cabinet. I scour Mrs. Richmond's other prescriptions, ones she never uses. My eyes gloss over the labels, hunting for anything like Xanax. The warnings catch my attention. *May cause drowsiness and dizziness. Alcohol may make this worse. Use care when operating a vehicle, vessel, or dangerous machines.* I select a random bottle, then shake it in my hand. I yank off the cap.

Every bottle is empty.

Did I use all of them?

No. She hid them from me.

Why would she do that?

I text her: *Can you order more Xanax?*

No, she responds immediately. *It's not due for a refill.*

Emergency, I text back. *Please, Mrs. Richmond.*

It takes a minute this time. Then her response comes through: *What could you possibly need it for now?*

I slide down, slithering to the floor. Collapsing like a heap of dirty clothes until I'm completely flat against the cold tile.

There was a time when I used to want to please my grandmother. I didn't understand why she wanted me to follow in her footsteps, but I took every class, did every extracurricular, even dated the man she wanted me to marry. Hid those dark desires deep inside of myself, only letting them out when I was alone and couldn't hold them back anymore.

It took me a long time to realize that I would never measure up to what she wanted. And even then, I was in denial about it, until she finally forced me to drop out of the doctorate program just to silence the rumors about why my fiancé broke up with me.

The cool temperature of the tile calms me, but the tears still stream down the sides of my face as I stare up at the white ceiling. Why am I still here? Still alive, when my life has no purpose? I burn bodies; anyone could do that. I'm paying Mrs. Richmond back for the tuition; she doesn't need the money though.

I think about death a lot. It even seems like a fantasy to disappear like my mother. How quiet it would be, the weight leaving my shoulders, the tension gone. It's not that I want to die; it's that I don't want to wake up.

Defeat brews in my temples, a dull ache that builds until I can barely move without oscillating pain. I hug my arms around myself, keeping the screams inside. My mind jolts, the white noise —the air conditioning, the random creaking pipes, a neighbor driving by—reaches new heights as I try to *think.* To figure out another way.

There are so many ways to die, but I always imagine someone

else taking my life, watching me as I end it all. Maybe even fucking me as I die.

I judge our clients for needing that barrier between life and death, but I'm exactly the same. Even in my fantasies, I'm a coward. I can't do it by myself.

When I look down, my hands are on the steering wheel. I don't remember leaving the house or getting in the car. I don't remember if Mrs. Richmond came home, but I can remember her words: *Pull yourself together.* The same advice I always give myself.

My mind leaves my body, my consciousness is unaware of what I'm doing. I'm living in a carcass of myself.

I drive. I pass the medical spa. A light shines in the window, and a few cars are parked in front of the building. I don't stop. *Eternal Hope*—it's a joke where I'm the punchline. I probably couldn't get any medical assistance in death because I'm not terminally ill. Even in a medical setting, I'd have to fake paperwork to get what I want.

I'm not going there anyway.

The Souvenir Emporium parking lot across from the mortuary is barren. It must be after midnight by now. I park where I always do—on the side where they keep the garbage bins, a short distance from the margarita shack.

I know where I'm going.

Chapter 5

Ren

Stars speckle the sky, the rumble of ocean waves like a slow thumping beat under my skin. The mind is a funny thing. You can be clinically unwell, but as long as you can function, no one gives a shit. It's not like there's anything wrong with that. It's the easy choice; I understand that well. I coast in automatic patterns, and as I draw closer to the mortuary, I regain energy. I can come, then I can sleep. I can forget myself for a while.

By the time I unlock the front doors, the digital clock in the entrance lobby reads *1:27*. I clutch my bag to my hip, a length of rope with a hangman's knot tucked inside. I keep my composure in check, prepared with an excuse if Denise walks in: *I forgot my wallet. Sorry for bothering you.* Denise lives in Destin; she's never out here this late. She calls me or the embalmer to do nighttime pickups.

The refrigeration unit buzzes. I open the door. The cardboard boxes are like online orders: mindless products purchased during a late-night scroll, filling a person's life with meaningless junk, just to keep that person from drowning in their own personal hell. I don't judge: some people fill their emptiness with shopping; I fill mine with come. In the end, dead bodies are property, nothing more, and what I'm doing is simply *borrowing* clothes.

I check the labels and dates. The names. My hands flutter with anticipation, momentarily losing track of the emotions, and that bliss keeps me going.

I find the one I'm looking for.

I slide the cardboard box onto the gurney, then open the top. The body isn't fresh; it's probably in limbo while the family decides what to do with it. The sweetly sour scent of death lingers in the air, dulled by the cool temperature. The important part is that the corpse is *my* age. Her flat, cloudy eyes bore into the ceiling, her skin purpled and yellowed. She's thinner than me, but with the same long, dark hair. A flimsy, white cotton dress covers her body, and I run my hand across the material. There are no signs of trauma here. She's beautiful. Still in perfect shape.

I wonder how she died.

I scan the permits next to the refrigeration unit and find hers. *Avery Smith.* Some of the boxes on her form have been scratched out and rewritten—the family wanted her embalmed at first; now, she's off to the crematory, into my care. Embalming tends to be more expensive, and the shock of the subtotal probably swayed their decisions.

In my mind, I warp her story until it fits into another version of me. Her family *wants* to get rid of her. To pretend like she never existed.

Just like me.

I bend her knees and elbows in strange angles until I remove her dress, bra, and panties. I leave her body out, still thawing to room temperature, then head to the crematory with her clothes. I undress and place my own clothes on the table next to the retort, my body tingling with anticipation. The conveyor belt calls like a siren song, languid and stretched out, waiting for me.

I slip into her dress. Her underwear. Her bra. *Embodying her.* Little scales of her skin flaking onto mine. The conveyor belt moans with my weight, and I raise my head slightly, then wrap the rope around my neck, cinching it until the pressure is light, like a choker necklace.

I pull the canvas bag over my head, erasing my own existence. No one can see me like this.

The stranger's clothes press into my back, the rubber on the conveyor belt heating with my skin. With one hand keeping the noose tight, I use my other hand to slip into her underwear and glide my fingertips over the tender, hairy skin between my legs. I think of the pills. The weight of them in my throat, choking them down like rocks falling to the bottom of a pond. That serenity swallowing me whole. Ending my life.

It's not enough.

Those visions transform. I see a figure—a man so overpowering that I don't have a choice. His dick impales me, tears bursting from my eyes no matter how hard I try to keep them inside. He puts a gun to my head. My eyes roll back and I pant as I reach my first climax. I tighten the rope slightly, my fingertips skimming across my mound, circling that sensitive bundle of nerves, the slickness of my sex dripping down between my legs. I'm not dead, *damn it*, but he's going to kill me because he wants me, and there's nothing that I can do about it. My imagination finds more clarity—his gaunt features look down on me, more skeleton than man, his light blue eyes haunting me like the hottest part of a fire. Like Blaze. I stand on the edge of the abyss, near that pleasurable peak I'll never escape from *unless* he pushes me in. Unless Blaze—

Do you like knowing that you're going to die, little cunt? he asks. My core pulses, my need fixated on him. Pleasing him. Only him. *Once I come, once I finish using you, I'm going to kill you exactly the way you like it—*

A raucous bang jerks me from my fantasy, the backdoor slamming against the wall. A whistling tune fills the air. My chest stiffens, my body twitching with nerves. Every part of me trembles. I bite my lip.

Who the fuck is in here?

Chapter 6

Ren

The flute-like whistling floats down the hallway, my skin crawling the louder the tune gets. Closer. Counting down the seconds until the stranger finds me. Until I'm exposed.

I'm fucked. *I'm so fucked.* I'm lying on the retort's conveyor belt with a bag over my head and a rope around my neck, all while I'm wearing a dead woman's dress.

If Denise finds me like this, I'll be fired. My grandmother will never forgive me.

I picture my body disintegrating into the floor.

The cheerful whistling mixes with the heavy pound of boots, the power in each footstep shaking me to my core. No—the steps are too loud to be Denise. And Emily, our embalmer, is quiet; she's not the kind of person who would even *hum* to herself.

My heart throbs in my ears as I try to think. The steps grow louder, masculinity permeating the air. Salt. Sweat. Earth.

The gravedigger. *Blaze.*

He's close now.

I can't run.

I can't go anywhere.

A last chance at survival surges into my mind: *if I don't move, maybe he'll think I'm a corpse.* In theory, I—that stupid crematory operator—could have forgotten to store the body. Blaze will come to that conclusion, skip over this room, and leave. And besides, he's new, right? It's unlikely that he knows that we keep the bodies —even the cremation orders—in the refrigeration unit. He's a groundskeeper. A *gravedigger.* He stays outside. He doesn't do anything indoors.

So why is he here?

The footsteps still, the boots stopping on the tile outside of the doorway, the whistling tune fading to silence. I hold my breath, mentally crossing my fingers that he loses interest.

This is nothing, I think. *I am nothing. Don't look at me.*

Seconds pass. Minutes. A damned eternity.

A groan of approval escapes his lips.

He comes closer, his steps delicate, like he doesn't want to scare off a frightened animal. His weight shifts across the floor, each movement wringing my chest, weighing it down like a sack full of sand.

"What do we have here?" Blaze asks, his voice a low rumble rippling over my skin. His hand presses into my ankle. His skin is warm. So damn warm that a chill slithers up my legs to my core. The pressure of his touch balloons inside of me. Unwieldy, like intoxication.

"Still warm," he says. "I can work with that."

What?

A zipper rips through the air, my chest seizing all over again. The unmistakable slapping of skin against skin fills the room. *Friction.*

He's rubbing his erection. Masturbating to my lifeless body.

My legs part slightly, saliva building on my tongue. I *should* be scared. Panicking. I try to tell myself that I *am* scared. That I'm only frozen because I don't know what to do. I bite my lip, my pussy pulsing, and he *moans.*

My thighs tense reflexively. But corpses don't jump. They don't *need.* They're just bodies.

I'm just a body.

He touches my ankle again, and my pussy constricts at the contact, the hairs on the back of my neck standing with sensitivity.

It's everything I want.

"Who left you here naked, Ms. Smith?" he taunts.

He knows. He knows I'm not dead. That a body isn't supposed to be here.

He's playing with me.

Does he know it's me?

My skin prickles as he strokes my ankle bone, his fingertips riding up my calves. He gets closer to the valley between my thighs, his heat somehow frigid. Goosebumps crest over my skin.

"Our crematory operator knows better than to leave you here like this," he says, his voice barely above a whisper. "I apologize for this disrespect. Really, I do."

My face heats. With one fist still running up and down his dick, he reaches under my dress, into my bra, then captures my breast with his free hand, hard and unforgiving, pain shooting to my temples. I squeeze my eyes shut, so grateful for the bag over my head. My eyes blur, need swelling inside of me.

I'm a toy that he's using. A sex doll. A body without a brain. An inanimate object.

Why does it feel so good?

"A body is a body," he murmurs. "And you've got such a nice pair of tits for a dead girl."

Tension coils in my gut like a wave rolling across the beach, meeting back at the center between my legs. I try so hard to stay still. To be numb.

I can't help it. I feel everything. The touch of his fingers. Soft, then *rough*. Like it doesn't matter how I react, only that he gets what he wants.

He takes. Exploring. Pinching. Skimming my body, open land that he owns.

My body responds. Arousal weeps between my legs, forcing those needs out into the open. Goosebumps spread, chills whipping across the sand of my skin like the wind before a hurricane. I internally plead that he doesn't notice, but it's a game I'm playing with myself.

He knows I'm awake. He knows I'm alive. He knows that I'm not just a dead body.

And we're both playing along.

He kneads my areola between his fingers. My skin flushes, my nipple pebbling. I clench my jaw and will my body to *stop*.

But it refuses.

"I didn't know 'dead girls' still responded to physical stimulation," he says, a hint of sarcasm in his voice. My stomach sinks to the bottom of the pit.

He's toying with me. Playing with our predicament. Using me. Pinning me down to where I have no choice.

And I like it.

"What an interesting discovery," he says. "I really must investigate what else a corpse is capable of."

My body heats, small beads of sweat gathering on my upper lip. I should be scared. Any sane person would run. They'd probably have a panic attack. At the very least, a normal person would feel guilty about being caught by a coworker. Scared about the repercussions. The coworker turning them into their boss or the police. The thought of dealing with that drama doesn't thrill me, but the idea of being with him—Blaze using me until *he* comes— makes those thoughts evaporate.

A normal person wouldn't get caught stealing a corpse's clothes and masturbating at all. And a normal person definitely wouldn't fuck a woman who's pretending to be dead.

We're both still here.

He pulls down the top of the dress, yanking my nipple from the small bra, his mouth wrapping around my areola. Each slurp of his tongue is greedy, sucking the life out of me. My head rolls to the side, and I scrunch my eyes closed, telling myself it's the natural movement of a corpse. If he touched *any* dead body like this, it would move from the impact.

It doesn't matter though. He knows, and I know, and my body yearns for more, so badly that I want to scream.

Abandoning his cock, both of his hands grip my breasts as he pulls them both out of the bra, smashing them together, his mouth switching between my nipples, suckling them like they're candy. Like he's ravenous. Guzzling and wet. Moisture pooling on my chest. It's disgusting. Sloppy. And my whole body is on fire. My legs spread. My toes tilt out. My body willing him to enter me. My tongue is dry, and all I want is to stop thinking about how I need more. More of this degradation. More of *him*.

He stops, standing up quickly. The shift of fabric fills the room. My skin hardens everywhere. Is he zipping up? Finished with me? I can't see anything under the bag. Please, oh please, don't tell me he's zipping up. Not until he comes. I want him to fuck me. I want—

"You can't do a damn thing about it, can you, little corpse?" he says.

Little corpse.

He's taunting me. Daring me to tell him to stop.

And I should. I really should. There has to be a reasonable explanation for this, or at least a lie I can tell so that *he's* at fault and I'm free of blame.

My pussy won't let me say a word. I stay still, panting and waiting for him.

He laughs softly, a mix of condescension and amusement in his tone, like music meant for someone special. Not me. My body churns, my chest tangled with knots.

"You're nothing but a lifeless cunt for me to use," he growls.

He mounts the conveyor belt, then shoves my thighs wider, my legs crashing to either side of the belt. His mouth knocks against the canvas bag, breathing through the fabric, his heat broiling my cheeks. The rope slides along my neck, and with one quick movement, he pulls my damp underwear to the side, then his cock parts my pussy lips, his dick sliding into me, thick and hard. There's no resistance; I'm wet, but it *hurts*. Tears burn in my eyes. I haven't had sex in years—but he moans, moans like a madman, like he's possessed by my grip—and that pain melts away, giving me the chance to experience how hard he is inside of me.

I bite my tongue, holding back my response.

I shouldn't like this. It's wrong. It's—

"I love it when they're fresh," he grunts. His cock hammers inside of me, heat building in every pore. His masculine sweat circles me like a vulture. Needing more from me. "There's nothing better than a dead cunt. Freshly killed. *Fuck*—" He shouts,

33

breaking the rhythm of his thrusts. "The only thing that would make it better is if *I* had been the one to kill you. Don't you agree, little corpse? I could've killed you right when you hit that peak. That's the best way to die, isn't it? The climax to end all lives. You would've loved that; I can tell."

He resumes his brutal thrusting, and I try so hard to stay still. My body strains against the friction, each nerve ending desperate for more. I want it all so bad. Every depraved second. Every horrible thing he could do to me. Heat swells, the muscles between my legs constricting, blood flowing until everything is sensitive. I thrust my hips toward him, willing him to impale me. To gore me until my intestines are spilled all over the floor, until I'm truly dead. It's insane; he's pretending like I'm dead, like he wishes he would've *killed* me, and it's so messed up that I can't stop myself from enjoying it. From experiencing every deranged ounce of his pleasure. Of his cock. Of finally being useful for something. Because I've dreamed of this since I can remember. For *years*. It's the *only* way I can come.

He must know *exactly* how much power he has over me.

Why do I like this?

His thrust goes deeper than before, ramming against my cervix, nearly tearing a wail out of me. A deep pain ricochets through my stomach, and then I feel it. His cock gushing with come. I try not to moan, but my body clenches and I come noiselessly as his cock shoots his seed into me, a primal groan full of glee leaving his chest as he marks his territory. Filling me up with him.

His cock twitches one last time, and I flinch in response. He pulls out slowly.

I bite my lip.

If he leaves now without either of us speaking, we can pretend like it never happened. I can deny it. Even if he has a camera and is recording the whole thing on film, my face is covered. My hand tattoos are by my sides, out of view. He can't see me.

The rip of latex snaps through the room.

My jaw drops.

A condom. He's taking off a condom. The final nail in my coffin.

"Dead girls don't get pregnant," he mutters. "But you can never be too sure, can you? Not when they respond like filthy little sluts."

I don't move. Neither of us is supposed to be here, and if we both leave separately, we can still pretend like we didn't know the other one was here.

His boots clunk away, and soon the backdoor to the mortuary clicks shut. I'm alone. Probably. My stomach clenches as I hold my breath, waiting for the confirmation of stretching silence that he's really gone.

The keyhole jiggles; he locks up after himself.

My chest deflates. It's *over*. I get off of the conveyor belt as quickly as I can. I scan the room for my clothes. The side table is empty.

Didn't I put them there?

I search the room. The darkness invades the crematory, keeping everything in a constant shadow. Not a single thing is out of place.

Did he take my clothes?

I grab an oversized pullover sweater and some jeans out of the lost and found bin, panic swirling in my temples. I take off the corpse's dress and underwear—the panties wet, the bra soaked with Blaze's spit—and I get dressed in the spare clothes quickly. I glance at the sprawled gurney in the refrigeration unit and place the body back inside of the cardboard box, shoving the dress and underwear on top of it. I'll take care of it tomorrow and burn the evidence with the body. Right now, I need to get the hell out of here.

As long as I get out of here without facing him, I can deny anything happened, and I'll never, *ever* do this again. Besides, soon it won't matter. The corpse I took the clothes from—no, *borrowed* from—will be burned tomorrow, and no one will know a thing. Then I just need my grandmother's prescription refilled. That can't take more than a month. I'll swallow them all, and it'll be fine. And until then, I'll stay as far away from the gravedigger as possible. It's not like he needs to come inside of the mortuary. Avoiding him will be easy.

I open the front door, the key in my hand, ready to lock up. I check the side of the building to make sure I'm alone, but when I turn my head, the gravedigger steps around the corner, peering down at me, his presence looming like a storm cloud, threatening to break. My clothes dangle from his fingers like strings of fate. A lifeline he's cradling. My only chance at survival.

His lips curl in a smile. "Hello, little corpse."

Chapter 7

Ren

Pinpricks trickle across my spine, paralyzing me. I fixate on my clothes in Blaze's hand, not daring to look him in the eyes. My vision blurs. A dryness swirls in the back of my throat.

This isn't happening.

"The little corpse is speechless," Blaze mocks.

"You stole my clothes," I finally say. Invigorated by those small words, I ball my fists at my side, willing myself to appear brave, when inside I'm shitting myself. This isn't supposed to happen. We're not supposed to talk like this. "You stole my clothes, asshole!"

"Might I point out that you stole Ms. Smith's dress and underwear?" He lifts his shoulders. "I suppose we're all criminals in some capacity, aren't we?"

My body tenses in response. I keep my face stoic, the same expression I use with Mrs. Richmond and Denise to pretend like I don't care about a thing. But I'm freaking the hell out. Everything we just did in the crematory is *real* now, and we can't pretend like we don't know each other.

What do I do now?

"Give me back my clothes," I demand, still gawking at the clumps of fabric.

"No."

My cheeks redden. I grit my teeth. "What do you mean 'no'?"

"We need to talk about this…" His upper lip twitches. "This *situation* of ours."

Ours.

Finally, I meet his eyes—those cold, light blue eyes, like glass shielding against a snowstorm. Except Blaze *is* the force of nature that's going to destroy everything.

I grumble, but it comes out like a growl, and it startles me. I don't *growl*. Growling is for animals, and I've worked hard to get my emotions under control. It's like another person is taking the reins, almost like my survival instincts know that I have to get out of this predicament as quickly as possible, even if it means growling.

And then what? a voice inside of me asks. *What life will you go back to?*

The gravedigger grins as if he can read my thoughts, then motions to the side of the building. Reluctantly, I follow him. Keeping my distance. Always wary.

We lean against the exterior of the mortuary, facing the parking lot with a view of the east end of Front Beach Road. The Souvenir Emporium directly across from us is dark; the lights on the gas station illuminate the margarita stand next to it. A bizarre mix of death, tourism, and the beach.

And here we are: a gravedigger and a crematory operator. Recently fucked. And bound by the knowledge that we both *aren't* supposed to be here right now.

Blaze angles toward me. I stay facing forward and stare as intently as I can at the Margarita Shack. I would chug three giant glasses of sugary slush just to pretend like what we did was a dream.

My skin itches at his proximity. I don't do well with people. Not like this. It just doesn't work. And Blaze is like everyone else. He will one day realize that he never should've wasted his time on me, even if it was only a quick screw at work.

"I'm Blaze," he says, eyeing me up and down. "You're Ren, the crematory operator, yes?"

I blink. My stomach tightens. This is our first conversation, and though we've been working together for weeks now, this is only the second time I've seen him.

He knows my name. Says it like he knows me.

It's unnerving.

"Is Ren short for anything?" he asks.

I don't say a word. Why does he want to know?

"Your name means 'water lily' in Japanese, doesn't it?" he asks. "Could mean plenty of other things, but that's the meaning that fits *you* best. Do you want to know why, little corpse?"

I narrow my eyes, still focusing on those odd pink and green lights shining from the shack's windows. It's in the middle of the night, but you can't get rid of the tourist theater of this beach town.

"No," I say.

"Did you know that water lilies can be poisonous?"

I startle, looking at him briefly. His skin is pale, the stark corners of his cheekbones like the caverns of a skull. His eye sockets are in shadow, those light blue irises glimmering like dying candle wicks. I shouldn't even give him the dignity of a response.

Before I know what I'm doing, I shake my head.

Water lilies are poisonous? Why is he telling me this?

In the sky, a few stars dig themselves out of the darkness. It's too bright out here, too developed for the rest to share their light.

"What do you want most out of life, little corpse?" he asks.

A diatribe about life from a funeral worker? How original.

Not.

"I don't know," I say.

"Try."

I shrug. "I want to go home?"

"Why? So you can sneak out of your grandmother's house again?"

My cheeks burn. I jerk my head toward him, and he smirks at me, so damn smug my skin crawls. How does he know that I live with my grandmother? Is he making fun of me?

Screw this.

I angle toward the parking lot, ready to get the hell out. He grabs my arm.

"You can't leave. Not when I've seen you here," he says, his words slow and methodical. "You broke in after hours."

I keep still, facing the street. A car passes without the driver noticing us.

"So did you," I say.

"We both know that *you* were the one who broke into the funeral home first. *You* were the one who vandalized Ms. Smith's body for your own sexual gratification," he chuckles. "I just happened to find you. It's not your first time now, is it?"

Ice floods my veins. He knows.

He's been watching me.

Why?

What does he want from me?

A million thoughts war in my mind. My consciousness bounces back and forth, trying to find clarity in it all, but finding none.

Anger throbs in my temples, melting the fear inside of me.

No. This *isn't* over. He doesn't get to decide how this ends.

"You fucked me, pretending like I was a corpse when you *knew* I wasn't dead," I rasp. "You *raped* me."

Pride lingers at the corners of his lips. He lifts his chin, looking down at me.

"Rape," he murmurs. "Such a strong word for what we did. The way you were so compliant. So willing. So *reactive* to everything I did." He licks his bottom lip and my eyes betray me, following his rough tongue against those pale pink lips. "Go ahead, love. Tell Denise that I raped you after hours, and I'll tell her exactly what you were doing here. How you've been sneaking into Last Spring for weeks now. For all I know, it's been months. *Years* before I even stepped foot into this town. What have you been doing all of this time? Stealing? Changing payroll? Making more work for yourself so you can keep your job? Oh no—it's worse than that, isn't it? You've been desecrating bodies, and if the clients find out, you'll be burned alive. You know how this town gets." He clicks his teeth. "Is that what you want, little corpse? To destroy everything in your wake, including yourself?"

A shudder ripples through me. Stubble marks his jaw, his facial structure angular, almost like he's been hacked from a thick piece of wood. Splintered. Frayed. An old tree carved into the shape of a body, the core rotting inside.

Cloaked in black, towering over me, he's not a handsome man; he's frightening. The kind of man you'd cross the street to get away from him. A violent ghost shrouded in a human's skin.

He's got me pinned under his claws, and we both know it.

"What do you want from me?" I whisper.

He grins, his head dipping down just enough to meet my gaze. "You want to die, don't you?"

My jaw is tight. "What?"

"I see it in your eyes. The way you stare at the retorts while the bodies burn. The jealousy in your eyes when you see the corpses in the caskets. How you long to be one of those cooled bodies in the refrigeration units. Be honest with me, Ren. You want to die, but it's not that simple, is it?"

Visions of the open caskets flash before me—

The embalming botched like a caricature.

The bloated body I put into the retort yesterday.

The dead woman my age—Ms. Smith—how bruised she was when she died.

The images I've conjured of my mother.

My cheeks tense. *This is insane.* He doesn't know anything about me. How could he?

I'm letting him dig into my head.

"Have you been stalking me?" I hiss, carving the anger out of my chest, focusing on the fact that he invaded my privacy. I don't focus on the fact that he sees me. That he even seems to know me. I don't want to acknowledge what that would mean. "What is wrong with you?"

He chuckles, the sound skittering across my core.

"Stalking would imply that I'm obsessed with you," he says, leaning forward. "I'm afraid what you are to me is more of a curiosity, Ren. You live with your grandmother in a nice neighborhood, and most nights you force yourself to sleep with pills and alcohol. Nothing out of the ordinary." He winks. "Yet, that's not every night, is it? You spend nights here too, dreaming of death.

Getting off on it. Pretending like someone's hands are wrapped around your neck. Telling yourself that life would be better if someone killed you, if you just had those final breaths *your way*, taken from you, like you always dreamed of. Your killer driven so mad by desire that they can't help but fuck you until you're dead." He licks his teeth, his eyes locked on mine, and I shiver. "Tell me, though," he continues, "if you're so infatuated with death, why haven't you killed yourself yet? Are you afraid, little corpse?"

Tears well in my eyes. His words are like a knife digging out my guts, shoveling them onto the ground while he walks all over them. Because he's *right*. Almost every day, I imagine disappearing. The world would go on, and my grandmother and Denise—everyone in my life, really—would keep thriving. My life *and* death don't make a difference.

I imagine driving into the ocean, and the water taking me down. A noose brushing my skin before it snaps my neck. A gun resting on my temple as the trigger is pulled.

I know I won't do it.

Maybe I am afraid. Maybe I think I want death *only* because I don't know what it will be like. The nothingness. An absolute void.

There are no guarantees to how it would *feel*. No true indication if I would regret it, or if I would welcome it.

He has no right to know those thoughts within me.

"Fuck you," I hiss.

"You *are* afraid," he murmurs. "And why wouldn't you be? Death is the only unknown we have. Even for the untouchables like us—the ones dealing with the dead all day long—that *death*, that inevitable end, is still an unknown, ominous presence."

I clutch my purse to me. My own noose is inside of it, like a safety blanket comforting me. My clothes dangle from Blaze's hand, swaying like palm branches.

Even if he is cornering me like this, I can still get out. I can still leave. None of this *has* to matter.

His thumb flicks over his lip, and my thighs clutch together. The memory of his body against mine floods me. His mouth on my breasts. The pressure of his weight. His thrusts. His complete power over me.

Even when he made it clear that he *knew* I was alive, I gave it to him. I know that. And now, it's like he's holding up a mirror, forcing me to face myself for the first time in years.

"Just give me my clothes," I beg in a whisper.

"You want someone else to take your life when you least expect it. To do it *for* you. You want someone to lead you into that darkness. To lock you inside and never let you out."

I scrutinize him. His eyes twinkle with longing, his jaw loose. The slight dip of his chin.

Maybe he's not making fun of me. Maybe this is real. Like he's seeing those hidden parts of me, the ones I rarely openly acknowledge myself.

My stomach sinks. Am I that obvious, or is he actually curious?

"Would you slip off in your sleep?" he asks. "Would you take a bullet to your head? No, not *my* little corpse. That's too easy for you." He winks, a sigh dancing on his breath. "You want to feel the rope close around your neck as your vision and hearing starts to fade, don't you, love?" His eyes dart down between my legs, his tongue skating across his lips. My neck flushes. "You want to feel every last second fade away as someone powerful takes that dripping cunt of yours for the last time."

A small drop of arousal dampens my jeans.

I straighten myself. He's playing with me. There's no way that this can be as good as it seems.

No one wants the real me.

"What do you want?" I ask, louder this time.

"It's simple," he says. He tilts his head. "You want to be dead. I like torturing women. Let's be honest; I like killing them too. It's fun to fuck corpses, but you know, they don't *react* quite the way the living do. And I haven't been able to find a woman as satisfying to kill as my first. I'm changing my hunting criteria, I suppose. And that leads me to you."

My heart pounds in my chest. He's definitely screwing with me. This isn't real. He's trying to see what I'll believe. To prove how stupid I am.

I blink rapidly, as if the action will make Blaze disappear.

He studies me.

"You just admitted to murder," I say.

"We've all got our secrets. Now, we both know each other's." He beams. "You're a sexual vandalizer of corpses, and I'm a murderer. But there's no proof now, is there? Words are words. Try holding that up in court."

I grit my teeth. "Which means your threats of outing me to Denise are full of shit."

"Ah," he sighs. He pulls out his phone. "But I do have video evidence of *that*."

My eyelids flutter, narrowing in on the device. How can he have evidence of what I do here at night? I've been careful, haven't I? He *has* to be messing with me.

That's what this is: It's all a joke. It has to be. Besides, if he's a murderer, why doesn't he kill me right now? We could have ended this unnecessary conversation with my death an hour ago. Instead, he's *talking* to me. Showing me that he knows me.

"You're psychotic," I say flatly.

"Perhaps I am. That doesn't mean I can't help you though, Ren. Like I said before, I've killed my fair share of unwilling women. Trust me; they all get wet—it's a coping mechanism—and yet, they don't always come, you know? Perhaps that's the change I need. Where *you* come in. Killing a woman right as she comes, to see that ecstasy frozen on her face, melting into the pure emptiness of death. Conditioning her to *want* that release." He steps forward, and I shift a little further to the side, my spine prickling with nerves. "You like playing with that blurred line, don't you, Ren? You could be that woman for me."

The hairs on my arms rise. His lips pull up into a smile, and my insides quiver.

He's serious.

"Be my fuck toy, and I'll kill you when you least expect it," he says. "Teach me to use the retorts while we're at it. That way we both get what we want: You don't have to endure this fucked-up world a moment longer, you get that finale you've always wanted, and *I* get to kill you." He cracks his neck, and I gnaw on the inside of my lip. His tone is matter-of-fact, like this is a normal arrangement, when it's anything but. "Are you on birth control?"

I blink. He's asking about birth control *now?*

"Who cares if I get pregnant if you're going to kill me anyway?" I ask.

"I imagine morning sickness is a hassle. If I'm being honest, I don't particularly like cleaning up vomit," he says, his entire demeanor calm. I clear my throat, trying to stay centered, but he's creepy, like a sunken ship at the bottom of the ocean, swarming with fish that will never see the light of day. "It'll be easier for both of us if we work together, don't you think?"

My lips part, my thoughts racing with the reality of the situation. Blaze doesn't want to get caught. That's why he's asking for *permission* to kill me. He wants my cooperation so that I can teach him how to get rid of a body without anyone knowing, and he can have his sick little fantasy come to life.

And I can have mine.

The bottom of my stomach heats, temptation floating to the surface. I could disappear. Mrs. Richmond would think I finally ran away. Maybe she'd even pretend that I found a husband to take care of me. She'd make up another lie to cover up my disappearance like she did with my mother.

I'd simply cease to exist.

"You could save a life," Blaze says, his voice airy. "Think of the potential. You could give yourself purpose. All by giving *your* life to me."

I huff, my nostrils flaring. He wants me to think of myself as a hero?

I've honestly never cared about anyone else. Mrs. Richmond's life would be easier if she didn't have to think about me. I tolerate Denise. The only person I might've cared about is my mother, and dying won't bring her back. What do I care if I save a stranger's life by letting Blaze kill me?

If Blaze truly likes killing women, then my death isn't going to change anything.

"You turn twenty-six soon, yes?" Blaze asks. I furrow my brows; how the hell does he know that? He must have looked

45

through my employment files or something. "How about this: if I don't kill you by the time you turn twenty-six, I'll give you barbiturates, or at least some kind of concoction, so that you can drift off to the other side while you masturbate and dream of dying, as seems to be your habit. Until that fateful day, we'll use our time to tease that masochistic pleasure out of you. Force you to face death. We can use it like a test run. Practice. Guiding you into that oblivion, figuring out your preferred sensual end. Then, I'll kill you. And if I don't, you'll have the power to kill yourself. In the end, we both get to indulge in our darker desires. You help me, and I help you."

My heart drums, beating against my chest. He's serious. So damn serious, it scares me.

"This is crazy," I whisper.

"It is, isn't it?" he says. "Honestly, Ren, we're two sides of the same coin. We could make each other—dare I say it?—*happy*. We belong together: the killer, and the corpse. We complete each other."

Complete each other?

I consider the possibility; I imagine it. His hands wrapped around my neck, my vision spotting, his cock plunging inside of me, using me to get what he wants as he takes my life.

My hands shudder. The only thing more insane than his proposition is the fact that for a few seconds, I actually thought he was making a real offer.

He's *mocking* me. Playing with my desires. Acting as if my whole life is a joke.

I ball my fists.

"Go to hell," I say under my breath. I shake my head, finally stepping away from the wall. There's nothing left to talk about. I cross the main road to my car.

"Already there. You know that," he shouts. "And remember, little corpse: if you tell Denise, I will too."

I twist around and stand on the edge of the street. The moonless sky casts Blaze in an eerie glow, a blue mist shadowing his pale face. A black, long-sleeved shirt hugs his shoulders, highlighting his broad chest.

I have no idea what he did before working at Last Spring, but it's clear that he's physically strong. And a part of me—buried underneath everything sane—wants to know what that strength feels like.

He winks, then uses the back of his hand to shoo me away.

"Give me your final answer soon, love," he shouts. "I'm getting impatient."

I shake my head furiously this time. This is *stupid*. There's no reason to even entertain the idea of us working together like that.

"There is no final answer. I'm not doing anything with you," I yell.

He lifts his shoulders, his lips pulled into an irritating smirk. "You're still here, aren't you?"

Still here.

I bite my lip, breaking the skin, the tang of metal spreading over my tongue. I spin away, then run to my car. He's right. By arguing with him, I've considered his idea for too long. *It's insane.* I don't need him. I don't need anyone. And no one needs me.

Not even Blaze.

I pull out of the parking lot, then glance over my shoulder. Blaze slants against the mortuary, lazily watching me drive away. He raises his hand, my clothes dangling in the air, the pant legs swaying like the rope of a noose.

Chapter 8

Blaze

My little corpse goes home, so sullen and shocked by the entire affair. It's intoxicating, knowing how much she's affected by this. She knows what she wants, and eventually, that chaos inside of her will dominate her decisions.

It always does.

Once I'm sure she'll be in bed, I drive to her house and park two streets down. I hop the fence until I'm outside of her bedroom window. Inside, her hands are at her sides like a corpse in a casket. Her chest rising and falling. Unconscious. Asleep.

An empty bottle of vodka rests on her nightstand. My corpse always has a backup plan to get her to sleep. I open the window. Crawl over the ledge. Her legs are spread—this time not covered by a dress—and the scent of her musk overwhelms me: the sourness of her adrenaline masking her inner sweetness. The hunger settles inside of me, eating me alive. She's not a traditionally attractive woman by any means, but *fuck*, my dick gets heavier just smelling her. Ash and rancid fear. Sweet and coarse. A need to have her, to use her cunt, to make her die for me, controls me like a finger pulling back the hammer of a gun.

My boots crash onto the floor. I roll my eyes at the excessive noise; my horny self is getting the best of me. I need to be more careful. Ren groans as she flips onto her side. My cock hardens.

Soon, she'll get that never-ending bliss. Soon, she'll be mine forever. *Soon.* Whether she likes it or not.

But fuck me—I want her to *choose* me. I want to know what it's like to fuck chaos until it submits. Until it gives me exactly what I want.

A door creaks, muffled by the walls. The grandmother's bedroom. My veins throb as the staggered footsteps of the grandmother leak through the house. I slide under Ren's bed, my shirt scratching against the hard carpet.

The bedroom door opens, socked feet shuffling forward. The grandmother scans the area, analyzing whether there's any danger.

A few seconds pass. Then she closes the door, leaving me alone with Ren. She doesn't care about the open window. The empty bottle of vodka on the nightstand. The barren pill container. The grandmother only cares about herself. I can hear it now, the calming thoughts she must tell herself: *I must have heard the neighbors. Ren is sleeping. Everything is okay.*

Ren's sleeping breath levels. She's found her serenity again, and she's so vulnerable that my cock twitches awake. I unzip my pants. My fat dick springs forward, the tip scratching against the jagged bed springs above me. I rub my palm along my length, using the dry friction, my fist pumping into the coils each time I reach the head. I picture Ren with a bag covering her head, like a prisoner waiting for her torture. Only aware of the distorted world in her bubble.

I imagine her blood spilling onto the fabric. Drenching her in it.

I grunt as the vision changes: I rip that canvas bag off of her head, see her expression as she comes before dying and leaving this fucked-up world, and it pushes me over the edge. Forces the orgasm out of me. Come drips over my hands. The liquid oozes down, coating my skin.

One day, I'll coat her in blood. Just like that.

My little corpse continues her steady breathing, so drunk that she doesn't even know I've come right underneath her. I sigh and reach around me, searching for something to clean up. I find an old sweater. I wipe my fingers on the fabric. She rolls over on the mattress again, the coils squeaking with her weight. I look at my hands.

A drop lingers on my forefinger. Like a dot of honeysuckle, waiting to be licked up.

Carefully, I slide across the ground before getting on my knees. Reaching over, I put a soft finger on Ren's lips, coating those dry slivers of her skin with my come. It reminds me of a fish, and I briefly think about the salmon skin salad my mother's boyfriend once brought over from a Japanese restaurant. The idea of skinning Ren alive like that intrigues me.

In a way, I'm doing it now. Eating her alive.

Ren licks her lips, her nose wrinkling at the salty taste of my come. Then her face loosens, falling back into deep sleep. My dick twitches, my balls tightening against my groin all over again.

I don't give in.

I want to kill her. I want to see that pleasurable ecstasy in her eyes right before she dies. And in order to make it the *most* satisfying kill, I need that connection. I need to see if she's truly like my first, like my instincts tell me she is.

And that takes time.

Once I'm home, I swing the door open. Moonlight floods in from behind me, illuminating the hardwood floors. I bring my fingers to my nose, inhaling the scent. On the head of it, you can smell my come. Then there's something else, something *divine* beneath it all. Ren's pussy. Sour. A hint of sweetness. Smoke. The flakes of the dead lingering on her skin, enveloping her every breath, heavy with lust. A hint of the bitter taste of her adrenaline. Knowing that she wanted exactly what I gave her.

Leaving the lights off, I walk through the dark house like Ren walks through the mortuary at night. I find my way to the spare bedroom, then unlock the old chest and stare down at the locks of hair. Yellow. Creamy white. Strawberry gold. All different shades of blond. A simple way that Ren is different from them.

I open the small compartment inside the trunk's lid, revealing Ren's black hair. It's separated from the rest now, and will continue to be that way until she joins them.

With one hand, I clutch the blond strands in my palm. With the other hand, I pinch her black hair, rolling it between my fingers, relishing in the thick strands. I close my eyes and cast my head toward the ceiling. The strands ripple between my fingers, the tension ripe. The need to fuck and kill her conquering me.

Just like I'll destroy her.

Ren will be my fourth kill. She'll be the marker of a new era, one where I find exactly the violent high I'm looking for, a time where I practice my craft until I'm an expert at murder and disposal. A phase where I find my eager little victim, and we plan her body disposal *together*, where we use this opportunity to perfect my system.

Ren is perfect.

I drop the blond hairs into the trunk, then carefully tuck Ren's black hairs into the hidden compartment in the lid.

Heat boils inside of me as I realize what I just did.

I was gentle with her hair.

Hair is nothing more than dead pieces of skin, and yet, I'm still cautious with her.

It's aggravating.

Ren is still alive. And now, she knows about my habits. That's a problem. A liability. I confessed to her that I like torturing women. Fucking them. Killing them. That I'm curious about doing that with someone like her, someone who is already attracted to the violent side of depravity. Someone as unrestrained as me.

I could've killed her tonight in her own bed. Instead, I wiped my come on her lips.

I'm setting myself up for a trap.

I shove those thoughts out of my mind. As long as my secrets die with her, it doesn't matter.

In the master bedroom, I take out a small container from the nightstand drawer, marveling at the little white pills. Her precious benzodiazepines.

I lick my lips, keeping myself in check. This *will* work. It has to. Ren will come around, and she'll see that we can work together. That we both want something from each other.

51

We're all animals, and Ren, as interesting as she is, is simply another woman to torture, fuck, and kill. She might not be a *willing* victim—at least, not at first—but her cunt *will* be wet for me.

I don't care if she's still alive or if she still has a brain. She's just a body. And if she doesn't comply, I'll kill her anyway.

I pull a heavy-duty dog's choke chain from the bottom drawer of the nightstand, placing it on my bed. Next, I take out a metal leash, displaying them next to each other. I bought them for her the other day on instinct. With the others, I had specific ways I wanted to torture them, and I followed those instincts to the last, intimate detail.

With Ren, it's slightly different. She's not going into the shipping containers like the others, but I still have plans for her.

I want to keep her like a pet. A good little toy, ready to be used. My corpse doll.

I add my knives, my gun, the rope, the duct tape, and the rest of the metal instruments to the collection. There are so many options for us. So many ways for me to play with her. I'm going to condition her to come for me, exactly at the time I want, and then I'm going to kill her.

Ren wants to die mid-orgasm?

I can give her that.

Chapter 9

Ren

In the morning, my head pounds. Sunlight blinds me from the open window. I'm almost positive that I kept it closed on purpose as if *that* would keep Blaze out.

Maybe I left it open like I always do. I don't know.

I stare at the ceiling as Blaze's words repeat in my mind: *If I don't kill you by the time you turn twenty-six, I'll give you barbiturates.*

The way he said it was simple. A deal. My end, for his pleasure. We both win.

Until that fateful day—his voice vibrates inside of me—*we'll use our time to tease that masochistic pleasure out of you. Force you to face death.*

A chill runs down my spine. He sees me. Knows what I want. And he wants that from me too.

He's been watching me, and I never knew he was there.

In the walls, the pipes stretch with hot water, their groans vibrating through the walls. Shortly after, an electric toothbrush hums. The tea kettle clatters against the stove. Then the front door slams shut.

I don't move.

At nine a.m., I call in sick. Denise covers up her annoyance with sympathy, like she usually does. It must be a huge pain in the ass since our embalmer is still out.

There's no way I could do anything today. Not with him on my mind.

Blaze. A fire incinerating any chance at a normal thought. My savior, and my killer.

It's like he thinks he's an executioner, performing a civilian task, eliminating a lost soul. Giving a mortal like me freedom in the afterlife.

No—he's a *villain*. A demon in human form. He admitted to murders. To killing women. Women like me.

That's *not* normal, and either way, I don't believe him. I refuse. He's messing with me, using my own desires against me.

Maybe I'm not normal either. People don't masturbate in crematories. They don't put on clothes of the dead, and they definitely don't *consider* an offer of suicidal assistance from a self-proclaimed killer.

Eventually, I drive. Going past Last Spring. Searching for something, though I'm not sure what. My eyes glance over the building, over the gardens, over the cemetery, not daring to see anyone inside. Afraid to see him. To know what his existence means.

And it's then that I know: I'm looking for evidence of last night. Proof of Blaze. As much as I try to deny it, I want to know that last night was real.

When I blink, I'm parked in front of the medical spa, Eternal Hope.

Medical assistance in dying is illegal in Florida, but that doesn't mean it's nonexistent. I've looked it up before; knowing the right people or the correct terminology can get you the death you want. As far as I can tell, if you say you're terminal—and you have the paperwork to prove it—then in their minds, they have enough guilt-free permission to indulge in their own righteous proclivities.

I see through it, though. The doctors may be more professional, but they are just as heartless as Blaze.

Suddenly, I'm in the waiting room. A painting of a pink lotus flower hangs on the wall, and a small, tranquil water fountain trickles in the corner. The receptionist peers up from her desk and smiles, as if she's been waiting for me.

It's all so fake.

"Can I help you?" she asks.

If the rumors are true, then she *can* help me in a more humane way than Blaze. She can put an end to my life in an illegal—but *clinical*—way. There will be no embarrassment. No pain. No memory of my life whatsoever. She can help me achieve the death I *should* want. It won't be scary. It'll be peaceful. Most people want that easy kind of end.

It's never been only about dying for me though. It's about that journey *into* the void. Being torn from my own skin. Seeing my soul fucked outside of my body. Giving myself to someone.

Someone like Blaze.

A stack of blank forms lies on the counter in front of the receptionist. A paper trail that could lead back to me.

If Mrs. Richmond followed those clues and found out that I had ended my life here, she'd always be the woman with the daughter who committed suicide. With the granddaughter who killed herself too. A matriarch that causes her followers to lose hope.

Doing it like this—the right way—doesn't seem fair to her.

That's what I tell myself, anyway.

"I'm sorry," I say, my voice faltering. "I thought this was a salon."

The receptionist nods with a sad smile, reading my lies. "We get that a lot. This is actually a medical—"

I don't let her finish her sentence. The door jingles shut behind me.

The next morning, I go to work. I stay in the crematory, skipping my usual lunch in the garden. Ash coats my skin, and I think of my own body burning into chunks of bone in the retort.

If Blaze put me into the retort, there would be no record of my death. All that would be left is extra cremains for another family, and that dead person would have company in the afterlife.

Mrs. Richmond would never know. No one would. The only

person who would know what had happened to me would be Blaze.

This should be *my* choice, my end, my decision. Somehow, Mrs. Richmond is still affecting my thoughts. Determining how I end my life.

I don't want to be that person anymore. I want to do something I want for once.

And deep down, I know what I want. It isn't what society wants.

Another day passes. Then more.

On the fifth day, my missing clothes are stacked in a folded pile on the side table in the crematory. A metallic and earthy odor fumes from the fabric, as if Blaze bathed in my clothes. Tucked into the folds of the shirt, there's a note in scrawled handwriting. A phone number and an address. The only sign that he's still waiting for my answer.

This time, on my lunch break, I take my place outside again, staring out at the cemetery and the ocean waves beyond it. To the side—past the gravesites—a family of four builds a sandcastle near the water, far enough away that it's hard to see the details of the structure. No one—not even the tourists—want to enjoy the beach in front of the cemetery. It's as if they know that the invisible dead are sitting on the grassy hill, waiting to drag them down too.

They don't have to worry about the dead. They have to worry about people like Blaze.

People like me.

That night, as I lie in bed, Blaze's blunt cheekbones fill my mind and transform into a charred skull. I shake my head, internally enraged at myself for fantasizing about a man who wants my *consent* to kill me. As if *that* will make a difference in court. As if he has an actual moral conscience that needs stroking.

He has a motive; I'm not sure what it is. It seems too simple for this arrangement to be exactly what he claims it is.

Would a killer *ask* someone to be his victim?

More importantly, would I like being under his control again?

During the day, I imagine taking a handful of pills, slipping into a bath, and never waking up. But at night, with a hand on my pussy, those thoughts are different.

What if I *feel* something when I die? What if I come like I did the other night, right as it all ends? If I feel something *real* for once?

What if I let Blaze take my life?

I imagine him fucking me. Choking me. Impaling me. Slitting my throat. Shooting me with a gun. If he has killed women before, then he probably has a gun.

A gun.

I could use a gun. I could shoot myself. I don't even need Blaze to do that for me.

I could steal *his* gun.

I lie in bed with my clothes on my chest, breathing in his scent. Metals and dirt, like a shovel digging through the mud.

Soon, I'm parked outside of a small house. The lawn is plain and trimmed, and the window blinds are drawn. It's almost two a.m. A black cat roams in the next-door neighbor's driveway, judging me for my late arrival.

His house is completely dark.

I know he's awake. Waiting for me.

I knock on the door. My stomach knots, each bulb of pain churning inside of me. I shouldn't be doing this. I shouldn't trust a stranger like Blaze with my life *or* my death.

Maybe he's right. Maybe I am afraid. Maybe I *want* someone to help me. Someone who is more authentic than a doctor. Someone who admits exactly what they want from me. A person who can see me for who I truly am.

A person who can give me what I want.

I stare at my feet. Time ticks by, and nausea rolls through me. I should leave.

The door opens, and a gust of warm air rushes past me. Black boots enter my vision. I slowly look up.

Blaze smirks. His jagged jaw. The stubble on his skin brittle and hard. Plain black clothes covering his body, contrasting with his light blue eyes. And his posture—the wide stance, his chest thrust out—radiates superiority over everyone and everything.

Every detail about him demonstrates his power over me.

There are millions of reasons to say no. To tell Blaze to fuck off and leave me alone. To destroy his little note and never give him a second thought. To do this the *right* way and ask a doctor for help.

I don't do any of that.

"Okay," I whisper.

His smirk widens. I don't have to explain myself; he knows exactly what I mean. He steps forward, then closes the door behind him, meeting me outside.

"Okay," he says.

Chapter 10

Blaze

"Well," Ren says as she straightens, braveness growing in her chest, like she can finally stand up to me now that she's agreed to what she truly wants. She gestures inside. "Are we doing this?"

I chuckle to myself, then lick my lips, paying attention to the way her eyes flicker to my mouth. Filled with irritation and still starved for what I can give her. Her black hair shines, thick with grease like she rarely washes it. The bags under her eyes are deep now, confessing the sleep she's lost from this.

It brings me euphoria.

My dick grows hard.

"You think you get to decide when we start?" I ask plainly.

Her chin trembles, shocked that I'd decline her advances now. I can see her shove it down, forcing the emotions out of her body.

"You were the one who was waiting for me to agree to this whole fucked-up plan," she says.

I shove her against the wall, her body slamming into the exterior of the house, confusion crashing into her like a giant wave. Her pupils dilate, so full of fear and panic. That vulnerability is tangible as I corner her. Trapping her like prey. I press myself up against her soft frame, forcing her to endure every hard, hungry inch of me.

She might be hungry, but I am far greedier. And I *will* get what I want from her.

"You think that because you agreed to my game, you get to decide the rules?" I whisper, my words harsh on her neck. Her skin prickles with goosebumps, and I scrape my teeth against her flesh and tease her with their sharpness. "Make no mistake, little corpse. That's all you are to me: a fucking dead girl. You're mine; if I want to kill you right now, if I want to fuck you, if I want to leave you begging for more, then I'll do exactly what I want."

She bites her bottom lip, chewing on it. Her eyes dart away from me, hiding the lust glazing her expression. I suck in a breath, slowly letting her back down to her own two feet. Using my palms, I skim her shirt and smooth the wrinkles where I gripped the fabric. I take the cased syringe out of my pocket, then place it in her palms.

She blinks at the medicine. I've had it for a while now. It helps to avoid unnecessary accidents with your victims.

"Birth control," I say. "In your arm. Lasts three months."

Which will last until her birthday.

"You have birth control lying around?" she asks.

"I have a connection," I chuckle, though I don't give her the exact details.

Ren nods. She stares at my black shirt like it's a dark hole, waiting to suck her inside. I pull her chin up, forcing her to acknowledge me.

"Always look at me," I order. "I want you to know the face of the man that will kill you."

Her chin dips in acquiescence. She doesn't *want* to submit or obey me; she's selfish too. She knows I have what she wants. A reward only I can give her.

I wink, pushing her in the direction of her car. "Go on now. I'll call you when it's time."

"But you don't—" She stops herself, glancing down at her phone, then back up to me. "Do you have my number?"

I stuff my hand in my pocket and shift the strands of her black hair between my fingers. I knew she would give in tonight. Seeing her clothes. Smelling my scent on them. All I had to do was wait.

Oh, my little corpse. I have so much more than your phone number.

"I do," I say.

"And you'll get me the barbiturates if it doesn't work out?"

I laugh. *If* it doesn't work out. I'll *make* it work out. She will too. There isn't any need for those promised barbiturates, but to satiate her, I'll play along. I'll get her the drugs she craves, just like I got the birth control.

"Don't you trust me?" I ask, my cheeks tight with sarcasm. She shakes her head, and I chuckle. "Good." Then I forcibly turn her shoulders until she's facing away from me. "Don't make me tell you twice," I warn.

She stays still for a moment, then moves forward. Inside of her car, she looks back at me. I lock eyes with her. Her days are numbered, and we're both glad for it.

I step back inside, then sit on the trunk filled with my victims' hair. I dial my brother.

"What?" he asks.

Brody is technically my older half-brother. He's a physician and has access to some of the best substances that medical science can offer, especially when it comes to the products I need or the drugs my little corpse wants. We've never gotten along—not since our mother died—but Brody knows that I've got him exactly where I want him. I committed murder; he helped me cover it up. He will always be tied to me.

"I have a situation," I say curtly. "A—" I stop. How do I describe my next victim, as willing as she may be, without upsetting someone as delicate as Brody? "A *friend* of mine wants to end her life. I need barbiturates."

He grunts, reading the subtext. "You want to use drugs and not your hands this time?"

I laugh, the condescension in my tone matching his. He's so full of shit. He's done the exact same thing I have with his glorious *medicine.* The only difference is that he has a guilty conscience that keeps him in check; I don't. I don't give a shit who lives or dies. I only care about the power killing gives me.

"I'm helping her out," I explain. "She hates her meaningless life, so why not help her? I'm finding a way to help the public. I'm moving up in the world, just like you, big brother."

"You're a twisted fuck."

"You're not any better."

He stays silent, angered by that comment. I smirk to myself, enjoying his disgust. Brody thinks he's charitable because he provides pharmaceuticals to those who can't afford the retail prices. Even when his patients pay under the table, Brody takes his cut. *Profits* off of his dying clients. They are *clients*, after all. Customers. Not people. He provides various drugs, even barbiturates that are hard to come by in the States. He's even helped assist people to their ends.

The saint is as guilty as the rest of us; he just happens to be better at camouflaging it.

"Why are you helping her and not doing your usual thing?" he asks, his voice hoarse. *My usual thing.* It fills me with glee. He can't even verbally admit that I kill people. I slouch in boredom, the wooden trunk creaking underneath me. "Who is she?"

My jaw ticks. Why does he want to know about her?

"Why do you care?" I ask. "She doesn't matter to you. None of the others did. We both know that."

"You're hiding her."

Irritation floods my veins with ice and fire, the accusation maddening. There's nothing about Ren that I'm hiding. Her tumultuous desires intrigue me. Remind me of my first, in a way.

I'm not protecting her. I only want her death.

The prick probably wants to help her. He thinks his methods are better than mine. More *humane.*

He can find plenty of others to profit off of, but not *my* little corpse.

"What's her name?" Brody asks.

"My. Little. Corpse," I say, growling out each word with punctuation, emphasizing that she's *mine*, and mine alone.

Brody mutters something about how I'm a sociopath. I ignore him. He didn't try to stop me with my first, second, or third. He has no reason to care now.

"I am a client. You are the seller," I continue. "You can

pretend like I'm helping someone terminally ill if it makes you feel better; I don't give a fuck. But you *will* give me the barbiturates like the good doctor that you are, or you can force me to use a different contact in your industry. An untrustworthy source," I tease. "Take your pick."

The audio crackles, irritation simmering on the other side of the line.

"I won't be in town for another six months. I'm out of the country," he says.

"Ship it," I command. "Find another contact here to deliver the goods for you. I don't care. Six months is too long, and if you don't want to help her, then I will have no choice but to take matters into my own hands."

"I can't tell you what to do," he says, raising his voice like he has power. "Nothing I say or do is going to change anything. But we both know that if you want barbiturates, *I'm* your best bet. And if you want it, you'll wait." He shifts, the phone scratching with static. "I've got six more months at the hospital here. I can't leave any sooner."

"Don't forget what you did for me."

The connection between us is invisible but tangible, the history clutching onto us like a spider's web. I've never let him forget that we both benefited from her death and that he *never* turned me in. Even when he found out about the second and the third, he kept my secrets, and with that knowledge, they became his secrets too.

He's as bad as I am.

"Make it happen," I say. "Two months."

I hang up.

In two months, he'll give me those drugs. Ren's birthday is in three months, give or take. Which gives me enough time to play with my morbid little toy before I discard it.

Chapter 11

Ren

The text arrives midday without any context or explanation. I know it's him. No matter what I do, I can't stop thinking about it. Maybe it's my sore arm—the birth control must be working—or the fact that he admitted, *or lied*, about being a killer. He invades my mind and penetrates every thought.

The minutes count down, racing toward his demand.

Come to the crematory at midnight, the text reads.

I stare at the phone's screen and avoid him at work, staying in the crematory for lunch and my break. It doesn't give me clarity though. In fact, it stirs tension inside of me like a stormy ocean.

Midnight comes. I practically run to him, telling myself that I'm only doing what he says because I'm afraid of the alternative. That I'm scared for the other potential victims. That I want to help them.

The truth is I'm desperate for his attention. His approval. His desire.

If life is one big game to Blaze, maybe it is a game to me too. He likes killing women, and I want to be tortured until I die. Why *not* do this?

What's stopping me?

I unlock the front entrance of Last Spring Mortuary, then slip inside, leaving the funeral home dark. It's better this way. You never know if another staff member will unexpectedly show up.

Like Blaze.

"Hello, little corpse," a deep male voice says from behind me.

I spin around. Blaze emerges from the shadows, dressed completely in black. He takes my hand and pulls me toward the crematory. My fingers buzz, and nerves flutter in my stomach.

Inside of the crematory, a dim candle flickers in the corner. The flame dances over his skin, his cheeks even starker than before, as if he's sunken in on himself. Dead already. Evil.

And somehow, I feel myself going toward him. Yearning to embrace that darkness.

His shoulder brushes me as he passes. He stretches into the chair on the opposite side of the crematory, slinking into the seat like he's in charge. Comfortable. Taking up my space.

I don't know what to make of this, so I go to the screen next to the retort. The oven is off and has been cooled down for hours, but I still check the dials like I'm working. Give myself something to do. At least this way, I don't have to question why my skin heats whenever he's near. Why my body tingles, anticipating his next move.

His hand comes into my vision and pushes something forward.

A glass flute in my hand, filled with a bubbly liquid, the drink light pink in the shadows.

He's giving me champagne?

I raise a brow. "What are we celebrating?"

"Our arrangement."

I flinch my head slightly. Does that mean he wants to kill me tonight?

"Think of it as practice," he adds.

I take a sip. The bubbles pop on my tongue, and a sudden dizziness fills me up. Champagne always gets me drunk faster than other alcohols. I grip my purse, the canvas bag and the noose inside of it. Waiting for me.

For *us*.

"Why do you wear a bag over your head when you touch yourself?" he asks.

My cheeks boil. It's like he can read my every move, even when I hold my purse against me for comfort. I quickly find the other seat in the room, sitting across from him. He knows everything about me, doesn't he? At least, it feels like that. I should hate it, but the fact that he knows so much thrills me. He doesn't think of me as a freak; I simply am what I am, and he wants to understand me.

I roll my eyes. "None of your business."

"Are you ashamed of yourself?" he asks.

I jut my chin forward. In a way, I am. It's protective. If I can't see anyone else, then they can't see me either, and I don't have to endure their dismissal of my existence. I don't have to acknowledge the video proof from my past that spread like wildfire, proving that I wasn't the normal person I claimed to be. That I've always been *this*.

"I've always done it," I say. It's partially true. Since I dropped out of the doctorate program, it's one of the things that has helped me come. "It calms me, I guess. If I can't see what's going to happen, then I can forget."

"Forget that you're being brought to the executioner's block," he says.

Our eyes meet, his piercing blue irises like an icicle ready to impale me. It's not lost on me: Blaze *is* my executioner. What we're doing—me eventually teaching him to use the retorts and him fucking me until I'm comfortable coming for him while I die—it's like being blindfolded. The way blinders calm a horse as it races to the finish line.

"When I kill you, you won't have a bag over your head," he says, looking down his nose at me. "I want to see your face when you die for me."

My insides twist, the heat lowering to my core. It's fucked up—so *completely* fucked up—and I can't stop myself from enjoying it. From wanting more.

I want to see his face when I die too.

"How do you dream of dying?" he asks.

I flick my thumbs over the tattoos on the top of each hand. As long as my neck didn't break, a noose would make those last minutes count. I would be *forced* to feel something. The will to fight. To resist.

That answer seems too private.

"I didn't know this was an interview," I mock.

"It'll make your death more fun for me," he drawls.

I cock my head to the side. The blinds over the window are open, and the parking lot beyond the glass is empty. Any car that drives past will have no idea that we're in here.

"A gun," I say.

"There's no art in a gunshot, love," he says.

I widen my eyes, facing him. "It's instantaneous," I argue. "You can't fight it. A gun to my head while I'm being fucked? That's something. It's—"

"Why do you want to die?" he asks, cutting me off. His tone is matter-of-fact, as if he's asking why the sky is blue.

I finish the champagne, my stomach grumbling in response.

I should stop now.

He hands me another glass. I down that too. I don't answer his question; I don't owe him an answer. Instead, I unlock the door of the retort. The oven's cavern is empty, scattered with dust flecks from the previous bodies. There's no way you can truly clean an oven like that. It doesn't matter what you do; we always leave a part of ourselves behind.

"Because life is meaningless," I finally mutter.

"Why is *your* life meaningless?"

My throat swells, my temple pulsing. Why does he keep asking me questions? It's not like he actually wants to know.

"Why do you like killing women?" I snort.

He pauses, then spreads his legs, relaxing into his thoughts. His fingers rub at the bottom of his jaw as if he's actually considering the question.

"Possession," he says.

The word sends a shiver down my spine. It's authoritative. Like he knows that he owns me.

"You want to possess them?" I ask hesitantly. *You want to possess me?*

"No one else gets to kill them. Only me," he says.

67

Only me.

The way he phrases it is almost like he's claiming someone's virginity or a person's hand in marriage. In reality, he's claiming someone's freedom so wholeheartedly that they won't be able to decide anything ever again.

There *is* power in that.

Eternal Hope flashes through my mind. The blank walls. The generic pictures of flowers. The babbling electric fountain. There's an emptiness in the medical spa that is both familiar and distant.

Blaze isn't like that. Whatever this is, it's deeper than a doctor and a patient. He's not just caring for my life. He'll be caring for my death too, in whatever way *he* thinks is best.

"It's sexual, isn't it?" I ask.

"Did you read that online?"

"Possession *is* sexual."

"Everything is sexual when it comes to power, love. Control. Manipulation. Fear. That's why you come here night after night, imagining someone who wants you enough to kill you. Someone who doesn't care if you live or die. Someone who only wants to use your holes like you're an inanimate object."

My cheeks redden. He's not…*wrong.*

It's more than that though. My fantasy continues *after* me. Whoever he is—whether it's Blaze or another faceless man—he never stops fucking me after I'm dead. Not even when my body is scraps of decaying meat. He finds me *useful.* Pleasurable. There's value in my corpse.

Even in death, I'm worthy.

"Have you ever watched someone die?" Blaze asks, interrupting my thoughts. A misty expression takes hold of him, like he's imagining a paradise where he rules over his corpses. "There's a look on their face in the exact moments before they're gone, where they know—without a doubt—that *this is the end.* It might be milliseconds, but everyone gets it, even when it's a shock to them." His eyes narrow, his focus aimed off in the distance. "There's another layer to someone who's being killed though. Dread. The extreme emotion. The will to live soaring like lightning cracking across the sky, like fire whipping through dry leaves. It's the most exquisite expression of free will."

His pants twitch, his cock jerking against the fabric. His arousal is obvious. *Potent.*

Heat flushes through my body. Death like that is sexual to me too.

"Then why kill someone who wants to die?" I ask.

He smirks, knowing what I'm actually asking: *Why me?* Why kill a person who would rather be dead anyway? Why does murdering a person who doesn't care if they live or die appeal to him?

"I imagine there's another layer to someone who wants to die," he says with a smile. "You want to know why I chose you, Ren? Because you're *special.*"

I roll my eyes. "Now you're just being a dick."

"The fact that you want death makes it easier for me to perfect my methods."

His methods. Body disposal. Torture. It doesn't matter what he means by that; it's *there,* lingering between us like ocean spray.

I tilt my head. "You're not telling the whole truth."

"I never promised that I would."

He pours another glass of champagne into my flute. I suck it down.

He pours another.

"You told me you've killed women," I say between glasses. "And you act like I should be grateful for what you're doing for me. But you're a coward, aren't you? You tell me I'm afraid, but you, Blaze, are *afraid* of getting caught. You need to 'perfect your methods' because you know you're not smart enough to do it better each time."

This time, I'm the one grinning. It's insane to be taunting a killer like him. To be honest, I don't believe that he's an actual killer. He may be crazy, but I'm crazy too. And until he finishes the job, I *won't* believe him.

"You're scared of prison, aren't you?" I cackle. "You just want your next kill to be easy."

His smile drops. I've hit a nerve. I don't care though. I don't care about the lies. About pretending. About being someone respectable. About being what my grandmother wants me to be. I don't care about any of that when I'm with him.

We both simply *are*.

"Fear exists in every corner of our imagination, love," he says, his voice low and measured. "It takes a fucked-up soul to actually face that existence and know that one day, it'll consume us all. Just like it's already consumed you."

He stands, coming toward me. He puts his hand under the glass and brings it toward my mouth.

The room spins around me. I drink it all. Finishing it like he wants me to. Is this glass number three? Or four? Champagne gets me drunk easily.

This feels different though. Too easy. Like he put something else in my drink.

Is he going to kill me tonight?

Or is this the 'practicing', like he promised?

"Did you drug me?" I ask.

"You fear not being good enough," he says, ignoring my question. He cups my face, taking me in his palms like a snail with a crushed shell. "Don't worry, little corpse. I already know everything about you. I already know how low you really are, and you're exactly what I want. I'm going to take your existence and give it meaning. You are nothing but a pleasure toy for me to fuck and kill, and when I'm done with you, that's all you'll be. That brings you comfort, doesn't it, love?"

My cheeks heat, every part of my body tingling, tension surging to the points where his hands cup my face. My body reacts every time we touch. It's been ages since I had a sexual or romantic relationship with anyone, and part of my attraction to him is that primal need for attention. For someone who actually wants me. To know what it's like to feel *anything* again.

And yet, there's something else inside of his words too. A swelling pain that eventually feels good. A sensation that numbs you. A raw hunger that scoops up my organs and flesh and muscles and every soft thing about me and makes me *his*. Hard. Unrelenting. Inanimate.

There is no such thing as failure when you don't have shame. Only existence. *Nothingness.* It gives me the safety of being. Of not thinking anymore.

"Drink," Blaze orders, his eyes fixated on me, looking down into the depths of my soul.

And I do. Every last drop.

The room swirls in shadows of gray and black. My mind buzzes. Tries to make sense of it.

This is all part of his game. My game.

Or is it?

Is Blaze really a killer, or is he saying that to mess with me?

What if he's worse than a killer? What if I'm making all of this up in my head?

What if he doesn't kill me, and I have to live with myself after this is over?

Is he just trying to humiliate me?

I need something—anything *real*—to grasp onto. Like a weapon. A gun.

"Let's go to your house," I slur.

"You think you're safer there? As if seeing my home means that you're truly worthy?" he asks. "You don't want to get burned alive tonight; is that it?"

I shake my head, a smile forming on my lips. It seems silly when he puts it like that. Like I'm causing a slight inconvenience for him.

"Open it up," I say, nodding toward the retort's control panel. "I'll give you my password. Your only lesson in body disposal. First —" My head droops to the side, full of drink, or… whatever this is. Lust, maybe. *Need.* Or is it drugs? "First, I want to see your house."

He stares at me for a moment, his jaw tight.

"Why do you want to see my home so badly?" he asks.

For a second, I think about lying. A story that sounds believable.

I opt for the truth. Even if I don't know if he's being honest with me, I don't have any reason to lie to him. Not when he can see right through me.

"A gun," I say. "You have a gun, right?"

"I do."

"I want it."

"You want to shoot yourself, love?"

I shrug. There's an appeal to it. You put pressure on the trigger, then it's over. You don't have to question it because the chances of living are so slim, they're negligible.

He claims that he'll give me what I want. But those are just words, and words won't kill you.

Maybe I want that guarantee that this will be over before I turn twenty-six.

"You want me to shoot you?" he asks.

I lift my shoulders. The final state of my corpse doesn't matter. I simply want it to be over, and I want to enjoy it.

"I want to make myself clear," he says, his countenance darkening. "The only person who gets to take your life is *me*. And like I said before, there's no art in a gunshot. I won't waste your final moments with a bullet."

This time, I laugh hard. He thinks he's better than me because he won't use a gun to kill me?

He's crazy.

"It's hardly 'art' to let me burn alive in an industrial-sized oven that you can't even see inside of," I say, mocking him. "Where's your big talk, Mr. Killer? Was this your plan tonight? To burn me alive and be done with it? To hope that you can hear my screams? Where's your talk of torture when your only method is to burn your victims alive in a funeral home?"

He laughs, but everything about the sound is forced. Menacing. Pleasureless. My skin crawls, and as I meet his eyes, he licks his lips, staring at my mouth.

"You're right. I'm not finished with you yet, little corpse. I so rarely make my victims die this soon. I'd rather play with my toys." He leans forward, bringing us eye-to-eye. "Are you feeling it yet?"

My vision fills with dots, each black spot trickling upward like the bubbles in the champagne.

"Think of this intoxication as practice for when you're dead.

Drinking until you're unconscious. A body without thoughts," he says.

Fear flickers through me, but I'm already gone. It's like my head has disconnected from my body, floating like a balloon. I don't know up from down; my control is spiraling, lost in the darkness.

Blaze clutches my arms, keeping me together. Holding me down.

"Now," he says in a low voice. "Spread your fucking legs for me."

Chapter 12

Blaze

Her mouth hangs open, her cheeks redder by the second. I play with that silence. Simmer in it. Basking in the fact that she craves this as much as she tries to deny it.

I keep myself still while her knees quiver in anticipation. Waiting for me.

This power she gives me? It's invigorating.

"S-spread my legs?" she stammers.

I come forward. Grab her knees. Push them apart. She gasps, my touch electrifying.

"Drink," I order, an evil grin on my face. The drink is a passive aphrodisiac; it'll prime her for me, make her feel *like* she's losing control, when it's just champagne.

We both know she wants it to be more. She *wants* me to drug her.

She downs the rest of the glass.

"Last time, you gave yourself away before I even touched you," I say. "I indulged in your fantasy, knowing that you wanted to play dead. This time? It's more than that. I need to know you, Ren: what makes you tick, what makes you"—I lick my lips, the taste of her desire practically dripping over my tongue already—"*hunger* for more. I need to know everything about you."

Her fingers dance across her leggings, searching for clues

about what to do next. Gray fabric. A white shirt. A matching gray hoodie. She's already dressing in the colors of a corpse.

"You knew," she whispers. "You knew I liked pretending to be dead. Even before that."

I smile. "Before what, love?"

"Before you—" she stops, unable to decide how to frame it this time, now that her truth is out there. "Before you had me."

Had her. Like an object.

Amusement rises inside of me, threatening to bubble out in maniacal laughter. Of course I fucking knew. She's so stuck in her own head that she hasn't caught me following her around. Hasn't noticed her missing hair. Ren is so far gone that she suffocates herself in her own little world.

"Will you kill me, then?" she whispers.

Her glassy eyes are enraptured, hunting for details. She wants to know every gory little aspect of her future death. To get off on it.

My kind of woman.

"I drugged you," I tease in a guttural voice. I tilt my head toward her empty flute. In reality, if I wanted to make her unconscious, she would *know*. There's more fun in a victim knowing exactly the kind of fucked-up things you have in store for them. It's a manipulation tactic, using honesty as a means to control the other.

But with Ren, I can play pretend.

"In seconds, you'll be gone," I murmur, continuing our dirty talk. "And it'll feel so good, won't it, love?"

I pull her up to her feet until our bodies are pressed against one another, the heat of our skin melding us, bringing us closer. Showing us that we're made of the same exact materials.

I tilt her chin until she's gazing blankly into my eyes. She doesn't see me. She sees her final hours. Her salvation.

My balls contract, desire filling my cock with blood.

I am her salvation.

"You're just a body now," I say. "No mind. No soul. Not even a fucking heartbeat. And I'm going to use your cunt." I growl, then bring my mouth to her ear. "The only reason you exist right now is to please me, Ren."

"I—" she slurs, but it's hard for her to keep her words and thoughts straight now. The bitch is too drunk to keep herself together. "We can't—"

I pinch her chin, then lick the side of her face. The salt on her skin. The sweetness of her moans. She melts into my touch, at the fact that I'm treating her like a toy.

She's such a deviant little slut.

"Be a good little dead girl and shut the fuck up for me," I murmur.

A shiver runs down her spine. I hoist her up, forcing her to straddle me as I carry her through the dark building. In the showroom, I lay her down in an open casket and marvel at the thud of her body weight, the casket wheezing into the bier. I pull off her hoodie. Her eyes close. There's a smile there, like she knows exactly what's coming, like she welcomes it.

Tonight, her hair is shiny, as if she took a shower for me. Anticipating what I'd do to her. Perhaps doing it for her final night. The little corpse wants to look good in her final hours. It's entertaining.

I run a hand down her dull, sand-colored arm. She's nothing like the typical blonds I've destroyed. The big tits. Tanned skin. No—Ren is different. But that's not what makes her so fucking right. Why I can't stop myself from what I'm going to do next.

It's the fact that we both know that she got ready for me. For herself. For *this*. That she craves this as much as I do. Displayed like this, a nearly unconscious body inside of a casket, she looks like an offering. A sacrifice. A human doll for me to use.

My dick hardens, my mouth wet, every nerve ending alive with the need to control her. To conquer her until she's nothing more than a handful of pebbles.

I yank down her leggings and underwear, clear to her ankles. Ren hisses, and I slap her pussy. Her eyes widen, pools of darkness calling to me. I inhale in her arousal, her sour smell, tasting it on the back of my tongue like salt skirting over the skin of a fruit. She cries out.

"Dead girls don't talk," I howl.

She whimpers. Her legs spread, and I roll my neck in blatant satisfaction. *Fuck*, she's exactly what I want right now. A cunt. A willing slut. A bag of meat for me to destroy. To take everything I have and to open her legs for me willingly.

"This is something different, even for me, love," I say, lowering my voice. "Tonight, we discuss *your* preferred method of reaching orgasm. Next time?" I smirk. "Next time, it's *mine*. And trust me, cunt, you will scream for me."

She moans, forgetting my warning. I don't care. Each noise buzzes with power inside of me. I explore her wet folds, her meaty pussy thick in my fingers, giving me exactly what I need. She's damp with sweat. Arousal. The freshly trimmed pussy hair tickling my fingertips. Her scent wafts between us. Musk. Sweat. Smoke. The faintest hint of sharpness.

"What makes my little corpse react so *well?*" I hum as I tease her sopping slit with my fingertip. She twitches against me, eager for more. Such a willing little cunt. I skim my finger upward, under her shirt, painting her with arousal, my touch leisurely as I near the bells of her breasts. She sucks in air, bracing herself for what comes next.

"Is it your breasts?" I graze her nipples with my palm, the little peaks rising for me. "Your pussy?" Without warning, I dig two harsh fingers into her cunt and curl my fingers until her knees shake, her pussy gripping me like a fucking vise. She jerks forward in surprise. Still, she doesn't tell me to stop. "What makes you *come*, slut?"

"I—" she stammers. I rub the sensitive flesh inside of her, molten and sloppy, her eyes rolling into the back of her skull.

"Too empty-headed to talk?" I tease. I ease my fingers out of her. Her hips roll forward, so eager for more. My cock strains against my pants, aching to answer her call. To fill her up. "You know what you want. I've seen you do it here plenty of times, love." She bites her bottom lip, still humping my fingers, then she whimpers, admitting that gyrating against my hand is not as satisfying as when I take what I want. I chuckle. "What? Were you too carried away to notice me watching you in the corners of the mortuary?"

"I—"

"Too fucking gone to sense my knife inches from your neck?"

"Blaze—"

"To see me plotting this very moment?"

I lick my lips, then slant down. Her breath coats my chin in hot bursts.

"I don't—" she tries. I wait, giving her a chance to answer. Her cheeks redden. I angle slightly away, studying her. Her entire body is flushed with arousal. My dick twitches; it's hungry for more, hungry to spill her blood.

She turns to the side and avoids me. Irritation floods me like ice water. I crack my neck, containing myself.

She *will* give me what I want.

"You want so badly to give everything up," I say, a hint of frustration evident in my tone. "And yet, you let this one thing stand in the way of our arrangement: what makes you come. Which do you want, little corpse? The freedom of death, of getting that final orgasm that you want, or to drown yourself in these ideas of what the rest of the world thinks is right?" I click my tongue, my jaw clenching. I pull back my fingers, my hands dangling at my side. Judging her with narrowed eyes. "Are you embarrassed by what I think of you, little corpse? Surely, you'd never let a concern like *that* get in between what we both want." I get in her face, this time breathing on her, forcing her to feel my heat. Arousal and fear mix in her eyes. "Now answer me: *what makes you come?* Because I intend to kill you while you come."

Her lips move. Her answer isn't audible.

"Answer me," I growl.

"I don't know!" she yells. She tosses frantically, her head twisting like a serpent swimming across a lake. Finally, she meets my eyes, those dark brown gems glistening with tears. "It's been a long time since I've been with someone else. I honestly don't know! I only know what works when I'm by myself. It can't be nice. It has to be rough," she rambles. "Otherwise, I don't feel anything. It has to be like I don't matter. Like it's unforgiving! So that I don't have to think—"

Unforgiving.

The word hangs in the forefront of my mind, even as she continues to explain. It has a certain flavor to it. Bitter, like regret and petulance. Like she needs to be punished for the things she knows she's done wrong in her life. The shame. An escape from her own reality.

It almost disgusts me that she thinks these things matter.

The saltwater in her eyes builds, fueling me. My dick throbs, so damn eager for her warmth, I can hardly contain myself now. Whether it's blood, come, or tears. I want her heat.

For now, I can play with that shame.

Her attention falls to the side, once again unwilling to endure me. I unzip my pants, letting them fall just enough for me to access my cock. I pull it out, letting the heavy length slap down to the side.

I mount the bier, using my body weight to pin her in place.

"You know what *I* enjoy, love?" I ask. I grab my dick and place it against her wet slit. Her pussy hairs tickle the head of my dick like fingernails scraping along my neck, and the bitch writhes against me, the drink in her system giving her the courage to do exactly what she wants. "I crave women's tears." I tease in an inch, and she moans underneath me. Thrusting herself against me like an animal. Madness fills my skull. Fire swallowing me up like a sinking ship.

"This isn't about what I want tonight though, is it?" I chuckle, the sound low and deep. Goosebumps rise over her flesh, and I lick her ear. "It's about you and your greedy cunt. How fucking needy you are. How desperate you are for someone to take what they want from you."

"Please, I—"

I thrust inside of her as I slap my hand over her mouth and nose, cutting off her air. I use my dick like a knife to gut her from the inside out, and she's so wet that she takes every inch. Compliant. Giving herself to me.

Her eyes widen, and she pulls at my hands, anxious for air.

Her legs spread wider, willing me to take more of her. To stab her repeatedly with my cock. To end her fucking life. I move my hips slowly. Teasing it out of her. Knowing that she's losing the last bits of oxygen. Soon, she'll pass out.

She writhes, her eyes rolling to the back of her head, the whites exposed, and *that's* when I thrust even harder inside of her, using her body as a vessel. She's a passed-out cunt. A fucking hole. I force her over to that other side and bask in the unconscious state of her body, using her pussy like a whetstone, honing the blade of my cock until it's fatal. I'm close—so fucking close, it hurts—but I give her back her breath, anchoring my hands against her breasts, twisting her nipples, willing her to wake up. She gasps, and I dig my fingers into her flesh.

Tonight isn't about me. It's about learning *her*.

"So fucking pathetic," I growl, my words vibrating against her neck. "I promise you this, little corpse: I may have asked you what makes you come, but don't for a single second think that it's because I care about your pleasure, about fairness. I don't." A guttural groan rips through me, matching my thrusts. "I'm going to take what I want. And what I want right now is to learn exactly what makes you come so that you die right as you hit that peak. You hear me, you little bitch? You're going to come and die for me like the whore you are."

"Please!" she cries.

I remove my cock, then prop myself up on one elbow, dipping my fingers into her gushing hole. I lube up my long digits, taking my time. She pants. So fucking impatient, my head spins.

Then I massage her back hole. The ridges pucker and flex against me, knowing what comes next. I ease a finger inside, and those rings of muscles cling to me, begging for more sensation.

"No..." Ren whines as her ass presses deeper against me, pushing her body onto my fingers. As much as she tries to deny it, she wants more. *Needs it.* "Please. I don't—"

I remove my fingers violently. Glare down at her. Forcing her to accept what she just asked me to do.

Her mouth gapes with need. I let the silence eat away at her.

"Do you need me to teach you your place again?" I ask. "You

exist for me to take." I slap her face, humiliating her like a child, her juices marking her cheek. "And if I want to fuck your tight little ass simply because *you don't want me to*, then I'm going to do it."

Her lips tremble, her mouth open and waiting, her tongue noiseless. I skim my fingertips over her asshole again.

It's drenched. Her arousal is seeping out of her cunt. There's enough to coat her ass *and* to lube my own dick.

I press the slick head of my cock against her back hole. Ren shakes her head, her lips stammering.

"Blaze, please—"

It's unforgiving, she had said. *Like I don't matter. So that I don't have to think—*

My head is dizzy with lust. She has no idea what lies ahead of her.

Her asshole puckers against the head of my cock. Tight. Wet and willing. But unprepared.

She might be an anal virgin.

My chest expands. "You're barely ready," I say, condescension dripping in my tone. "Poor little thing."

She thrashes back and forth. So scared. Her lungs swelling with fear.

"Please," she cries. "Please don't do this."

"Dead girls don't get choices," I murmur.

I force myself inside of her. Her ass is like a glove, and I gasp for air, relishing in that painful constriction. She sobs, so frantic for it to stop, so needy for me to take everything I want from her. I don't care. I thrust in again, deeper this time, claiming her ass like I'm stabbing her with a knife. I grab her chin and force her to look at me. To witness this. To see exactly what she asked for. To experience every sensation of what I can do to her, even as she claims she doesn't want it. I move my hips the barest amount and glare deep into those plain brown eyes, and she wiggles against me, spreading herself, taking me deeper. Shoving her ass onto my dick. The tears pool on her skin, painting her in a glossy shadow.

And she moans.

I bite into her neck, growling into her, and she shudders

against me. My dick carves out her ass, forces her to take me until she relaxes. It doesn't take long. She wants it; the little bitch knows it too. Her legs and arms sew around me like a cocoon, nearing that peak. I press my lips to her ear.

"Come for me," I command.

Her cries rip from her lungs, and I grab her throat, choking her, teaching her to associate her peak of pleasure with the loss of oxygen. She twists, her skin rubbing against my palm with the finest friction, and I savor the pain like it's the last thing she'll ever give me. And when her eyes roll back from the ecstasy, I dig my fingers deeper into the muscles of her neck, forcing her to choke while she comes for me.

The pleasure ceases; I keep squeezing. Keep choking her.

Her eyes roll to white, and her body loosens. I let go, giving her air again; I don't stop fucking her. I use her body. She doesn't *take* my cock right now, because there's nothing *willing* about her. She's a toy. Inanimate. A used up carcass.

She comes back, coughing. I keep moving my hips, my dick sliding inside of her, against that smooth oasis of her ass, and she cries like a lost little lamb.

My dick twitches, and I groan, nearing that peak myself. Damn near pushed over the edge hearing her cry like that. That sound that shows me *it hurts*, truly fucking hurts, and that she wants it even more. She whimpers in that absolutely mournful way, and my dick pulses, and I can't take it anymore. Each spurt of my come fills her ass.

I pull out as soon as I'm done, my dick still hard at my side, and I curl two long fingers—dry ones, the ones that aren't wet from teasing her ass—and I carve a cavern back into the spot in her pussy, where she craves unrelenting pleasure.

She shakes her head. "I can't. It's too much!"

I rub that tenderness inside of her, forcing her over the edge. Her muscles contract.

"Come for me, you little bitch," I growl.

"Please, please, please—" she begs. Her body begins to twist, ready to convulse for me.

"What, cunt?" I bellow. I don't stop my fingers. I keep thrusting. Keep jamming my fingers into her sensitive flesh. "Make it stop? Is that what you want?"

"No. I—"

"You're already in a casket," I shout. "Beg me to kill you."

"Please," she rasps in a hoarse voice. "Kill me—"

And her body contorts in pleasure and she gasps, her come squirting out of her like a fucking geyser. I clutch her throat again —not enough to knock her out, but enough for her to *feel* it—and she gags, choking on me, twisting and fighting. As my fingers massage her cunt, pressuring her from the inside, she relents, letting me take her throat, melting into me.

The pleasure ceases, and she moans. Tension lifting from her shoulders. Another forced orgasm.

Our breathing settles. I angle myself to the side and lean on one elbow. Her chest steadies, her face glistening with sweat. A hint of a feeling grows inside of me, like the embers of a dying flame.

There's no reason to be proud of her. I'm not. I tell myself that the only thing I'm feeling is pure fucking selfishness in finding whatever this is.

Because Ren is what I need right now. She isn't like my first, but my dick loves gutting her all the same.

I rise from the casket, my boots landing on solid ground again. Ren's shirt is drenched with sweat and come. The air reeks of sex and booze, the champagne oozing out of her pores. She's dripping from both holes.

One day, some asshole will lie in this same casket, and they'll find their eternal sleep on top of our come stains.

The thought makes me smile.

Ren studies me, trying to decipher my amusement. To understand herself too. Her brows relax, signaling that she understands enough. She's not fighting me or what we have anymore. Still, she still looks away and blushes in shame.

Then she faces me again, her eyes full of need. Still so fucking full of the desire to be hated. As if that's the only affection she's ever known.

And maybe it is.

Perhaps her masochism is a coping mechanism. A way to survive. The will to come breaking through the surface of her desire to die. A way to find promise, even as she struggles to stay above water.

I don't know if my assumptions are correct, nor do I care. Only two things are certain: we all die, and Ren will die *for me*.

I zip up my pants, then offer her my hand. She stares at my empty palm, a question in her eyes, as if she knows there's another deal we're making. As if she's afraid of shaking hands with the devil.

Eventually, she takes my hand, using my stability to help find her balance. For the first time since I laid her in the casket, we stand on equal footing. After pulling up her leggings, she zips her hoodie up over her wet shirt. The cotton jacket is loose, swallowing her whole, and she seems so fragile like that. Like the world could devour her in a single bite.

I won't let the world conquer her like that. I'll be the one to consume her entire world.

"You're not a very good corpse," I say with a dull expression. Anger flicks through her eyes at the insult, and with that, a smirk prickles my lips.

"And you're not a very good killer," she snaps.

I grab her by the throat and shove her against the wall, a rack of caskets rattling next to us. I tease her neck with my fingers, knowing that soon she'll yearn for my fingers around her throat, just to know that I can make her come. That I own her every orgasm until her dying breath.

"I've killed three," I say. "You will be my fourth. And when you take your last breath, you are going to wish you could use it to thank me for giving your cunt meaning."

She blinks, her eyes glossy again, and it's obvious we *both* want to go at it again just from those words. Ren probably has no idea that she's a physical *and* emotional masochist, nor that I absorb more power over her in every single fucked-up thing we do. Call me her sadist. A hedonist. A deranged killer. All of it applies, and yet none of it holds any weight.

In the end, we both have a use for each other.

I let go of her neck, then wipe my hands on my shirt dismissively.

"Your shift starts in eight hours," I say. I check my phone. "Make that six."

She holds her neck. The purple and red ovals are vibrant on her skin, even in the shadows.

"Six hours?" she whispers.

I point back to the casket and lick my teeth.

"Sleep it off. That's what you usually do, isn't it?" I say. "Drive home when you're sober and use your grandmother's makeup to hide the evidence."

Ren stays in place, unsure of herself. I shake my head with annoyance at her hesitation. Why does she care about sleeping at work when she knows she's going to die soon anyway?

I angle her back toward the casket. It must be wet with our fluids now. She climbs in, her eyelids heavy with exhaustion and drink. I push down her shoulders until she rests in the comfort of the casket again, and her eyes close. She'll fall asleep soon. The good little cunt. I don't need to stick around to confirm it.

It's pathetic how wrapped up she is in my words. How desperate she is to do whatever I say, even if that means taking her ass when she begs me not to. I can't decide if I hate it or if I enjoy it.

I know I enjoy manipulating her. I don't have to lock her in a shipping container to know that her death is mine. I can leave her here, free to run away, to do whatever she wants, and she'll still be my next corpse. There's power in that, though a part of me wonders who holds the reins.

Perhaps that's why I want to kill her. She's not my usual sort. She's different.

I won't kill her yet.

I glance in her direction. I should set an alarm on her phone, but I honestly don't care what happens to her at Last Spring. We've already made our arrangement; it's not like she *needs* this job to survive or to pay her grandmother back for her wasted college tuition. As long as I can sneak Ren in after hours, she can teach me to dispose of her body, and I can fuck her until she begs me to end it all.

Her chest moves subtly in a steady rhythm. I arrange her hands and fold them across her stomach like a corpse, chuckling to myself at her resting state. In a way, she's predictable. Moldable. A willing little doll.

What's not predictable is my curiosity surrounding her. Why I insist on keeping her alive.

"Can't kill you if you're dead from drunk driving," I say in a low voice. Then I leave her there, dead asleep.

Chapter 13

Ren

I flip over and bury my face into the pillow. I swat the sides of the narrow bed, searching for a blanket, but all I get are pillows and cushions. A damp scent like body odor and salt fills my nose, and I huff into the bed. It stinks, but I'm too tired to care.

Metal jiggles. A doorknob, maybe. Then the pressure in the room changes, traffic and ocean waves singing into the building. The doors close, and a feminine hum fills the air, a song I'm familiar with and hate because of how annoyingly cheerful it is. My grandmother doesn't sing songs like that.

My eyes widen, anxiety filling my chest like a balloon. I grit my teeth.

Shit.

Denise. That's *Denise* humming.

I'm still in the casket.

Denise sniffs loudly, obviously smelling the same stink: my ejaculation soaking into the coffin. The scent of sex. It's been hours since Blaze left, right? I'm right by the stains, so I should smell our sex.

How can she smell us that far away? Are we *that* potent?

I bite my lip, then lie still, hoping she doesn't see me. Playing dead *for real* in a mortuary for the second time.

I pinch my sides and groan internally. Fuck my life.

Heels clack on the tiles, the taps dissolving into the hallways of the building. I wait, holding my breath. The coffee machine beeps, and frantically, I stumble out of the coffin and trip over my legs. I steady myself—or try to—and the room spins around me. Damn it. That champagne. How much did I drink?

My thighs contract, squeezing together, the thrill of last night throbbing in my core. Arousal pulsing in my cheeks. My neck.

How does he have that much power over me? It's like his ghost is haunting me, even now.

By the time I get home, Mrs. Richmond's car is gone, probably already at the school. There's enough time to wash off, and for once, I can't skip the shower. I dry myself off quickly and tussle my damp hair. I debate whether I should use texture cream or oil to dampen the flyaways, then I see my reflection.

A blue oval. Four little circles, purple and red.

A handprint on my neck.

Blaze *isn't* a ghost. He's there, written in my skin.

I shake those thoughts away and grab old makeup to cover up the bruises. When that doesn't do anything, I dig through Mrs. Richmond's foundation and find something thick. I scrutinize the cover up in the mirror; it looks like I let an amateur apply cosmetics to my embalmed body.

I find a clean hoodie and zip it up. Chalky makeup or not, my bruises aren't visible dressed like this.

Back at the mortuary, the first part of the shift passes in a whirlwind. There aren't any bodies lined up for cremation, which helps when you're running late. So when Denise gets a hospital call, she sends me to do the pickup. I speed to the city. Pick up the corpse. Sling it into the refrigeration unit. A headache lingers on the bridge of my nose, but at least my vision is steady now. I walk briskly to the break room. I *need* coffee. With cream. Lots of sugar. And—

"It smells like piss in here," a male client grumbles from the showroom, his voice carrying down the hallway. I pause, glancing in his direction. An older gentleman pinches his nostrils, his sweater clinging to his bulky chest. A white-haired woman holds his elbow, her dainty fingers wrapped around his upper arm.

My skin heats. He's standing right where Blaze and I had sex last night, where he choked me while I came.

Where I squirted all over him.

Is female ejaculation urine?

My cheeks flush. It's mortifying; it must be obvious that it's me. But for some reason, even with the embarrassment, I can't shove away these feelings. My body races, reaching for those memories. Wanting more. *Needing* it. I wish I could say I blacked out, but my clit throbs, and I can't deny it. Gushing that liquid. The uncontrollable urge to give in to his pleasure. How he took complete control of me.

Is it wrong that I liked it?

"Shh," the older woman says. "This is a funeral home. It's going to smell bad. They can't—"

"It reeks like a gym locker. Like the owner of this building thought an air freshener could hide the stench of a bunch of sweaty—"

I scurry into the break room, out of sight. The coffee pot is cold, still full of this morning's burnt brew. I exhale carefully and concentrate on the task in front of me. Irritation bubbles under my skin, and my neck tingles. Why do I need coffee so badly? It's not like it's going to change what I did.

Or that I liked it.

I breathe as slowly as possible. It's just coffee; I don't have to make *that* the thing that sends me spiraling into a hole of shame. I can do this.

I dump the pot, then start another brew. I scan the refrigerator for cream to make Denise's go-to beans more palatable, but there aren't any cartons. An empty jug lies in the trash can, and I cross my arms over my chest.

It's my luck, isn't it?

I brace myself, holding my breath. This is it. The last straw. The thing I *don't* need right now. The tipping point where I start crying, and then I wonder why I'm even alive anymore if I'm going to cry over not having creamer for my coffee.

That tension never forms. Instead, something else lurks in the background, swimming around my neck, dragging me into its current. I turn to the parking lot window and glaze over the asphalt, trying to figure out what that feeling is. It's not unpleasant; it's warm. Almost like a small creature is burrowing inside of me, urging me to keep searching.

I focus on a black sedan in the farthest parking spot: Blaze's car. He must be on shift right now.

A jolt of electricity runs through me.

He's here. On property.

The hopelessness isn't boiling over. No, it's curiosity. A frenzied seed growing, sprouting from the earth, anxious to see the sun again, to see *him*—

A fist knocks into the doorframe. I startle, a hand on my chest.

"Hey," Denise says. She rests a hand on her hip. There's tightness around her eyes, like she's struggling to be nice when she knows she's too annoyed to be sympathetic.

"Are you doing okay this morning?" she asks.

I bite my lip and nod. How much can I say? Did she see or hear me this morning? What does she know, exactly?

Do I even care if she knows what we did and fires me for it?

"Mrs. Vee is in the refrigeration unit," I say. "I'll get her queued up for this afternoon."

"Good," Denise says, scanning the room. "Have you seen any rats?"

"Rats?" I ask, trying hard to act normal. This is a *normal* conversation. She's asking about rats. That's all. It's not about me, or how she's going to fire me for sleeping at work or for screwing Blaze in a coffin.

Even now, even with the anxiety churning in my stomach, I wouldn't take it back. I liked the way he fucked me too much.

Why did I like it so much?

"You hear those clients talking about the smell?" Denise asks. She sighs, then continues: "Blaze thinks a rat probably peed in one of the caskets. We've never had rats before. Still, I'm having him set traps."

The silence pools between us, and the subtext becomes clear.

She knows the smell has to do with me.

If I get fired for this, I can't work with Blaze. I don't know why that bothers me, but I don't want to screw up our arrangement. I just want to hold on to what I can for now. Because I haven't cried yet today, and—

Screw the coffee. I need to get out.

I keep my head down, scurrying to the crematory. Denise follows me. My face burns, and though there's no one in the retort right now, I twist the dials on the side of the machine to pretend like I'm working.

"Ren?" Denise asks.

Finally, I meet her eyes. I fill myself with a blank expression, crossing my fingers that she can't see the shame or longing locked inside of me. I don't even want to see it myself right now.

Because I know I liked every single moment with Blaze, and now everyone can *smell* it.

"I know you slept here last night," she says slowly, her eyes never leaving mine. "Did something happen with your grandmother again?"

Again? I wring my fists together. Are there cameras I don't know about? Motion detection sensors linked to her phone? Does she know that last night wasn't the first time I've stayed here after hours?

"Maybe you were drinking and... had an accident?" Denise asks.

I don't move. She tilts her head, then straightens.

"You have your reasons," she says sheepishly. "I get that. I can only imagine what it's like to have a grandmother like Donna."

I widen my eyes. "You know my grandmother?"

"Your grandmother came by when you first started working here. She—" Denise shakes her head. "It doesn't matter. But call me next time, okay? It'll be easier if you spend the night at my house. You know how the clients get. I want to avoid any"—she shrugs her shoulders—"*issues* if I can help it. Anyway..." She heads toward the hallway, then gives me that warm, practiced smile. "If you need anything, let me know. If it happens again, I will have to take disciplinary action."

I nod, my heart beating so loudly that it thrums in my ears. Denise leaves me alone, and I'm left with my telltale heart.

My boss knows.

Does she know exactly what happened, or does she just have a feeling?

Blaze thinks a rat probably peed in one of the caskets, she had said.

My stomach flutters with knots. Why would Blaze say that? Did he say that to throw Denise off of our scent—my *literal* scent—or did he say that to tease me, knowing that she'd bring it up and ask me about it? Is he disgusted by me? By the fact that my ejaculation smells *that* potent?

Does he know she saw me here this morning?

Work. That's all I can do right now.

I transfer the hospital corpse from the refrigeration unit to the crematory. The family wants the body cremated as soon as possible; they need closure, I guess. Nobody wants to see a body in decomposition. Unless you're me.

I hoist the body onto the conveyor belt, memories of last night flashing across my vision. *Blaze lying my body down in the casket.* The corpse goes into the chamber. *Blaze's palm reaches up, gripping my throat.* I switch the dials and increase the temperature of the retort. *The blinding light in Blaze's eyes as he forces me to fight for my life and fight to come.*

Does Blaze think I'm crazy? Or does he actually get off on it like I do?

Am I as messed up as a self-proclaimed killer?

We both came, didn't we?

Knuckles wrap on the doorframe. This time, I whip around, ready to attack. Blaze leans to the side, holding a steaming mug of coffee. I blush. He chuckles, wiping a thumb across his dirt-speckled chin, his patronizing attitude shining through the friendliness. I scowl, but my grunt is empty. I don't mean it. Maybe I even like the fact that he's always judging me, because no matter what his final opinion is of me, we're still connected. He still wants to kill me. He won't give up on that.

Unless he's a liar.

This is insane. I shouldn't be questioning whether or not he's a real killer, or even finding comfort in the fact that I can give my life to him.

I turn back to the temperature gauge, pretending like he doesn't affect me. He's an annoyance. A business partner. Someone I made an arrangement with.

It's work.

Chapter 14

Ren

Blaze lifts the cup of coffee in his hands. "Morning to you too," he says.

My shoulders drop, the confusion pushing down on my frame. I don't usher him in, nor do I tell him to leave.

"You brought me coffee?" I ask.

He rolls his eyes. "No." Then he puts the mug in between my hands. Steam rises from the surface. The heat radiates through the ceramic, like the heat of his body warming me from the inside out.

Does this coffee mean Blaze is taking pity on me?

No—he's *mocking* me. Showing me how pathetic I am. That I can't even get my own cup of coffee without his help.

"Thanks for sharing," I say flatly. I ready myself for the burnt aftertaste of our break room's coffee without cream and sugar to cover it up. The hot liquid splashes against my tongue, washing over my taste buds. I raise a brow. It's earthy and sweet, with a hint of acidity. It's black, and somehow, it still tastes good.

I sneer playfully, pretending to accuse him. "Did you drug this?"

"You wish I would," he says.

"It doesn't usually taste this good."

He angles his head toward the break room. "My personal stash. Buy your own beans. It's not hard."

My lips tingle. I didn't *ask* him to get me coffee, nor did I request his secret stash of freshly roasted beans. All I know is that we had sex last night, he choked me to unconsciousness, he made me come multiple times, and now, he's being *nice* to me. Sharing coffee with me. It's weird.

Is he trying to get me to like him?

My skin is on edge, my nerves vibrating with his nearness. He licks his lips, and I remember his tongue on my cheek. Licking me like prey.

If he truly is a killer, then all of his decisions have a hidden motive behind them.

We agreed that he could kill me. That we would have sex in the meantime, too. There's nothing to discuss, but the words come out of me before I can stop them. As if I *want* to talk to this insane man who wants to kill and fuck me.

"You told her the smell was a rat?" I ask.

"I couldn't tell her you came like a burst pipe now, could I?"

My cheeks redden, my teeth grinding. It's like he knows how much it embarrasses me.

"What?" he asks, stepping forward. "Are you ashamed of your pleasure, little corpse?"

I look away from him. "Isn't squirting like pee or something?"

He grabs my chin, pinching me. I meet his eyes, and my body fills with heat.

"Did you enjoy it?" he asks.

He knows how much I enjoyed it. He can probably tell that I'm craving it right now.

I nod, barely enough for him to see it.

"Then who cares?" he asks.

"You called me a rat," I mutter.

"I say that in the most endearing way a predator could call their prey a rat."

My nostrils flare, and he snickers to himself, the smug bastard. I take another sip—damn, it's good coffee—and I put down the mug on the side table next to the control panel.

I tap my foot. Even if he brought me coffee, even if he told me there was nothing to be ashamed of with the pee and the mess of ejaculation, I don't need to put up with this bullshit teasing.

And yet, I don't tell him to go away. I play into his game.

"I'm not a victim if I'm *asking* you to do it," I say dryly.

"I called you 'prey.' You called yourself a 'victim.'"

I scoff, fire building in my cheeks. He's right, and it's irritating. It's like he wants me to know that *I'm* the one who got myself into this situation. Like he's mocking me.

"Why are you such an asshole?" I hiss.

"We are the way we are, Ren. Of all people, you should understand that."

"Try me."

The retort beeps. There's nothing I need to do right now; the alert only means that the retort has reached the desired temperature. I settle my gaze on the dials anyway, focusing on anything to avoid Blaze.

He comes up behind me and takes my mug off of the table, bringing it to his lips, drinking it like it's his own drink. He sets it back down.

The print of his lips stains the rim of the mug. We're sharing a drink. Saliva doesn't stop us. Come, spit, maybe even blood aren't real boundaries anymore. Like we're truly connected somehow. One and the same.

Then it dawns on me: I *do* want to know why he's like this—why he has these urges to kill women. Knowing his past or his "reasons" won't give me any clarity on *my* end of the bargain. Yet my mind reasons that if I know him better, it'll be a hell of a lot more personal than a medical practice where the physicians are required to act like their patients are zoo animals, caged and dependent.

In a way, I'm like that with Blaze. He has me locked in his trap, and I need *him* to get my treat.

Using the medical spa to end my life? It's distant. Detached.

Blaze isn't like that.

"There's a reason you're—" I start, but I don't know how else to put it while we're at work and someone could walk in on our conversation. "There's a reason *why* you're helping me. Why you do the things you do."

He smirks, and I roll my eyes. He loves messing with me, forcing me to refer to his murders like this. At least, the murders he *claims* to have committed. I'm still not convinced.

"Why?" I ask.

"You're asking why I do it?"

I shrug. Neither of us wants to say *that* word aloud. Not right now, anyway. He stares at me for a second, his blue eyes almost grayish-white and analytical, evaluating whether or not to give a real answer.

I'm curious, I guess. Or bored. Maybe I want to understand my killer. As if those answers will give me a clue to myself. Why I'm drawn to the other side of that darkness. A place where I don't come out alive.

I don't say any of that, though.

"Tell me about your first," I say.

He peers out the window and rests his palms on the windowsill. A new group of mourners crosses the parking lot, the stream of black clothing like dark clouds rolling over the beach, warning us of an oncoming hurricane.

When I first started working at Last Spring, groups like that made me jealous. I was young when my mother died, too young to remember her funeral. And even when I was old enough to ask, my grandmother refused to share the details with me. She wouldn't even tell me if she was cremated or buried. So I pictured her as much as I could. Tried to envision her body decaying with dignity.

Now, I'm so used to death that I hardly even notice when a funeral is going on unless I'm on my break in the garden. I'm numb to it, and everything else, really. Whenever I do *feel* things, it's like I lose control. I drown in my own shame and anxiety.

Blaze makes it different though. He sends energy *through* me until I'm feverish. I always yearn for what's coming next.

I give him a dull look. "It's not like I'll tell the police," I say. "You're going to kill me anyway, right?"

Blaze huffs, and this time, I'm the one who snickers. I adjust, getting a better view of his face. Brown dust collects near his temples, lingering from his work outside. A faint smile lingers on his lips.

He knows I'm right.

"Some people love their mothers." His eyes gloss over, a sheen covering them with darkness. "My brother might have loved her once. He was the good one. The one she wanted. The one that eternally connected her to the sonofabitch she once called a husband. Me? I was the fucking parasite that broke them apart. The rodent that shit all over her house. The one from a nameless man I've never met. The child who got sick constantly. Who got kicked out of school. Who caused her trouble when she had better things to do than to take care of a piece of shit like me."

A chill prickles over my skin, creeping across me like growing vines clinging to a rocky cliff. I grab the mug and take another sip, desperate for something to do. Blaze's eyes stay fixated on the window, like it's a portal to his memories.

"She worked at this pizza shop in town. Crappy little place, but the boss sold drugs, and that meant she got a discount on her habit. Plus, his other regulars became her boyfriends. They all got high together." He glares into space, irritation seething in his shoulders. "The thing was that those fuckers had needs. My brother was older, smart enough to stay in his room. I got in the way. Tried to stop one of them from hurting her once. She started locking me in the closet for hours after that and would forget I was there. Until finally, I learned to watch them take her like that. To get *hard* from it."

The back of my throat seizes, a dry tightness that unnerves me. How can that be real? It's unbelievable to think that a mother would lock her own child in a room, probably starving him, until he learned to watch her have sex.

It is believable, though. The most horrible things are usually true. People used to say things like that to me, back when I was in high school: *I can't believe you saw your mother hanging there when you were a toddler. She really killed herself? No way!*

"She made you watch?" I ask.

"And then she let them have me."

I shake my head rapidly, but it's real. I know it is. Blaze scowls, his rage funneled into that furious expression, the veins bulging from his face.

"Make no mistake, Ren. This isn't about justifying what I did. My brother insisted that we did this the right way. All I had to do was wait until he graduated from high school, then he could take care of me. He would take care of it *the right way* if I just waited a few more years."

A sharp breath fills my lungs.

"As you can guess, I didn't wait," he continues. "She held these 'parties,' right? Orgies where they were all blasted out of their minds. When I was fourteen, they all left, and I went to go find her. The cunt was passed out on a lawn chair in the backyard. So drunk that when I kicked her, she didn't even move." He grits his teeth, and my stomach lurches. I cross my arms over my chest. Still, I listen.

"Her legs were spread so fucking wide that I could *smell* her cunt. Smell what they did to her. How they used her like they used me. And this thought hit me." He cocks his chin to the side, and for the first time since he started sharing his story, a hint of amusement sparks his lips. "What if I fucked her? What if *I* was the one who took *her* power for once?" The smile spreads, his teeth exposed like the jaws of a predator. His eyes widen, bloodshot and shocked, suddenly aroused by the memory unfolding inside of him. "She was my biological mother, but I didn't care. She wasn't my protector or my nurturer. She was a cunt who had controlled every part of my life since the day I was conceived. Fucking her was exactly what she deserved."

Footsteps tap down the hallway. A child laughs and a mother whispers, guiding the child to the bathroom. Blaze looks at me, his jaw loose, those innocent sounds a reminder that he never had that sort of carefree past.

"So I fucked her unconscious body," he says. "Treated her like a corpse. It wasn't about the sex, or the lust, or some Freudian bullshit about wanting my mother to care about me for once. It was about forcing *her*. Making her pay. Giving her all the rage in my soul, taking back what she had *stolen* from me. Her warm cunt gave me strength, made me realize *I* was the one in control now. *I* was the one who could do whatever the fuck I wanted, my future be damned. Because what kind of life is worth living if you're getting stepped on by the people who are supposed to love you?"

I try to swallow, but my throat is dry. Blaze's eyes flicker to my neck, settling on my bruises. I gulp instinctively again; I'm not swallowing anything.

People who are supposed to love you.

My grandmother never locked me in a closet. She always made sure I had food to eat, even when she refused to speak to me. And my mother left before I could remember her. Sometimes, I'm angry at my mother for abandoning me like that. Leaving me with a caretaker that she must have *known* was the kind of person who would beat your soul until you had barely enough strength to breathe for yourself.

Sometimes, I can't understand why my mother did it, and sometimes, my mind reminds me that I *do* understand. I wasn't enough to keep her here, and I'm not enough to keep *me* here either.

Blaze turns away again, and I lean forward, examining him. He probably hasn't told many people about his past, and I don't want to interrupt him. Our pasts are so different, and yet his pain seems familiar. I want my grandmother and mother's acceptance, their unconditional love, and I'll *never* get that. Maybe that's how he felt once too.

"She woke up," Blaze continues. "And when she saw it was me, she screamed. Punched me in the nose." He flicks a hand over his face. "I knew that if I was caught, I'd never have a fucking chance. So I covered her mouth and nose until she passed out again. Rendered her unconscious."

I focus on the toes of my flats, processing it. Blaze covered *my* nose and mouth last night. Made me unconscious. When I woke up, he was *still* fucking me. Just like his drunk mother.

Why didn't he kill me too?

Maybe I don't want to know.

Blaze is probably only telling me about this because he knows he's going to kill me. I can understand that. It's part of why I can let go with him. There's nothing holding you back when there's nothing at stake.

"What happened then?" I ask.

"I dragged her into the woods. Adrenaline is a funny thing; you can be high out of your goddamn mind, but your will to survive kicks in, and suddenly you've got the power of a giant." He forces a laugh. "So I stabbed her in the stomach. That did the trick. And as she bleed out, I kept fucking her, and you know what? The bitch came. Came like I was one of those men that she fucked while she was high. She got this look in her eyes after that, almost like she was *relieved*. Like she knew that death was the best thing for her." He taps the window, and an insect flutters off of the pane outside. "She died, and I didn't stop. I used that cunt," he snickers, then scowls to himself. "But I wasn't going to get caught because of her."

The control panel beeps, signaling the next stage of the burn. I scan at the dials and confirm everything is correct, then stare at the back of Blaze's head. Taking the same chair he used last night, he spins it around until it faces the window, then he sits. His thumb traces his chin, deep in thought. The retort hums with fire, and I glance at the metal door, imagining my corpse inside of the oven, the flames devouring my flesh until there's nothing left. I don't imagine his mother could've been incinerated like that.

"What happened to the body?" I ask.

He smirks. He hears it too—my choice of words: 'the body,' *not* 'her body.'

"Buried her in the backyard. When my brother came back from college, all he had to do was look at me, and he knew what happened."

"Did he ever try to turn her into the police like he said he would?"

Blaze shakes his head. "The guilt was too much for him. In his mind, she was good to him. Sometimes, he tried to tell me it wasn't *that* bad. She was nice to him, right? I must've done something to deserve the way she treated me."

Heat flushes through my body. How could his own brother say those things to him? I clench my jaw, my lips flattening. The man was supposed to protect his brother, and instead, he told his brother that he was freaking out over nothing?

You would know if your leg was broken, my grandmother told me once. *You can walk, can't you? Stop feeling sorry for yourself.*

People who are supposed to love you. Protect you.

Blaze stands, still facing the window, his back to me. His fingers tap the windowsill in a steady rhythm, like a heartbeat. I tuck a piece of hair behind my ear.

He jerks around, his bloodshot eyes bulging as he seethes at me.

"You think I'm weak, don't you?" he snaps. "That I'm some fucked up, insecure little boy who needs to kill women to feel good about himself."

I blink rapidly. My lips quiver, fear clawing at my skull, trying to climb out, but I keep it tucked inside of me. I think of the reasons I should be afraid of Blaze. He claims he's a killer. He's choked me unconscious before. And he just told me he killed his own mother.

I'm not scared. Apprehensive, maybe, but this is what I wanted, right? To know the man who is going to kill me. To prove that he isn't clinical.

Blaze is anything *but* clinical.

"I know," he pauses. "You must think I'm a misogynist."

He says it plainly; a statement. His judgment bestowed upon me. My face twitches. Misogynist? Why does that matter? Does he care about what I think?

No, this is a test to see if I'm like everyone else. If I'll blame it on him like his brother did.

"I think you don't trust *anyone*," I say. "Why would you? Your own mother and brother betrayed you." I lift my shoulders. My mother didn't kill herself to hurt me; I was too young for that. In spite of that, it always felt like she must've done it because she didn't care about me. Like I wasn't enough to keep her alive. Like I need to do the exact same too, because if I can't keep my mother happy, then why am I making my grandmother's life miserable? It's not like she wants me around. I'm a burden to her.

"I don't trust anyone either," I say.

Blaze's upper lip twitches, almost curving into a smile. "Not even yourself?"

I look down at my flats. "Especially not me."

"And you're not baffled by my sadism."

I shake my head. I don't know if it has to do with my mother's death or my grandmother's lack of physical affection, but I can't have normal sex. I can't cuddle. I can't let anyone hold me. Even when I was having sex with my ex-fiancé, we *never* touched outside of the bedroom. It's like I couldn't take his touch without imagining my mother's body hanging there. How loose her arms must have been as she swung from the noose.

By the time I was in college, I knew it was an addiction, and that fantasy grew until I started dreaming of a man who would fuck me while he killed me. As if that would make my mother's death make more sense. As if I could finally understand my own impending doom.

Blaze's sadism makes sense to me.

"I don't judge people for what they like," I say. "I know what I like is fucked up. I know I'm a freak."

His eyes sear into me. Studying me. Reading something below the surface that I'm not aware of yet.

"You truly think that," he says slowly.

"Who pretends to be dead? Who wants to get killed while being fucked?" I laugh nervously, my throat thick with shame. "It's not normal."

"I just told you I fucked and killed my own mother, then fucked her corpse."

It's so far away from my own experiences that it's hard to accept it as fact. Or maybe I'm numb to everything in this world, and I'm glad to hear his messed-up story. It's comforting, in a way. We're more alike than I thought.

"You aren't disturbed by me," he says.

"Why would I be?"

He chuckles slightly. "*You* intrigue me, Ren."

My throat tightens, my breath hitching in my throat. His pale eyes hold me, captivating me, keeping me pinned in place. I bite my bottom lip, longing for his mouth, for his hand around my throat.

His tongue flickers across his teeth as he watches me.

"At least I interest someone," I say quietly, playing it off like a self-deprecating joke.

"Do you kill people while you fuck them?" he asks. I stifle a laugh, then shake my head. He grabs my chin, his eyes flickering across mine, making sure that I'm focused on him. "Then you're *not* that fucked up."

He lets go. I rub my face, my skin melting from his touch. It's unnatural how much I want him, even after this. There's no judgment between us, because we're both fucked up.

It's liberating.

"I didn't realize it was a competition," I say, my voice raspy, a hint of flirtation mixed in my tone.

"You want your prize, little corpse?" he asks. "Will that make you happy?"

Happy.

The feeling always eludes me. Happiness is a construct of our society, and yet it's what every person reaches for. Happiness. The ultimate dream. Success. A family. A life partner that will make you feel loved until the day you die.

The word "happy" coming from Blaze—it's like he knows what I'm thinking about.

My fucked up, pleasure-filled death.

His eyes glimmer, like he's holding my own torture in front of me. A reward. A treat for a pet. A trained animal. A rat collared and caged, bound to him.

I don't care if that's all I am to him.

I want to feel *him* come while I die. I want to know that I had something to give before I let go and never think again. I want to feel powerful. *Free.* Even if I only feel it as I'm dying.

Blaze steps closer, the distance narrowing between us. The air in my lungs thins, my pulse increases. His fingertips skim over my hoodie, and even though there's fabric between us, goosebumps flutter across my neck, so in tune with his touch.

There's something about Blaze that's different. Something

that's mesmerizing. Even when I'm at home, I think about death, but I don't only wish for it lately; I wish for Blaze too. I anticipate his next move. I wait for *his* final touch.

I roll my shoulders and peer at the timer on the retort's control panel. I want to pretend like he doesn't have that much power over me. But inside, I know how much I want to surrender to him again.

"You're such an asshole," I whisper.

His fingers dance up my arm and snake past the opening of my hoodie, tickling my neck. My pussy constricts, and the bruises throb with pain. The core of my body heats.

Denise's signature heels clack down the corridor.

"Ren? Have you seen Blaze?" she asks. "We need him in the garden."

Blaze steps back with a wink, then disappears down the hallway. He greets Denise, chatting playfully with her, and he sounds *normal.* Like he's not hiding this screwed-up past. It's confusing, and...intriguing. He doesn't let those memories stop him.

I grab the mug of coffee; the steam is gone now.

I glimpse back at the empty doorway. Denise gives Blaze instructions, like this is any other day.

I touch my neck. Blaze was teasing me, wasn't he? Touching my neck to tease me with the memories of last night, to make me want more.

My fingers find his bruises, the pain snaking through me. As I wait for the body to finish burning, I don't think about my mother hanging in the void. Instead, I wonder how much pressure it would take for Blaze to break my neck.

I fantasize about him asphyxiating me as he submits to his own desire to come for me.

Chapter 15

Blaze

The doorbell rings, a single chime erupting through the house. Without even seeing the unwanted visitor, I know who it is. I curse, then wrap a towel around my waist. The inconvenient fucker.

Brody stands on the porch with his hands in his pockets, checking his sides as if someone's going to report him to the police for simply talking to me. His dirty blond hair is cut short, his eyes as light blue as our mother's, like mine. I'm tall and built; he's average, both in height and weight. He's tan, while I'm pale as snow. Even his blond hair is common; mine is nearly white.

The fucker always comes back to me like a mindless sheep.

"You said it'd be months," I say.

"Figured I'd make my favorite client happy," he says.

Not brother. *Client.*

I motion for him to follow me, then return to the bathroom. Brody slants to the side, taking a peek into my bedroom.

"What's with the leash? You get a pet recently?" he asks.

I angle toward the metal leash on the nightstand. For a moment, I picture Ren wearing it. Her bruised body. Her tear-stained face as she crawls to me. So obedient. Like a fucking dog. Lower than me. A chain around her neck. And with some more conditioning, all it will take is one little tug of the choke chain, and the bitch will come for me.

No, Ren isn't a pet. A pet has a will of its own.

She's my object.

"A side project," I say. I raise an eyebrow. "And?"

Give me the fucking drugs.

Brody sighs, then pulls out two plastic pouches. The first contains a case with several individually wrapped items—thin, plastic wands with caps on the end. The other pouch has the typical orange prescription bottle with a few pills.

"These are like lollipops. Tell her to put them in her cheek," he says, angling his head toward the case with the wands. "There are sixteen hundred micrograms in each, so you shouldn't need many. And these pills?" He nods deeply. "Got them from Canada. She probably only needs one, but you can give her more if you want to be safe."

Safe. Because overdosing on pharmaceuticals is *better* than death by primal violence.

I turn the pouch with the orange container in my hand, reading the label: *Brody Barwick*. He must've gotten some friend in the field to prescribe them. It's funny how *noble* he thinks he is—doing the right thing, getting "medicine" for the people who can't afford it. In reality, he's a glorified drug dealer. People die from his medications, just like they do from street drugs.

"What's her name?" he asks, cutting into my thoughts.

Instinctively, I glance back at the chains. *Her name.* It's an odd question, especially coming from him. A detail he doesn't need. Still, my brain rattles off answers: A dead girl. A rat. My object. My toy. My little corpse.

I could say any of these answers to Brody, and it wouldn't make a difference because it wouldn't give him what he needs.

Ren Kono. That's her name.

Aggravation settles on my shoulders, then drips down to my chest. Does he think he can protect her? That he can save her from me? I crack my neck both ways, leveling myself, forcing the emotions down. Brody isn't better than me, nor is he better than Ren. He's the same as us.

And he doesn't deserve her name.

"Jealous?" I force myself to chuckle, to act as if it doesn't bother me. But the anger seeps into my veins like poison. I ball my fists and stare at him coldly. "Why? Because she's not one of your little patients? Trust me; you'd never be able to help her. Not like I can."

"You need to make sure you know what you're doing," he says, lowering his voice. "Assisted suicide isn't the same thing as murder." I pretend to gag, and he shoots me a glare, then angles his head in the direction of the street. "They have a medical spa on Richard Jackson. Why not send her there?"

It doesn't take a genius to hear the true meaning behind his words: *Why does she need you?*

I grind my teeth. We both know the answer. Ren *doesn't* need me. It's obvious to all of us, even to her. And it's laughable that we both keep clinging to this thin connection between us, like it means something more than two people using each other.

That's all we are: a killer and his prey. We agreed to that.

I study the plastic bags. The cases are light, almost airy. Somehow, my hands sink with their weight. It's all Ren truly needs from me.

And at the same time, she wants the excitement. The *meaning* I can give her.

"I'm helping our fellow civilians just like you, big brother," I smirk. I usher him toward the door, patting his back. "You get money. I get pussy and blood."

"I'll be in town for a few weeks," he says, ignoring my quip. "Staying at my condo in Rosemary Beach."

Rosemary Beach, another expensive getaway for the one-percenters living in the South. Of course he has a condo there. He's too good—too high class—for Panama City Beach.

"Thanks for the invitation," I say. "But for me to miss these little get-togethers of ours, I need the distance. Years, really. I'll call you."

He looks over his shoulder. "Call me if she needs anything."

Not if *I* need anything. If *she* needs anything.

Ice pumps through my veins, my limbs cold and rigid. I don't like that he's taking an interest in her. I narrow my eyes at his fake righteousness.

"Right," I say.

Then I slam the door.

The coolness extends to my fingertips like a flu spreading across a sickly body. Returning to my bedroom, I toss the plastic bags, then pick up the choke chain and leash, the weight satisfying in my palm. There's a tangible nature to Ren's death. She's another insignificant blip on humanity's timeline, like we all are. A way to perfect my technique. She reminds me of my mother—chaos, all immediate presence—and yet, she's different too. She sees herself. Drowns in her shame.

There's no reason to give a shit if Brody takes a personal interest in Ren. I don't pretend to help other people, nor do I act like I'm a superior being that deserves the grace and adoration of my followers. I help *myself.* I know who I am. We're all rats crawling around like vermin on this god-forsaken earth.

Disease. Shit. And *death.*

And thank the fucking dirt under our hands and knees, Ren knows who she is too.

Chapter 16

Blaze

An hour later, I park outside of Ren's picture-perfect home. To anyone else, it seems as if Ren is living with her grandmother to take care of her.

Ren is the one who *thinks* she needs help. Who never moved out. Who tortures herself by living with a grandmother that's way too fucking stubborn and judgmental for a woman in her sixties.

My little devil can get what she wants; she simply hasn't unlocked her true potential. And if she wants sex and death, she knows she can get it from me.

Still sitting in the car, I text her: *Come here.*

Be right there, she immediately responds.

I scroll through my phone, scanning over articles from Blountstown, waiting for news that they've discovered one of the bodies there, but it's a small town full of secrets. Every once in a while, there's a missing persons report, but the journalists would rather promote the seasonal festivals than to remind the citizens that some of their loved ones have disappeared. They can't rub it in, or else the townsfolk will be up in arms. How dare an outsider destroy their sense of safety? They're all just good families living in a small-town, America. They don't deserve something like this.

They don't realize their boogeyman was homegrown, just like they were.

The car hums underneath me. I count the stepping stones spaced out across the lush lawn in front of Ren's house. Then I count them again.

I slam my fists on the steering wheel. She's *making* me wait. The fucking slut.

Where is she?

I honk the horn. It's disrespectful, and somehow, I bet it's the exact kind of thing that would turn Ren on—treating her like she's not worth the effort of walking to the door. Like she's a trained animal that should *come* as soon as I call.

The bitch doesn't come.

Is she doing this on purpose? Making *me* come to *her?*

I power off the engine, irritation simmering in my chest like a hive of bees. I'm not going to her because she made me; I'm going to her *door* because I don't like waiting.

This better be good.

I bang on the front door like a madman, my fists crashing on the wood. Ren opens it, her chin shaking for me to leave. A stout, yellow-haired woman steps in front of her, blocking her exit. The old woman is smaller than me, yet her expression is filled with contempt. As if she's looking down on me.

"You must be Mrs. Richmond," I say.

Her eyes narrow, flickering over me, taking in my black clothes. My pale skin. White hair. She sneers, and I know what this is: I'm an untouchable. Someone who works with dead bodies. I don't *deserve* her granddaughter, even if her granddaughter is just like me.

It's as if Ren's grandmother thinks she's made from different material than *us*.

"I know you work at a funeral home," the grandmother says, turning to Ren. "And I understand that we need those services on the beach. But it's late, Ren. Our neighbors—they have children who go to my school. If they—"

The grandmother goes on a verbal rampage, stomping all over people like me, rubbing in the fact that I've probably woken up half of the neighborhood already. Mrs. Richmond can't have people knowing that her granddaughter is being picked up by a coworker this late at night. What would it do to her reputation?

I lean against the wall of her picturesque house. The grandmother sneers at me briefly. How dare I touch her things!

"He's just taking me to a work function, Mrs. Richmond," Ren says. "It's not like—"

"A work function? This late?"

A work function. As if our arrangement is simply a project we're working on together. Perhaps it is. As Ren explains away our plans for the night, pretending like there's an annual party we're going to, her black hair coats her face like a layer of paint, hiding her shame.

This isn't a new routine for the two of them.

"If you had only finished your doctorate's degree," the grandmother scolds, cutting her off. "Honestly, at this point, I'd even consider letting you work at the school *without* the degree. I don't want to see you waste your life away like your mother. What future is there in the death industry? Your paycheck hardly covers your monthly loan payments, let alone gives you enough to save and move out on your own—"

Loan payments Ren *owes* her grandmother, because she didn't finish the doctorate program like her grandmother wanted. As if Ren dropped out on a whim.

It's not as simple as the old bitch likes to claim.

The grandmother angles her body toward Ren, a fucking tsunami tearing her granddaughter apart layer by layer. Tough love. Tearing down her own blood, as if that will make Ren better, *stronger,* when it doesn't take a genius to see through the bullshit.

People like Ren's grandmother use "tough love" to make themselves feel better. Like it gives her a good reason to patronize her would-be successor.

My mind buzzes with white noise, the anger building in my chest. A blankness overwhelms Ren, the emptiness taking over her body: the tears that fill her up, emotions that she refuses to let go. Not here. Not now. Not in front of her grandmother.

It's irritating.

For a split second, I wish I would've killed that old bitch like I considered weeks ago. But that would've left Ren in a precarious state, and I wasn't about to risk the opportunity to manipulate my little corpse.

I don't give a shit what Ren's grandmother thinks of me, nor do I give a shit about her relationship with Ren. Damn it—I don't even care about *Ren*. She's my next victim. My fourth. A convenient arrangement.

But her grandmother is stepping into *my* fucking territory now. I don't care for mothers—or even grandmothers—like her. I won't let Ren be *her* next victim. The only one who can destroy Ren's sense of self is me.

Only me.

I step forward, my boots thudding on the pavement. The grandmother quiets. I tip my chin down and broaden my shoulders. The grandmother is small, and she knows it. Next to me? It's *funny.* I could eat her for breakfast.

I smile at her, letting her understand the falseness of my expression.

The old bitch flinches.

"Mrs. Kono—no, that's right," I say. "Ren's mother gave Ren her father's surname. *Not yours.*" I laugh coldly. "If I'm not mistaken, Mrs. Richmond, *you* could've been a great mother, or even a fantastic grandmother, but it's sad, isn't it?" I lower myself to her level. "You wasted *your* potential, didn't you?"

Her chin wavers, her posture dipping slightly. I've struck a chord, even without saying the exact truth I'm hinting at. The grandmother evens herself out, pretending like I haven't done anything to startle her.

"Excuse me?" the grandmother gasps. "You don't know anything about me! What I've been through. Everything I do for Ren, for this family—"

"You want Ren to fail, don't you?" I interrupt.

The grandmother gawks at me. *I'm right.* She doesn't want to admit to herself, but it's there, lingering in her silence. If Ren won't be her little carbon copy, then she's worthless to her.

"If Ren fails, then at least you'll always be better than her. Better than your daughter too, right?" I snicker.

I know about her daughter's death; gossip is easy to come by in a small town like this. Ren's mother was supposed to take over her school too. They had a falling out *right* before the grandmother disqualified her own daughter from the job.

"You have to be better than *everyone*," I say. "Even those school children you help—they need you because you're *so* much more capable than they are. You're even better than their parents, aren't you? You break down others just so that you can see how small they are compared to you."

The old bitch sizes me up. "You don't know what you're talking about," she says.

"Ren does." I turn toward Ren. She gnaws on her bottom lip nervously. "Don't you, love?"

Ren shifts her stare between the two of us, analyzing how she's supposed to move. If she's supposed to be the submissive granddaughter, or if she's supposed to be my little corpse.

Her choice doesn't matter in the long run. Even if she bows to her grandmother right now, I'll still use her. Still, the urge to push her in *my* direction churns inside of me like a water spout twisting down from a black cloud.

"What do you have to lose?" I ask Ren.

Ren's eyes meet mine, glimmering with the desire to act. To do like *she* wants. An expression I know well.

She knows I'm right. If she's going to die anyway, then why submit to her dictator's every condescending whim?

"She has a lot to lose," her grandmother beckons. "Ren is a good girl. She may have her tendencies, but she's—"

"He's right," Ren says, interrupting her grandmother. She straightens her shoulders, then confronts the old bitch head on. "One of the teachers told me that my mother never wanted to take over the school. You forced her to turn down that job in Georgia, then fired her when she still wasn't good enough for you." She shakes her head, her cheeks tinting red. "Just because you want to mold us into miniature versions of you doesn't mean you can. I'm not going to fall in line because I'm worried about disappointing you or about letting my mother down. My mother would've been proud of me for doing what *I* wanted, for not letting *you* tell me what to do."

"You didn't *choose* to work in that funeral home!" the grandmother snaps. "You were desperate. It was the first job you applied for!"

"And it was *my choice* to apply there." Ren grits her teeth, then turns to me. "Let's go to that work function now."

Ren's chin trembles, afraid of the mess she's made and simultaneously exhilarated by the power of it. She's letting go of those shackles, finding a new way to move forward.

And, fuck me, my chest expands.

The grandmother opens her mouth, tries to find words, wags a disapproving finger at us, but she's unable to speak. I wink at the old bitch, then offer my elbow to Ren. She takes it, and I escort her down the driveway.

I don't open her car door like her grandmother probably expects a gentleman to behave; I let Ren help herself. The grandmother gawks at us from the front porch, floundering at the fact that her guilt and shame tactics have little power over Ren this time.

And that power swells inside of me. Hot. Like a helium balloon stretching up to the sky. I love doing the opposite of what society expects of me, and I know, unconsciously, *Ren does too*.

I drive immediately, not giving Ren a chance to buckle her seatbelt. Confusion sparks across her furrowed brow. I grin.

Finally, she straps her seatbelt.

I focus on the road, the reality sinking in. I have a problem now. Ren's grandmother *knows* me. When Ren disappears, she'll suspect me.

I can get rid of her if I need to. She's older than my usual type, but she's blond, and there's a certain satisfaction in watching someone insufferable submit to torture.

Ren isn't my usual type either. I'm more than willing to try different things to get what I want.

The highway darkens as we head out of town. A country song —the only music that comes in between the two cities—hums from the radio. The singer rambles about getting mud between your toes and how liberating it is to let go. To embrace the natural world and see the beauty in every living thing.

It's a bunch of bullshit, and yet I picture Ren covered in mud.

My dick grows in my pants.

A wave of nausea fills me, dread pooling in my gut, my mind swirling with frustration. Anger. Goddamn irritation. It's not the country song that pisses me off; it's me. I don't know what the fuck I was thinking when it came to Ren's grandmother. Family drama is the last thing I want, and exposing myself to her grandmother doesn't make this "arrangement" any easier for me. There will be loose ends that I will *need* to tie up now, and I'm not supposed to give a shit about Ren *or* her family.

There was something inside of me though, a hunger that sought out her grandmother. That wanted to disrupt the very nature of the manipulative games her grandmother was playing. To show Ren that she doesn't have to kneel down to anyone *unless she wants to.*

"Where are we going?" Ren asks.

Home. I could say that. But just because you lived somewhere once doesn't mean that you find comfort or safety there. It's simply a memorial of the little boy I once was.

"Blountstown," I say.

She lets out a sigh. Steadies herself. I quickly glance at her. Darkness covers her countenance, but the questions are palpable, drifting in the air between us.

Am I going to do it tonight?

Ren must think I'm finally going to kill her. Perhaps she *wants* to die now that she's finally stood up to her grandmother.

Pride burrows in my chest. I push it out. Ren doesn't mean anything to me. She's a vessel to fuck. A high I *need.*

Those two cases from my brother—the pills and the lozenges—are in my nightstand drawer. I don't plan to give them to her anytime soon. It's not her birthday yet, and I have other methods I can use right now.

An hour later, a junkyard shadows one side of the highway, a used car lot on the other. Another mile in, between the second-hand store and the family diner, a pizza shop blinks with an *Open!*

sign. Brent's Italian Restaurant. It's a small town—less than three thousand residents—and that detail is supposed to come with peace. Everyone knows everyone. My mother knew she could count on the sympathy of the men in this town, as long as they got to have their way with her. As long as they could use her youngest idiot child too. Me.

We drive down a dirt road, around one of the neighbor's pastures, to a single-story house guarded by thick barriers of longleaf pine trees. The porch light is still bright from my visit this morning, a lighthouse warning others of the invisible danger waiting in the darkness. Moths mash into the stained walls, cobwebs matted into the siding. The lawn grows in knee-high blades and clusters around my mother's old truck. I park in the weeds. Put on my black leather gloves, physically removing all evidence of humanity within me.

I walk to the front porch. Ren follows me.

In the foggy night air, the cicadas chirp and the frogs whine in chorus. Ren crosses her arms, holding herself, scanning the old truck for signs of life. As if a ghost will lurch out of the passenger seat. As if she can see the demon who used to drive it.

Our footsteps creak on the wooden porch. I gesture at the doorbell. Ren fidgets, hesitant to wake up the unknown occupants. I click my jaw. She can stand up to her grandmother, but she's afraid of a few strangers?

I bare my teeth at her. She inhales, settling those nerves, then pushes the button.

It's silent, though. The doorbell has been broken for years.

Ren turns to me, waiting for my next command. My lips peel back into a snarl, then I motion to the side of the house. She lifts her hand to stop me—this is a stranger's property, after all—then she thinks better of it. The little corpse doesn't say a word.

She doesn't know that this is where I grew up. All she knows is that no one is home right now. And for now, I'll keep her in that darkness.

Chapter 17

Ren

The moths smack against the side of the house like hail. My heart beats in my throat. I can't move. I can't do anything. I stare at the door like it'll tell me something real.

Is this where I die?

Blaze grabs my elbow, forcing me around the house. My breath hitches, the gravity of the situation suddenly bearing down on me. If Blaze really is a killer, what if it's not me that he's after? What if we're here so he can murder someone else?

I stumble behind him in the shadows, the overgrown grass scratching through my leggings.

Eventually, my eyes adjust. A heavy, warm fog hangs over the yard. Woods surround us in almost every direction, except for the area that leads back to the road. I think I remember seeing a farmhouse on the way here; I don't know how far away it is.

We're isolated out here.

Blaze stops in front of a hole in the ground. No, it's not a hole. It's hip deep—shallow compared to the graves at Last Spring. And when I look down, I lose my breath.

A wooden box. Rectangular. The nails jagged. The final wooden plank rests to the side of the hole, exposing the bare insides. No cushions. No pillows. No keepsake gifts stowed away for a loved one to keep in the afterlife. I know exactly what this is.

My casket.

"Take off your clothes," Blaze says, his voice ominous. "Underwear stays on."

My hands shake, so I ball them into fists to stop myself from reacting. My knuckles whiten. Weakness envelops me, and my knees buckle.

He wants me to get naked? Here? Why now?

Why can't I do it?

Our eyes lock. Blaze bares his teeth again, warning me of the consequences of denying him. I quietly remove my leggings, my shirt, my bra, my hoodie. It's humid, like the mouth of a monster. Still, the air on my skin exposes me and reminds me it's still technically winter. All of that heat is from *me*.

Vulnerability crushes my heart, trying to bring me to my knees. I try so hard to resist it.

This *is* what I wanted. To be buried alive. To have someone force me to embrace my death so that I don't have to be afraid of it anymore.

Isn't it?

"Get in," Blaze orders.

The hairs on the back of my neck stand on end. Hesitantly, I lower myself to the ground. My calves skim across the dirt, colder than I expected, each clump hanging on to the moisture in the air. It's not that deep; if I reach down with one leg, I'll be standing inside of the grave.

I don't move.

This is what I wanted. I know that. So why does this feel like a trap? Like I'm in the middle of some horrific joke?

Blaze pushes my back and I yelp and fall into the handmade casket. The wood creaks, and I spin around, looking for a way to escape.

There's nowhere to go.

"What? Are you scared, love?" Blaze laughs. "You were the one who asked me to kill you."

I never asked him for anything. "You offered," I hiss. "No, you *blackmailed* me into this mess!"

"I didn't threaten you with anything. We both had enough dirt on each other to keep silent. *You* were the one who came to my door and asked me to help you."

My shoulders tighten, each beat of my pulse rapid. There's some truth in that. I could've stayed away from him. I could've gone to that medical spa. I could've done this by myself.

"Now," he says in a gravelly voice. "Get in the box."

I kneel down, darkness closing in around me. The coarse wood scrapes my knees, a sharp pain shooting through me.

Blaze grabs the top of my head like a basketball and pushes me down, his gloved fingers so different from before that it scares me. The gloves are probably there to cover up the evidence, but it *hurts*. Like he doesn't want to touch me when he kills me.

Tears stream down my face. I lie down quickly. He jumps in beside the casket, snatching the wooden plank and lowering it to the top of the coffin. I'm small. An object. Stuffed inside of a container.

I'm nothing.

My teeth chatter, shock coursing through me like a tidal wave. I reach up, slipping my fingers between the wood, Blaze's force smashing them.

"Please," I beg. "I don't—"

Through the gaps between the wooden planks, I can see him grab tools from beside the grave. Angling down toward the coffin, his voice grows louder, echoing in that wood—

"The only way you're getting out of that coffin is if you come or if you beg for your life," he says. "Your choice."

Tears burst through me like an attack. I shove against the plank, and his laughter swallows me whole. He leans his full body weight on top of the plank, forcing me down. I wail. Like a dying animal. Screaming for the last time.

The nail cracks into the wood, the steady thud of the hammer mesmerizing me. The second nail. The third. The darkness drowns me, the heat of my own body beginning to suffocate me. He lifts the edge of the wooden plank, and I stick my foot through. The pressure of his weight pinches my foot; the pain splits me in half, and I tuck my foot back inside.

There's no way this is real. It isn't what he wants. It's not what we agreed to.

A fire stirs deep within me, forcing itself to the surface.

"Come, little corpse," he says, his voice distorted through the wood. "Come for me."

I close my eyes, willing myself to go to another place. Where I'm not being buried alive. Dirt taps against the top of the coffin, gentle like rain, like the fountain in the lobby of the medical spa. My hand squeezes between my legs. My slit is dry, and even that slight touch sends a shock through me. I'm too fucking sensitive.

I force myself to look to the side. It's all wooden planks. And I'm crying. It's irritating.

I have to come. I can't keep crying like this.

Why can't I get wet?

I suck my fingers, then rub my clit with one hand and penetrate myself with the other, my underwear keeping me bound to my own body. I could fake an orgasm, but somehow, Blaze would know. I dig into my flesh, mimicking the way Blaze made me come in the casket, how I squirted everywhere. How embarrassing it was. *The only reason you exist right now is to please me,* he whispered. His voice was so calming, it was like he was making love to me.

Does *this* please him?

Leaving me alone. Tucked inside of a coffin. Buried in the earth.

He can't even see me die.

And I can't see him.

I rub, and rub, and swirl my fingers. That peak is so far away. The more I try, the more difficult it is. The farther away it goes. I'm trapped in my own mind.

This *should* be my fantasy. This should be exactly what I want. Buried alive by a man who fucks me like he hates me. Who doesn't care if I come, as long as *he* gets what he wants.

If I die right now—trapped inside of the earth, alone, without him fucking me—then I did this to myself. I practically begged him for it.

How many women has he buried alive?

You're just a body now, he said. *No mind. No soul. Not even a fucking heartbeat.*

I try to convince myself that I'm there—on the surface, with him, that none of this is real—to push myself to come, but I can't. I just can't. I *need* to feel him. His wrath. His cruelty. His overwhelming *need* for me.

I cry, so much snot coming out of my nose that I can barely breathe. I shouldn't be crying; I'm losing oxygen faster, but I can't calm down.

He shouts, his voice dulled by the wood, but I'm alone. Lost. Discarded at the bottom of a trash can. Little segments of broken bone swept into a loose bin. A granddaughter who will never be what her grandmother wants. A child who wasn't good enough to stay.

A willing victim who wasn't tempting enough to fuck until she died.

The rain of dirt cracks against the top of the coffin. I reach underneath my panties, cupping my pussy. Trying so hard to concentrate.

But I can't.

"I can't," I finally cry. "I can't. Please. Don't let me die like this. Don't—" The dirt keeps banging down on the coffin. Beating into it. Burying me. "Please. Fuck me as I die. Don't do this to me. Not here. I need you. Your cock."

The overwhelming patheticness of my own voice fills me with shame, but everything I say is true. Even if it's sadistic, even if it's malevolent and degrading, I *need* Blaze's attention. His utter and complete rapture. To be possessed by him. A connection so intense that it *will* kill me. In the end, he'll come too. Just as hard.

Dying in this coffin isn't that.

The sobs take hold of me, my cries vibrate the box. The deep groan of the hammer's claw digs at the nails. I squeeze my eyes shut.

He's not going to leave me here.

The coffin lid lifts, dirt sliding down into the box around me. Cold air brushes my sweating body, and Blaze tosses the lid to the side of the grave. My body takes over; I kick my legs, so eager to do something. I suck in air, gasping for it. Desperate. Blaze leans down and I punch at him—not because I want to hurt him, but because my body is reacting. Rejoicing at the fact that I can do anything at all.

He grabs my wrist, holding me still.

"Tell me what you want," Blaze growls, his voice ringing through my chest. Dirt cakes his face and coats my skin in a light powder. We're covered in filth. "Tell me what you fucking want right now, dead girl."

I pant. I know exactly what I want.

"Make me come," I cry. "Then kill me with your cock inside of me."

He smacks me between my legs and grabs my cunt like he owns it. Because he does. He owns me.

"You couldn't bear to die without coming first," he says. "You're such a selfish little corpse."

He grabs the top of my hair, lifting me out of the grave, shoving me onto the leveled soil beside the hole. On my hands and knees. My nails dig into the earth, greedy for it, and he smacks my pussy from behind. The pain feels so good that I don't know what to do with myself.

I want to come. I do. I fucking do.

He moves my panties to the side, and his hands are clean somehow. Warm. Naked. Without those leather gloves. A new set of tears wells in my eyes. I don't know what it is. Is it relief?

Then I realize that he wore the gloves—and made me keep my panties on—to protect me from the dirt. Even if he killed me in the grave tonight, he still planned to use me.

And it's so damn comforting.

"Corpses don't get wet, do they, love?" he says. "But you? My willing victim. My unlucky number four. You get wet knowing that I want to fuck you as much as I want to kill you." He buries his mouth against my ear. "If you didn't get wet for me, you know what I'd do?" He digs his fingers into my pussy, another finger penetrating my ass, finger-fucking both of my holes. "I'd stab you in the gut and fuck the blood out of you."

I moan, the pleasure mounting in my chest. It's unbearable.

The disgust for myself and for him and the overwhelming need I have to take everything he has to give me. To let go. To give myself over to that need to come. And when his palm squeezes my throat and his fingers knead my pussy, everything inside of me constricts and I twitch on his fingers, and it's there. I can touch it. Taste it. It's everything I want.

And I don't hold back anymore.

"Yes," he howls. "Give me that sloppy cunt!"

I dive into the abyss, into the nothingness, the little death inside of me expanding into a void, a black hole devouring everything around it. I am nothing but pleasure and pain. Nothing but visceral emotion. Nothing but *his*.

Before I can catch my breath, Blaze twists me around and shoves me onto my back. The coarse dirt scratches my skin, ripping me away from the pleasure. I don't care. I stare into his pale eyes, seeing myself in him.

He kneels on my chest, his muddy black pants resting against my tits. He unzips, unleashing his engorged cock, so full of blood it looks purple. Veins wrap around it, contracting, threatening to come. He fists his length, an animalistic hunger in his eyes as he glares down at me. Bloodshot. Salivating. His throat contorts, and he smacks my cheek until I open my mouth. A string of spit winds down, drawing toward me. It misses my mouth and hits my chin, and he uses his free hand to rub it all over me. His palm is smooth as it massages my skin. The dirt and saliva blend together, caking me with mud. He spits again, and this time, I move, catching it. I swallow it down, tasting him. Swallowing his salt. His bacteria. *Him.* Tasting everything he gives me. Savoring it.

"Take my fucking come," he growls.

And I do. I open my mouth, panting, eager for it. His cock pulses, the head expanding with pressure as thick white fluid pours from his tip, over his fist and onto my lips. I lick it up—the dirt, the saliva, his come—and I'm ravenous. I need all of it. Every single drop.

A deep sigh splits into the frenzy as I finish eating his come. Blaze's expression is icy and calm now. The insects hum, and the frogs' cries suddenly filling my ears. It's like they started singing again, but they probably never stopped. They were always there, calling out to us. I just wasn't listening.

Blaze disappears inside of the house. The lights never flicker on. A minute later, he returns with a wet washcloth and water bottle. He offers them to me.

I rub my forehead and smear the dirt around my skin. I don't understand him.

"You just buried me alive," I say, hoping he catches the subtext, too tired to ask my real question: *Why do you want to clean me?*

"If I wanted to kill you tonight, I would have," he says. He nods at the wet towel, and I start using it to wipe my face. The hard granules of dirt dig into my cheek. Eventually, the air cools my clean skin. "When did I ever say that I'd kill you if my dick wasn't inside of you?"

My cheeks flame, my pussy pulsating at the thought. He knew I would freak out about being buried alive, didn't he? How many times had I fantasized about the prospect before him? How is it that he knows me better than I know myself?

Maybe it's not the dying that matters. Maybe it's the part *before* it, where I can see him. Where he sees *me*. Where nothing exists except for our primal hunger for each other. A connection so deep, we can feel it, even after we've come. Even now.

Perhaps Blaze will still feel me after I die.

He hands me a bottle of water, then gestures at my throat. "Wash. Drink."

I gargle the fluids in my mouth, then spit into the dirt. Blaze studies me, almost like he's as curious about the situation as I am. Asking himself why he's taking care of me if he's going to kill me anyway.

Did he take care of all of his victims like this?

"Your pussy needs to be ready for me," he says, reading my mind. "If you get an infection, we have to wait. And your time is already limited. I want you ready for me."

Reminding himself. Reminding me we both know where this

ends. Somehow, I know there's another part to what he's saying. Words we're both avoiding. The true reason behind this.

"Me too," I say.

He grits his teeth, then nods toward the shadowed pine trees.

"Come," he says. "I have something to show you."

Chapter 18

Ren

Blaze steps over the coffin lid like it's a tree stump. Like he didn't bury me alive and force me to beg for my life minutes ago.

My vision blurs as I try to focus on him.

He has something to show me?

"Where are you going?" I ask.

Exhaustion weighs against my shoulders, begging me to rest. Blaze prowls toward the trees, his large frame hunching forward like he's prepared to duck under the foliage. As if he has the energy to hunt. As if this is normal to him. Maybe it is.

I'm not used to this.

"Please," I whine. "Can we—"

He stops, then lowers his gaze to me.

"Do you trust me?" he asks.

I hold a hand to my chest. The moon is speckled white, the stars peeking around it like tiny eyes peering out from a cave. Blaze is a few feet away now, but I can see his smug expression clearly—his smile spreading like thin strings of kelp clinging to the sand, so confident under the direct sunlight, even when it's obvious that they will dry out too.

I twitch, and his grin grows wider, playing with our connection. The killer and the voluntary victim. All the words we don't say, because we both just know.

What do you have to lose? he had asked me, reminding me that I was already on the edge of the precipice. That nothing mattered.

I shouldn't trust Blaze. Not with my life. Not even with my death.

But I do.

I quickly put on my clothes and shoes, then follow him, our footsteps crunching the fallen leaves. The ground is moist under our feet, dipping with our weight. Branches and reeds scrape against our arms and legs, cracking underneath us, and each step deeper into the woods is darker than the last. My stomach churns; still, I focus on Blaze's white hair, the only beacon of light in the darkness. He's my guide, and yet we both know he's *not* a teacher. He's a devil, waiting to drag me under. Waiting to collect my soul.

Ten minutes into the woods, Blaze stops next to a live oak tree. He runs his palm across a gnarled branch, recognizing it.

"There," he says, then points behind a neighboring tree. "I dug it up for you."

It.

My skin crawls, anticipating what "it" is. I study our surroundings: the oak and pine trees, the soggy leaves on the ground, the dim moon. "It" could be a weapon. "It" could be a coffee tree, a thoughtful gift he knows I'll like. "It" could be a buried treasure for all I know.

Even with all of those possibilities, one thing is for certain: Blaze could have buried me alive tonight. He could have left me to die in that coffin. Laughed as I took my last breath. Claimed that it was what I said I wanted. There was nothing stopping him.

Except I begged for my life.

And he listened.

With careful steps, I circle the tree. A figure catches my eye—almost like a hollowed-out lifesize doll hunched against the trunk. Shoulders propped up, chin curling into the chest. Legs stiff before the body. Clumped blond hair. A leathered face, the layers peeling back, revealing spots of gray bone, still sticky with rotting flesh. The breasts are sunken and thrashed, the gnarled ribs broken in the middle; they were obviously hacked to pieces *before* she died. A palmetto bug skitters across the cavernous chest, then crawls between the thighs, disappearing completely.

And then I see it. The gash on her neck. Like he used a saw to take her last breath.

This isn't his mother. She'd be more decayed than this.

But it is one of the others.

Sharp pain stabs through my tongue, then copper slithers over my taste buds. I pinch my lips together, then glare at Blaze as if it's his fault, but he wasn't the one who bit my tongue. *I did.* And somehow that reaction reflects this realization.

Blaze truly is a killer.

I never truly believed Blaze when he said he had killed women. Even with the corpses I saw on a daily basis at work, his claims seemed so far out of the everyday world that I refused to accept it. He was a fantasy, a man who was pretending that he could give me what I wanted. And maybe one day, I could die pretending like I meant something to him, even if I had to kill myself to prove it.

A sour, dry scent wafts around us. I sniff it in, willing myself to understand it. It's different from most of the bodies that come through the mortuary. Slightly bitter. Old. Months—possibly years —have passed. I don't know how quickly bodies decompose in the Florida soil, but in the end, it's the same as the corpses at the mortuary, isn't it? A brittle, rotting body. Contorted. Forced into the right shape. Still submitting to the world around it. Like a seashell, washed up on a shore, the holes of past carnivorous snails unrelenting as they forced their mouths through the hard exterior, just to suck the life out of the mollusk within. Leaving the shell worn. A fragment of its former self.

As far as I can tell, this corpse was never submerged in the ocean. It was once buried here, in the earth. Laid bare to larvae. Worms. Rodents. Any scavenger—including Blaze—could use it for themselves.

It could've been buried right in the box where I tried to masturbate.

For a brief second, I see my mother. The deep sockets. Her

broken neck. A blurry image of a black-haired toddler watching a box get covered with dirt.

I used to wish I could've seen my mother's corpse. I guess there was comfort in it—closure, maybe. I thought it would give me the answers I was searching for. The reasons why I wasn't enough.

Now, I realize it wouldn't have helped me. Rotting flesh or ashes, I still would've been haunted by her death.

My mother must have felt like the world was walking all over her too.

"Who is she?" I ask Blaze.

"My third."

His most recent kill, then. She doesn't get a name; she's simply a number in a sequence, like the first grandchild in a hopeful lineage of many. Being Blaze's third seems more valuable than being the first in a big family. Even if Blaze kills hundreds after her, *after me*, she will always be his third. When he realized that he needed something different.

Someone like me.

"What about your first and second?" I ask. I hold my breath, my fingers itching for his touch. I don't remind him that his first kill was his mother; like the third, she's been reduced to a number.

"My mother is buried near your rejected grave," he chuckles. "I wanted to feel like I did when I first killed her. I tried to find blonds that looked like her."

I turn back to the corpse. Blaze's mother must have had blond hair too.

My hair is the exact opposite.

Will he still kill me if I don't look like them?

I shake my head. We need to focus on *us*. On our agreement.

"Why are you showing me her?" I ask.

"Why am I showing you *this?*" he asks, correcting me. He kicks the corpse's legs, and the head rolls to the side, barely hanging on to the spine. "You should know exactly what you're getting into if you're my fourth."

If.

There's a choice in that. A variable.

His murky eyes, shrouded in darkness, glimmer with the faintest hint of moonlight. And that soullessness pierces through me, beckoning me to see the truth behind his words.

I tell myself that this corpse is a legacy to him. A string of dead women are evidence of his power.

It's not.

Showing me this corpse is about reminding us what we agreed on. What we should want. This is about me. Forcing me to see my end. My future.

"It's just a corpse," he says.

"A corpse," I repeat.

"A corpse like yours."

A corpse like mine.

I stare at the body. The decay. The rot. The holes carved into the flesh, the homes tiny creatures have made in the body. Infestations and protection. I don't know if Blaze will burn my flesh and pulverize my bones, or if he will bury me with one of our client's loved ones in the cemetery. And I don't get that choice.

There's a chance that he'll bury me like he buried this corpse. In the ground. Where I'll rot. Insects and the earth will use my body for nourishment, and I'll be nameless. A number. Perhaps the only one who was *willing* to die.

But maybe I won't even have that.

A chill runs through my body, and I wrap my arms around myself. When I spin around, Blaze is right next to me, his breath cascading over my neck. His focus sears into me, digging past the layers of skin and between our barriers, hearing the question forming deep inside of me.

Will he kill me?

"Soon, I'll kill you too," he murmurs as he traces a finger down my throat. "Would you like that?"

All the heat in my body centers around that point of physical contact, reaching for it. Desperate for his forceful touch.

I don't think; I answer instinctually.

"Yes," I whisper.

His lips drop, and I understand that it's more than an instinct now. This isn't about the end—*my end*. It's not even about surrendering to the unknown.

It's about what Blaze does to me. What he gives me. How he guides me through this fucked-up world, and how for once, I want something more for myself.

He motions for me to follow him. The moon cuts through the branches, enveloping us in its light, our footsteps mingling with the cicadas and the frogs. Blaze walks around the hole in the ground and heads straight to his car. I match his footsteps, knowing that tonight isn't *the* night.

For now, he'll make me wait.

Chapter 19

Blaze

We find our rhythm after that. In Panama City Beach. In Blountstown. In the cemetery or the crematory. We fuck until I force Ren to fight for her life. Getting her to come gets easier every time. The touch of my hand to her throat—the slightest squeeze—and her body tenses, ready to rush over that edge. To close her eyes and jump into the oblivion.

In between those times, she shows me how to work the crematory. Her brown eyes light up, my pulse beating in my throat as I watch her. It excites her, having the ability to teach me something.

And when it comes to her, I'm a quick learner.

Ren flutters back and forth across the mortuary windows like a moth without a place to land, never quite seeing the light. Every so often, she glances in my direction. I doubt she can see me back here in the cemetery, but I know she feels what I feel—everything ahead of us, waiting for us.

It's not supposed to be "we" or "us." It's supposed to be about *me*. But that's not enough anymore, and I'm not sure why.

The sun sets over the beach. A bell gongs—a nearby restaurant celebrating the end of the day—and a figure appears in my peripheral. I stop the excavator and power it down. I turn slowly; I know it's not her. This person—this figure—is too proud, too sure of himself.

I'm face to face with my brother. Brody's blue eyes glisten, his cheekbones cut from marble. We're similar that way. If it weren't for how pale I am compared to him, we might be considered twins.

But I'll never be like him.

"You dig graves this late in your shift?" he asks.

My eyes flicker to the beach. Brody doesn't care about the details of my job. About the fact that I do whatever the director tells me to do, even if that means coming in late so that the machines don't disrupt an impromptu funeral service.

I tilt my chin at Brody, analyzing what the world actually sees when they look at him. His clean shirt. His ironed collar. He twitches, his shoes shifting against the lawn. Uncomfortable under my stare.

I want him out of here.

"What do you want?" I ask.

He scans the cemetery. A mourner stands over a grave, a bouquet of white roses in her hands. In front of her, six feet under, a corpse full of chemicals decays unnaturally, almost petrified in their doll-like state. I used to imagine Ren tucked inside of a stranger's casket, her natural body rotting on top of a perfectly embalmed corpse. I used to picture scattering her pulverized bones in twenty different plastic urns, spreading her out to be shared with those families, like a used-up corpse slut.

The idea is unsavory now. A bad egg. Her corpse belongs with me. In Blountstown with the others. Or shit—maybe I'll keep her in my house here, in Panama City Beach. I'm sure there are ways to keep a corpse from stinking up a place, and I'm willing to try new things.

It doesn't matter though. She's going to die, and I'm going to be the one to kill her. It's as simple as that. Her body is just a body.

Just like my body. Like theirs.

Like my brother's.

"Came to follow up on the recent business," Brody says.

It clicks into place, then. *The guilt.*

"Good" people use guilt as a way to hide their true motivations. In all honesty, Brody probably doesn't give a shit if my business associate—if Ren—lives or dies; he wants to know that he can't be traced to her death. That his secret will die with my transaction. He used his connections so our mother's death certificate read "natural causes", and I bet that's what he wants to do with Ren. He's anxious to play his part so he can't be implicated, and it pisses me off. He doesn't have the balls to be linked to anyone's death.

Until I die, Brody will always be under my thumb, frightened of my next move. And until Ren dies, both of us will be tied to her.

"Still alive," I say.

My gaze lingers over the building, knowing the exact spot where Ren is behind the walls. Sitting at the chair next to the retorts, probably finishing up a few infants we have in the refrigeration unit. She's been leaving them for the end of the day recently, as if she wants to be more productive and use every bit of her early morning energy she has on the harder bodies. The adults. Like us.

I hate that I know her habits.

"Here," Brody says. He hands me another pill bottle, this time *filled* with capsules. "I brought more secobarbital."

A door clunks in the distance. I shove the bottle in my pocket, then turn toward the mortuary. Ren floats along the side of the building like a raven, taking her perch against the wall. The white garden, orange in the evening light, waves to each side of her like glittering flames. There's not a single trace of dirt on her body, but I still see it there. Covering her. Her cunt raised in the air. The globs of mud caking her face. Her open lips.

The desire in her eyes when she said that she *wanted* me to kill her with my cock inside of her.

How I believed her.

"Who is she?" Brody asks.

Ren Kono.

Not a corpse. Not a number. A woman. A name.

"Ren Kono?" Brody repeats.

I run a hand over my face. Did I say that out loud?

Fuck.

"Crematory operator," I add, shoveling an air of indifference into my tone. I focus my attention back on the burial plot. As if Ren doesn't mean shit to me.

Because she *doesn't* mean shit to me. She's a future corpse. Any corpse would do. I can promise Brody that.

But it's not true, is it? She's the only one who doesn't question the order of the world. Who sees things for what they are. Including me.

"Ren Kono," Brody repeats.

His lip curls, and he tightens his arms against his body, locking himself in, guarding that name. I clench my jaw, a bitter taste rushing over my tongue, and for a split second, I imagine cracking my brother's skull on a headstone. Kicking him into a hole on top of a casket. Burying *him* alive this time, with enough earth to render him powerless.

I don't like hearing *my corpse's* name on his tongue.

"Don't you have a patient to protect?" I ask. He scoffs, then looks at the beach longingly, like all of the lonely tourists do.

Ren walks back inside the mortuary. The door clicks into place.

Brody sighs.

"It's her, isn't it?" he asks.

I lean forward sharply, getting in his personal space, then I bare my teeth like a fucking animal.

"You think I'd kill someone I work with?" I snarl. "You think I'm that stupid?" The bastard slants away from me, tension creasing his forehead. Scared like a child. I outgrew him in size once I hit my twenties, and I use that advantage over him now. He takes another step back. "I'll call *you* when my next victim is dead. You can be sure of that."

"Good," he says.

I wrench myself away from him. His attention lingers on my back. Hunting. Searching for what I want.

I *want* to kill him—to teach him a lesson for digging where he doesn't belong—but if I do anything now, he'll *know* it's her.

And I can't have that. I can't have him on my back any more

than I can have Ren still floating around, living her life, knowing who I truly am.

Moments later, I find myself inside of the building. Following her. She steps toward the exit, and I forget what I'm supposed to be doing.

Dead or alive, I need to touch her. To own her. To *feel* her.

Right fucking now.

Chapter 20

Blaze

I grab the back of Ren's arm before she reaches the door. Her plain brown eyes take me in, disarming me.

We stare at each other, neither of us saying a word. Thoughts float through my mind, screaming at me to get this over with. To stop wasting my time. To kill her like we *both* want.

But those thoughts evaporate, too weak to grip me now.

Ren and I stand in the hallway of the empty mortuary. Our only company is the dead. The familiar and the neglected. The corpses like us.

"I didn't know you were still here," she says.

I raise a brow, slightly amused. We both know that's a lie. She's been waiting for me, lingering in the building, so that we would leave at the same time. It's our pattern now.

I tilt my head toward the back door leading to the gardens and the cemetery.

"Sit with me," I say.

We walk to the edge of the graves and sit in the grass. Most of the plots have been reserved already. Many of the Floridian retirees like these plots on the beach, backed by swampland: you get the best of both worlds—the paradise and the home, escape and comfort. Even in death.

For a long time, neither of us says a word. The waves skim

across the sand, and the stars peek out of the darkness. I keep my eyes ahead of me on that bleak, ominous ocean.

Brody is gone now. That shouldn't give me relief, but it does. If he's gone, I can let go. I can focus on her.

"I broke my leg once. Masturbating in the shower, actually," Ren says. She laughs awkwardly, even though it's obvious that it's not a nostalgic memory. "I slipped, and it's not like I could tell Mrs. Richmond exactly what happened. She didn't believe I was really hurt, because I was walking—or limping, I guess. 'You would know if your leg was broken,' she had said. And when the school sent me to the hospital, she got mad. Said I was embarrassing her."

My lungs deflate, the tension ceasing. Ren isn't the type of person to volunteer information, especially about herself, and I don't know how to take it.

I should tell her to shut up. Remind her that dead girls don't talk.

I stay quiet.

I want her to talk. To tell me what's on her mind. I want to know, even if it's the last thing she tells me before she dies.

"I never really knew my mother," she says as she scans the dark waters. "I just knew that she hung herself. I guess I started using the noose because I wanted to understand her. To know what it was like when she died. Then I started having these feelings. This—" she motions in front of her, too ashamed to say the words. Her cheeks redden. "You know what I mean."

"Arousal," I say.

"Right," she nods. "Then Mrs. Richmond caught me. I came home, and my drawers and closet were empty. She replaced everything I had with new things. Items *she* chose. Ones that weren't tainted by my perversion. And for a long time, I repressed that need. Even when I got a boyfriend." She points to the beach. "My ex never got me wet though. Not like you do."

Instinctively, I lick my lips. Ren keeps her attention forward, a bashful smile flickering across her face. She's using the literal *wet* ocean as a transition into this topic, like we're on a romantic date where we talk about our pasts and our futures.

Why the fuck is she telling me this?
Why don't I tell her to shut up?

I wait for a response. For an explanation. For a connection between this story about her grandmother and the information about her ex. If she's randomly talking about her ability to become aroused as a way to break the silence, inspired by the body of water in front of us, then it's not important. It's a mere thought.

And if there *is* a goal to it—if there's a reason she's telling me this—then it means something. An uncomfortable rope holding us both in limbo.

The silence eats away at me, my own questions *needing* answers.

Finally, I speak up: "Oh?"

"We started dating in high school. Kept it going through college too. Every once in a while, he would tell me I was letting myself go. That I needed to wear makeup and exercise more. That I needed to love myself like *he* loved me," she says, her voice flat. I look closer and narrow my eyes. The only makeup I can see is dull gray around her eyes, left over from the night before. "Mrs. Richmond said stuff like that too. That maybe my ex would propose if I actually tried for once."

Of course that bitch said shit like that. I prefer it *this* way though. There's an appeal to fucking the makeup off of her face, but there's a stronger appeal knowing that this is the *real* her. That she doesn't hide herself from me.

"It made me feel like I was lucky to have him," she says. "Like I should be grateful, happy that we were together. Because *at least* he loved me, you know? And if I didn't change, then he'd leave me, and where would I be?"

She's small, then. Curled on the grass, her arms wrapped around her legs. Protecting herself, even though all of those memories are from her past. I doubt her ex or even her bitch of a grandmother ever laid a hand on her, but the damage is ingrained in her mind. That need for perfection. That desire to be good enough. The failure of it devouring her soul until there's nothing she can do to stop it.

"He'd chase away those insecurities by giving me a sliver of his attention. Asking me to suck his dick so that he could get rid of his migraine," she adds, her voice matter-of-fact. "Told me that I wasn't the prettiest or smartest girl he had dated, but I was the only one who could get rid of his headaches. Who would suck his dick without asking questions. And honestly?" Her voice falters, and my fists curl, eager to punch the life out of *someone*. But not her. "At first, it made me feel like I had a purpose. Like I was worthy." I force myself to stare at the black waters. To not let her words affect me. To just fucking listen. "Maybe there was something about it that made me useful, you know? Even if he never gave me the same thing in return."

"Because he couldn't get you wet," I say, anger simmering in my tone.

"You know, it's kind of funny. He got angry at me for that. Said that if I couldn't get wet, then there must be something wrong with me." She clutches her knees to her chest, practically coiling into an upright fetal position. "I even saw a doctor about it once. It was a condition of our engagement. We ran tests and everything. But my numbers came back normal, so the doctor said it was in my head. Told me that my *brain* needed work. That maybe I wasn't *there* with my fiancé." She turns to me, her eyes glistening with tears. "But that's not it, is it? It was about what I was repressing. What I wanted. I get wet with you."

My jaw loosens, and her brown eyes stab straight into my fucked-up soul. I rub a thumb over her bottom lip, pretending to wipe away a fleck of dirt.

Ren has caked my hand in dirt and come. Soaked me with her arousal until my fingertips wrinkled.

Ren *can* get wet.

The fucker never had it in him to give a shit about *how* to get her there. He was too self-absorbed in his own image of what he imagined a fiancé *should* be, that he didn't give a shit about her needs. Hell, there's a chance that if he had just *asked* what she wanted, she could've been okay with a good spanking every now and then, but he didn't even try. Her ex is like her grandmother, only *worse*.

And that irritates me.

"You know why I dropped out of graduate school?" She laughs. I grind my teeth; I highly doubt whatever she's about to tell me is funny. "I know it's stupid. I shouldn't have done it. But the only place I could masturbate without Mrs. Richmond or my fiancé knowing about it was in my office at the university. He snuck in though. Took videos on his phone of me with a rope around my neck. Shared it with our classmates."

She huffs in irritation, and it becomes clear to me.

That's why she wears the bag over her head. To cover her face in case someone takes pictures. She knows she needs the brutality to come; she doesn't want to suffer the shame. Doesn't want to completely give in to that vulnerability.

She doesn't use the bag with me. I won't let her. She knows she can look me in the eye, that I'll see her in all of her morbid depravity, and I'll *still* want her.

"Word got around to the dean. My grandmother," she says. "My ex said that's why he broke off the engagement with me. Because I was a pervert. And he couldn't be with someone who he didn't trust around his future children."

She shakes her head, gnawing her lip. Her chin trembles, and everything inside of me breaks. My nostrils flare. Sweat beads along my temples.

How could someone hurt her like that?

"The dean politely asked me to drop out," she adds. "My grandmother started making me pay her back for the tuition."

Conflicting thoughts war for dominance in my skull. I shouldn't give a shit about Ren's past or why she's telling me all of this. She's a victim. *My willing victim.* I've fucked and killed for much less. I've throat-fucked a woman until she passed out from the lack of oxygen. I've strangled a woman with a rope until her cunt squeezed around my dick from the will to survive. I've even fucked a woman while she cried, with a gun pressed to her temple.

Ren has *barely* tasted what I can give her.

These thoughts—these *needs*—swirl inside of me, filling me with the desire to show her everything that's possible. Everything I can give her.

It kills me that she thinks she doesn't deserve that.

"Is that why you want to die?" I ask, frustration obvious in my tone. "Because some dickless idiot made you *think* you weren't good enough? You realize how much he's like your grandmother, don't you? Telling you who and what you're supposed to be. Dictating your entire perception of yourself." With each sentence, the words become louder; I don't stop myself. "Is that what this is, Ren? Your need to die while fucking? You base your self-worth on what your ex and your grandmother say about you?"

She blinks, stunned by my words. Perhaps she's shocked by my honesty. That I would force her to see the truth of her situation.

Perhaps she's surprised that I raised my voice. That I got angry over the reasons she devalues herself.

Her grandmother, her ex, us? None of us are any better than the rest. We're insignificant. Animals. We don't matter. And it kills me—rips me to fucking shreds—knowing that she doesn't understand that.

"You think you aren't good enough," I say, my voice softening, the need to be tender with her overpowering the rage. "That's why you want to die?"

Her dull brown eyes meet my whitish-blue ones. There's an emptiness inside of her that reflects back to me. That sees me for what I am too.

I don't need to hear her words to know her answer; everything I said about her grandmother and her ex is true. The worst part is herself.

She is her own worst critic.

"There's no point, is there?" she asks in an emotionless voice. Her answer is as simple to her as the air we're breathing. "Why do you want to live?"

A light pain fills my chest, my mind radiating, unsure of which direction to run. Where to drag her with me.

There was a time when I was like Ren. Where nothingness seemed better than enduring. Where death seemed like a sanctuary.

Why *did* I keep going?

Ren's gaze holds mine, and I picture her lying on the gurney, her head covered in that canvas bag. How I may have known exactly who she was, but that I didn't truly understand how messed up she was underneath all of that.

I picture her in that dirt hole. In the broken coffin. Filthy and needy, doing exactly what I said, even when it terrified her.

I picture her when she comes—her beautiful, contorted face, struggling to give me what I want. Giving it to me anyway.

Some tiny part of her *wants* to survive. And I'm supposed to kill her.

I could do it right now. I could give her the secobarbital in my pocket. I could use the excavator to bulldoze her soft body into a grave, covering her with enough dirt that none of the mortuary clients notice her presence.

But then I wouldn't be able to make her scream and cry. I wouldn't be able to force that numbness out of her veins and *make* her see the reality around us. I wouldn't be able to make her suffer her own innate will to live.

My dick hardens, addicted to seeing that pure instinct in her face when she comes. Her eyes flick down to my bulge, and subtly, her knees spread, reacting to me so instinctively, that my skin tingles.

She touches her neck, waiting for me.

Why do you want to live? she had asked. There's an answer for that.

"I'll show you," I say.

Chapter 21

Blaze

In minutes, we're on Back Beach Road, taking the highway west into the Northern Florida woods. Darkness swallows the asphalt. Every once in a while, a lamppost illuminates a road sign, reminding us of civilization. Cars dissipate until we're driving alone.

About an hour in, there's a turnoff. A dirt road. *No Trespassing* is written in red letters on a faded, rusting sign. I'm familiar with the area. Private property, yes, but no one patrols the woods this far out.

And if we get caught, it doesn't matter.

It shouldn't matter. Not for me.

Definitely not for her.

The car inches forward and bobs on the dirt road, until eventually we hit a dead end. I curve the car to the side and angle the headlights into the trees. Ren gasps, her focus fixated on what I've left there for her. *For us.*

A noose.

I power off the engine, my chest rumbling, anticipation bubbling inside of me. It took some digging, but between the gossip and Last Spring's access to the county records, I knew about Ren's mother before she told me. *Ligature marks on the neck,* the medical examiner wrote. *Bruises on the fingers, signs of struggle. Death by asphyxiation.*

The tattoo of the noose. Her fixation with her own death. The details she told me in the cemetery. It's an obvious response to trauma. A coping mechanism.

I'm not against changing that.

Out in the woods, I pull a short stool from behind the trees and place it beneath the noose. Then I round the vehicle and open Ren's car door, surprising myself with those polite behaviors. Who knew I could be a gentleman? Leading her through her desires. Showing her the echoes of her past.

I hold out my hand, offering it to her. Waiting for her to take it.

You want to know why I want to live, love? I'll give you my reason.

Her pollen-tinted skin grays now, changing to wet sand as she stares up at that noose. Frozen in time. Ignoring my offered hand. Perhaps she's having flashbacks to her mother, too stunned to grasp the reality in front of her.

I should be sympathetic to that. Hold her hand. Let her know that I'll always be right here, waiting for her.

But that's not me.

I grab her by the fucking hair and wrench her out of the car, her body instantly tightening. She yelps. Her heart beats fast as she struggles against me, fighting me, resisting what she knows is coming, even if she's done it to herself a hundred times before. My dick hardens, ready for her, loving her struggle, *forcing* her to confront her own fear. It scares her—facing the past—and right now, it's waiting for her.

And she's been waiting for it too. She wants it. *Craves it.* Needs everything I can give her. Even this.

My head spins with lust, her ripe scent snaking into my nose. I get her locked under the crook of my arm, and I push on her head, forcing her deeper into the angle of my elbow as I squeeze the air out of her body. She pulls at my arm, so fucking desperate, it's beautiful—but my little corpse doesn't say a word. Doesn't tell me to stop.

Then she's unconscious. I lay her down. I've got a minute or so to finish the prep work. I slam the cuff on her wrists, then grab the rope from the tree and place it around her neck. I double-check my pocket for my switchblade.

Then, on my knees, I put my hand down her leggings, playing with her pussy. She's sopping wet, the sloppy little bitch, that fear driving her deeper into the madness. *Into me.* I roll my neck, desire shuddering through me. She's insatiable, my little corpse, and *fuck*, I want her.

She twitches, her abdomen clenching up, and she chokes on her own spit as she comes back to me. My breathing accelerates. Her eyes squint, the headlights blinding her. She yanks at her wrists; they're cuffed together now, and she whimpers. Kicks her legs. Whines as she pulls at those metal rings, tears welling in her eyes. And I laugh deep. My cock twitching against her.

"What the fuck?" she howls.

I smile. It's the first time she's questioned me tonight. Still, my girl doesn't say the words—doesn't tell me to stop—because she knows she wants it too.

I lick her cheek. Her skin smooth under my tongue, her lips quivering in revulsion. It disgusts her—licking her like an animal—and that's precisely why I do it. To remind her that this isn't about her. It's about *me*. What I want. How I can use her. What I can do to her and for her.

I take out my phone and record her in the harsh light. The dark night contrasts against the bright headlights like a black-and-white television screen. Synthetic against natural. Every part of our arrangement goes against our survival instincts.

And I love every second of it.

"Here's what we're going to do," I say in a low, taunting voice. She stills, like prey looking into the lights, trying to see the safety on the other side. But I'm all there is now. "You're going to tell the camera why you want to die," I continue. "List every reason. Don't skip any of it. And then, you're going to explain that you *asked* me to kill you."

"Why?" she whispers.

It's a simple question, and yet tension pulses in my temples. Her heart drums against me, begging for an answer. There's no reason to make her do this. It's not like it would hold up legally. The best option would be to kill her and get this whole charade over with. It's not like I *need* her anymore. I know how to work the retorts, and I know that killing her *will* be as satisfying as killing my mother.

But I *want* her to recognize those reasons. To see them in a new way. To see them through *my* eyes.

This isn't solely about killing her anymore. I need *more* than that from her.

"Think of it as a suicide note," I say.

Her face twists, fear and bravery struggling for dominance, but her shoulders shrink, that endless numbness washing it away.

Her eyes bulge, veins throbbing in her forehead. Anger surging ahead. My balls contract, relishing in the fact that she *does* feel. She's capable of so much, she just doesn't know it yet.

"Is this for insurance?" she hisses. "So you have evidence when you get caught? My wrists are locked behind my fucking back! Do you know how insane this is?"

"Are you asking me for the keys?" I ask.

Her face drops, all of that rage melting into the ground, dissolving into the truth. We both know her answer. Even these words—these requests for an explanation about *why* I'm doing this to her—none of it means anything because she doesn't want me to stop. Not really. She wants to go there *with me*.

She has to find her own truth.

"All you have to do is say it, little corpse. Back out of our arrangement. Tell me you want out, and I'll unlock your handcuffs." I motion for her to stand on the stool. On top of it, we'll be the same height, and the shifting power that it represents isn't lost on me. The deeper we go, the more power she finds.

But she's in *my* noose. She's still *mine*.

I take a seat on the hood of the car, then aim the phone's lens at her.

"Now, tell me, love. Why do you want to die?" I ask.

A tear slips down her face. Her head hangs low as she steps onto the stool. I shift the lens toward her body. The harsh lights wash against her like passing road signs, and she looks vulnerable like this. Powerless. Weak.

She's not.

Blood swirls in my ears, filling my cock with desire. The noose will go tight, and she'll come for me.

I can end this *right now* if I want to.

"Because I'm worthless," Ren finally says, her voice hoarse. "Because I don't do anything of value. My life doesn't improve anything. Or anyone. I'm a waste of air. I want to die. I want *you* to kill me."

I unzip my pants and pull out my dick. The veins undulate as I stroke the length, rubbing the head, teasing the tip—so fucking turned on by her internal struggle that it's hard not to come right now. Her *fear*. Her trepidation. The fact that she can't be numb; she *has* to accept this. She knows what she wants, and it's *not* easy.

I slide off of the car, my pants shifting down to my hips. The camera lens stays on her.

"Because I'm a burden. I'm useless," Ren whispers. "No matter how hard I try, I'll never be good enough."

I rip off her leggings and underwear with one hand, then kneel in front of her. On the stool, she towers over me, and it dawns on me—

This isn't a stool for me to kick out and watch her neck snap; it's a pedestal for me to worship her. She's a fucking goddess in her own right, taking control of her future. And I'll sacrifice it all to be inside of her as she realizes that.

I stand, slowly lifting her thigh with my free hand, exposing her juicy, hairy cunt. She's at the perfect height—high enough for me to fuck her, and high enough that there's a very real possibility that she'll break her neck. Even though I'm standing now, I can see the headlights shining on the glimmering arousal dripping down her inner thighs. My mouth salivates. Her scent snakes in through the pine trees: heady and sour, and so fucking addictive.

She has no idea the effect she has on me. I roll my neck, keeping myself even.

"Good enough for whom?" I growl.

"For anyone," she says.

I tease the tip of my dick into her slit, barely inside. Those soft hairs tickle the head of my cock.

"No, love," I say. "Try again."

"For you."

A guttural roar bursts through me. Ren gasps and twists back, almost tripping off of the stool. I grab her ass, keeping her in place.

"This isn't about me, and you know it," I snarl.

"For my grandmother. For my mother."

I lean my head down, my hot breath warming her through the fabric of her shirt. Her body erupts with goosebumps. She's sensitive, and so responsive to me. The trees surrounding us spin, and I know that I can't take much more of this.

"That's not it, little corpse, and you know it," I whisper harshly.

"I'm not good enough for myself," she cries.

I pull her off of the stool, then drop my phone as I plunge my cock deep inside of her. She screams, her pussy constricting around me like she could strangle me to death with that cunt. I fuck her hard, pulling her body with me so that the noose tightens around her neck. Her eyes widen, the blood pooling in her cheeks.

"Plea—" she sputters, losing her ability to speak. "B-blaze, please—"

I step back again, the rope choking her, her face blooming into a purplish-red, bright and fucking beautiful, even in these harsh lights. She bobs on my dick, swinging for control. Fighting against me. Against herself. Against her will to do anything at all. If the fall from a noose doesn't break the person's neck, then they can last up to five minutes asphyxiating like this. Swinging like a pendulum. Back and forth between life and death. And that's the struggle that I want: to see exactly what my little corpse does as those minutes count down, what she does when she sees the world darkening around her.

I hold Ren there, kneading her hips, my dick swelling, her cunt constricting on my length for dear life. Her eyes bulge, red vessels mixing with her irises, milking her focus into a muddy brown, and her cunt *squeezes*—that rippled velvet clutching against me one last time, the life in her pupils rolling to white as she loses consciousness—

I pull out the switchblade and cut the rope. She collapses into my grasp. We crash down to the ground, the twigs, the branches, and the fertile decay digging into our arms, our legs, every part of exposed skin. I loosen the noose enough to give her life again, but I don't stop fucking her. I thrust hard, *deep*, impaling her with my cock, goring her like a predator until I stab into her cervix, until I know I'm carving out a space for myself inside of her where she'll never be able to forget that I fucking own her.

She comes back to me, gasping for air. I thrust her around until she's lying on her stomach, burying her body into the twigs and leaves. She groans, the pain stabbing into her, and I fuck her from behind, relentless, not giving a fuck if she likes it, because she wants to be taken, used, to be worthy of something, and if it's the last thing I give her, then I'm going to fucking do it. Our bodies cut an imprint of us into the ground, marking our space, the first descending steps into our mutual grave.

"This is what you deserve," I say. "You're just a whore. My dead whore."

I fuck her, harder, and harder, teaching her everything I know. Everything about life and death and this fucked-up existence that we both crave and despise so deeply. How it numbs us. Forces us to hate the world around us. Tricks us into thinking there's nothing good worth living for, when reality is far darker than that.

"You think you're not good enough?" I growl. "You're wrong. You're nothing, little corpse. And nothing can't disappoint. Nothing can't be guilty. Nothing can't fail, because nothing doesn't exist. And that's all we are, Ren. *We* are nothing. And if you can't see that, then I'm going to fuck you until you understand exactly why I want to live."

I yank the hair at the top of her scalp, pulling her back like a chained animal, and she cries so loud, so deep, so *powerful* that I can't hold back anymore. I come inside of her, my cock jerking, my body convulsing. Ren's demons crawl into me and consume every last ounce of control I have. She dives over that edge too, her cunt twitching, come gushing out of her, mixing with mine, surrendering to that pleasure, needing it as much as she needs air.

We fall to our backs, collapsing from the adrenaline. I reach over and grip a fistful of her hair, dragging her against the twigs and branches until she's closer to me. She whimpers—it must hurt—but her clammy body finds its place on top of me. She curls into the fetal position, her breathing languid, finding her serenity in the aftermath of it all.

I brush the leaves and hair out of her eyes. They're closed now, so damn exhausted she might be asleep already.

"That's why," I say quietly.

Her chest rises and falls. There's a chance she didn't hear me. I'm okay with that. Relieved, even. A spiral of pressure claws up my chest, reminding me that none of this is what I planned. I already have that connection I crave. She should be dead right now, and that high from her murder should be satiating me, giving me the motivation to find my next victim.

It's a cruel game, playing with someone's sense of self, and that *should* fit me. It doesn't though, and I can't explain it. My dick is hard, but there's something else there too. A force that relinquishes my control of her. Of this. Of us.

It's like I can't control myself anymore.

I place a hand on her throat, then massage the bruises there, and impulsively, she spreads her legs. I don't squeeze though. For once, this isn't about forcing her to come; it's about letting her know that I'm here. That I see her. That I still want her, even after all of this. Even if she thinks she doesn't deserve anything—not even a fucked-up sociopath like me—I'm still here.

She nuzzles into me, her nose flaring against my chest, finding comfort in my touch. It must be painful for her to have my fingertips even skim across her neck—there's no doubt that the rope gave her a friction burn—but Ren's eyes remain closed, her body relaxing. Finding peace.

I let her sleep like that, the remnants of the noose hanging around her neck like a leash.

And for a while, I rest my eyes too.

Chapter 22

Blaze

I skip work the next day. It's a compulsion at first. A need to do something else. Something other than work with Ren. And yet my body aches—literally fucking hurts—like it needs her. I don't know if I strained my muscles fighting her in the woods, or if I'm just addicted. It's like my body craves her as much as it craves the high from my first kill.

It's fucking irritating.

I grab an old stash of sedatives that I coerced Brody into giving me. Need grows inside of me like a red tide blooming across the coast, the itch to kill driving me mad. I stare at the choke chain and leash on the nightstand, willing myself to picture strangling Ren to death with it. It's what I've wanted since the beginning. It should feel right.

It doesn't inspire me now. Not like that. My dick gets hard, but I'm not thinking of her corpse falling into me. I'm thinking about her cunt squeezing me in arousal. Coming for me. Her musk. That primal proof that she gives me every single time.

I can't stop thinking about her.

Once I'm sure Denise is out on a house call, I visit Last Spring. The new part-time assistant helps a client in the showroom, barely noticing me as I enter the building. I stand outside of the crematory. Ren works, a fluttering energy in her shoulders. A long-sleeve turtleneck shirt—probably to cover up the bruises—clings to her body. A scratch dashes across her cheek, red and scabbed over. Probably from the sticks in the woods.

My dick twitches *imagining* the deep purple bruises. Then I grunt in anger. These emotions are the problem. The reason why I'm slowly losing grip on what I want out of her.

Ren's eyes light up as she sees me.

"I thought you called in," she says, surprised. "What are you doing here?"

I search her face like I'll find something there. Evidence. Fuck, I don't know. *Proof.*

She smiles, and I know—whatever it is—it's not there.

Ren is okay.

I grit my teeth. Her beautiful, toothy, fucking smile, like a child in a toy store—it grates on me. Fills me with relief and annoyance and fucking pride when I see her happy like that.

I'm not supposed to make her happy. I'm supposed to kill her.

Fuck.

"I can take the hint," I mutter, forcing myself to seem offended, as if the rage will actually materialize inside of me and send me spiraling into some concrete action against her. "I'll fuck off, then."

"Blaze?" she asks. "What the—"

"Goddamn it, Ren. I'm talking to myself, all right? I just—"

I leave before I finish the sentence. The anger is *real*, real as the blood pumping through my cold, fucked-up heart. But the anger is not *for* Ren. *She* did nothing. It's *me* who fucked up. Me and my pathetic obsession with a woman who is more obsessed with death than I am.

It's not fucking right, and I don't know how to change it. To fix things so that they're back in place.

But I know, without a doubt, that I have to kill soon.

Not soon. *Now.*

I could kill her grandmother. She's an obvious choice. Then again, I get this stupid feeling that Ren would blame herself for her grandmother's murder.

But Ren's ex? Making her think she's truly worthless? Forcing her to be ashamed of her desires? As far as I can tell, she hasn't spoken to him in years.

I can work with that.

Panama City Beach is a small southern beach town, so it doesn't take long to flip through the high school yearbooks at city hall and find who I'm looking for. I find her graduation year, and eventually, I find her name. Ren Kono. My little corpse. The deviant little slut who is supposed to be dead right now.

I check her club pictures. She was in a few: yearbook, leadership, an honor society, even track and field. I'm sure her grandmother forced her into all of them; it's what a successful granddaughter would do. And repeating in all of those photos is one male face. The two of them stand together in every picture. Their names are even listed under the same university in the college announcements in the back of the book.

Arnold Weber.

Arnold, like Ren, still lives in Florida, though *he*—the big, strong, *successful* man that he is—moved to Tallahassee, the capital of the state. Apparently, after he got his doctorate, he switched gears and joined a startup social media marketing company, ditching his original plans to work in education. And because of the nature of his current business, he doesn't keep his whereabouts private. No—the idiot *likes* bragging on social media, checking in at every bar, every restaurant, every fucking *shop* that he visits, tagging anyone with him, using the line that he's "promoting" the company, when it's obvious that he's anxious for the reassurance that he's *worth* something. That people care about him.

Just like he bullied Ren into being his perfect, makeup-wearing fiancée, he's backed himself into a corner where he subconsciously beats himself up for not being good enough every single day.

I don't care about his battered ego. I don't care if he's changed. I don't care if he's a better man. If he'd apologize to Ren if he saw her now.

I want him to suffer.

Sure enough, in his usual form, Arnold checks into a tiki bar in Tallahassee, with some hashtag about influencing and meeting people in "real life."

The bar swarms in shades of rolling blue, a light projector in each corner to give the bar the appearance of being underwater. Arnold rests his forearms on the countertop, licking his lips at the bartender as he gawks at her cleavage. His button-up shirt is undone at the top, his chest hair poking out, and an oversized, gaudy smartwatch is on his wrist, so shiny it's practically a disco ball. The device glares, and the bartender flinches away. Arnold winks at her.

No matter how hard he tries to disguise it, Arnold is nothing. Just like we are. And I'm going to make sure he knows that before he dies.

"You're so pretty, you know that?" Arnold says. "You should smile more. A pretty girl like you? You'd make a ton of tips if you just smiled more. I can take your picture for the bar's website if you want. I'm a great photographer."

"Yeah?" the bartender says. "Do you want another drink from this resting bitch face, or are you going to keep giving me unsolicited advice?"

"Babe, you know I'm only trying to help you."

Annoyance flares in my veins. With anyone else, I'd be amused, idly watching to see how long the bartender will take it before she shuts him down for good. With *him* though, I don't see the bartender rolling her eyes and shoveling his bullshit back to him. I see a younger, more vulnerable version of Ren, tucking her black hair behind her ear, looking down at her stomach. Gazing in the mirror. Wondering if he thinks she's pretty enough now that she's wearing some makeup.

I keep an eye on Arnold, and as the night draws on, it's obvious that *despite* his advances, he's going home alone.

Makes things easier for me.

I follow him to his car—the fucker shouldn't be driving anyway—and I grab him from behind, then stab him with the syringe, the sedative filling his veins. He swings his fists, but quickly passes out, relaxing into me.

I move him behind the dumpster. A surveillance camera hangs

from the building's back wall, a loose cable limp on the side of it. It's all for show, like him.

Once the bastard is bound and in the trunk of my car, I take him to Blountstown. The grave is still there, the same one I half-buried Ren inside of, and there's satisfaction in imagining *him* taking her place. Near where my mother is buried. One pathetic excuse for a human rotting next to the corpse of another.

I drop him inside of the hole.

Stop crying, or I'll never let you out, my mother had said through the closet door, the memory of her words filling my head as I stare down at Arnold. His body is in a dark hole in the ground, where he can barely see. Where he'll fucking die. His strong jaw is set, a touch of gray in his brown hair. Dimpled cheeks. He was probably the star of the football team or something stupid like that.

It's annoying; I can see why Ren liked him.

My mind shoots back again, remembering why my mother preferred my brother.

Why can't you be better? my mother had said. *Your brother never complained like this, you know that? But you? You act like it's worse than death. If you just shut the fuck up and behaved like a good boy, we wouldn't be here right now, would we?*

Vibrations fill me, the rage coursing through each nerve. The same sensation I got after I watched them fuck my mother. After they took me too.

I told them they could do whatever they wanted, she had said later, like an afterthought. *They liked you. I guess there's a good reason to keep you around.*

My mother. Ren's grandmother. Even Arnold here, the fucking parasite. They're all the same.

I step on Arnold's chest, shifting my weight on top of him, my mother's words filling my head with steam. Each explanation she crammed down my throat. Each lie she told to keep the guilt from taking over. I should see myself in Arnold. I should take pity on him. Instead, I remember the time my mother watched as the first man gave me the cut on my side. How she watched as the other men reopened the wound, letting me bleed. How they all laughed. How I had to learn to take care of the gash, otherwise, it'd get infected again. I remember how she threatened to leave me in the closet if I didn't stop crying. Those times she said I'd never amount to anything worthwhile in this world. The times I believed her.

Perhaps I do see a sliver of myself in Arnold's lifeless body. I can see how his insecurities are like Ren's. Like mine once were.

But I'm not going to let him fuck over *my* corpse.

I move my boot, putting pressure on the fucker's throat. He coughs, then his eyes flutter open and widen as he comes to terms with his new surroundings. I lift my boot, letting him absorb the situation. He's in peril now.

Panic wrinkles his face, his lips quivering as if the shock has instantly cleared the sedative out of his system. I flick open my switchblade, heat snaking through me.

If only Ren could see him now.

"What the fuck, man?" he slurs. "What is this? Who are you?"

Usually, I enjoy a slow death, savoring every last heartbeat. With him, the rage fills my knuckles until I fall to my knees and stab him repeatedly in the stomach. I don't stop. My hands turn whiter than before, and the handle of the knife coats in red. Blood gurgles over his lips, and I laugh. I even pull the blade down and split open his stomach. Thread his intestines through my fingers like seaweed on the beach.

His organs are hot. Slippery like jellyfish. My dick throbs as I look down at him, but all I see is Ren: her blank eyes coming to life, then emptying back into that sweet abyss she wants to escape inside of. Her unconscious cave.

The fucker babbles, wheezing one last time, and I stroke the top of his head with a bloody hand, pretending he's her.

Soon, my love, I think. *Soon, my sweet little corpse.* I don't know what I'm promising, or why I want to give it to her. But right now, everything I have is for her.

A water bottle—probably the same one from the night with Ren—catches my eye. I jump off of Arnold and grab it, then dump out the rest of the contents. I scoop an arm underneath his shoulders, propping him up, then I hold the bottle to his stomach and fill it with blood and small chunks of flesh. The red liquid warms the plastic, and my hips pulse, considering all the possibilities. The ways I can use it to get off.

Power surges inside of me. It's *his* blood.

I cap the bottle, then use the extra blood on my palms to fuck myself. Red stains cover my pants, my dick hard as a rock. The blood is warm, like Ren's cunt. Like safety. Like knowing that I'm the last thing she'll ever need.

I come quickly, ejaculating on his corpse. Then the post-orgasm clarity comes to me, catching in my throat.

I've masturbated with blood before. I've even ejaculated on a corpse. I've done so many fucked-up things that would make a "normal" person wretch in disgust.

But I've never killed a man before.

Then, I realize I collected his blood *for her*.

Ren. The woman who was supposed to be my fourth.

I hold the bottle to my chest. It cools, adjusting to the late winter air. The fact that I killed *someone* should comfort me. It's not enough though.

I want *more*.

I drag the body inside, using the exposed beams in the house to hang it by the ankles so that I can properly drain it.

I don't let myself think about how much time I've already invested in Ren, nor do I think about how she should be dead already, how I should be moving onto my next victim. Shit, it's not going to be easy testing the blood to make sure it's safe for her, but Brody will have what I need, and he's too much of a chicken shit to ask questions.

There's the problem with the body too. I can bury it here, like I originally intended, with my mother.

But that doesn't appeal to me anymore.

The best option is to show my little corpse how much she's taught me.

Chapter 23

Ren

Hunger cinches my stomach. A rice bowl with teriyaki flank steak sits on the second shelf of the fridge, *Ren* written in black ink on the plastic wrap. I blink at it as if my name will disappear once my eyes focus. Mrs. Richmond never saves me leftovers.

Is this guilt? Does she feel bad about what Blaze said?

About what *I* said?

I try not to think about it. Understanding her motivations won't change what she thinks of me, and right now, I'm *really* hungry. I heat up the bowl in the microwave, then stand with the bowl burning my hands. It used to be my favorite meal. Supposedly it was my mother's too, something my father made for her once. Right now, I don't feel loss or sorrow though. There's something else inside of me, crawling up to the surface.

I picture Blaze sitting at the dinner table, eating the rice bowl. *It's okay,* he'd say dismissively. Knowing him, if I cooked it, he'd finish every bite to prove it to me that he could endure it.

And if my grandmother cooked it, he'd probably throw it in her face.

I glance at my phone. It's evening. Mrs. Richmond still isn't home.

It's been a long time since I've gone to the mortuary after hours by myself. I haven't needed it. Blaze and I have sex there, but I don't crave going by myself anymore. It's like Blaze has changed my habits. My way of thinking.

I sit at the dinner table, openly inviting Mrs. Richmond to walk into the house. To see me there. To join me. I used to dream of her finding me dead in her kitchen. To have that pain fill her. To force her to acknowledge the anguish I kept locked inside of me.

But I have this feeling that Mrs. Richmond would sweep me away like she did with my mother.

Once I finish the rice bowl, I scan the fridge for more food. I take a bite of watermelon. A pickle slice. I even open one of the sweet tea bottles Mrs. Richmond loves so much. For years, food has been nothing more than sustenance, but it's like drinking that bottle of water outside of the grave in Blountstown ignited something inside of me. I savor everything, letting the cold tea run over my tongue, the slimy pickled cucumber wiggle against my cheek, the watermelon crush under my teeth. I'm supposed to die soon, and maybe that's why my insides crave to experience everything and anything right *now*. Good. Bad. Ugly. Beautiful. All of it. Every bite. Every drink. Even every gulp of fresh air is like the best I've ever had.

It has nothing to do with food or the air though. I'm seeing the world in a new light, and as much as I enjoy it, I know it's all going to end soon. Going back to the way it was. It's distracting me from what's in front of me. Waiting for me.

Still, my fingers buzz with nervous energy, and I tap my cheek, my fingertips grazing over the healing scab from the woods. Feeling safe like this. Enjoying the world. The promise of it. It's a trap.

I check the medicine cabinet to keep myself grounded. Mrs. Richmond's old prescription bottle for Xanax is still empty, but another one stands next to it. A different benzodiazepine. It's full, like she got it for me, knowing that I'd need it.

Maybe she does care about me.

Or maybe she gets the medication for me so that I'll shut up.

My phone buzzes. I check the message from Blaze: *Meet me at the crematory at midnight.*

My heart flutters, like winged insects are humming in my chest. It's almost the same as his first text, back whenever this—this fucked up, invigorating thing we have—started. Last time, he *ordered* me to come to the crematory. Now, he wants to *meet* me there. It's a demand, sure, but there's a sense of equality there too. Like we're both traveling to the edge of our fate, our worlds colliding in the middle.

I shake my head. I'm reading too much into this. I'm his little corpse. I'm nothing. And you can't find value in nothing.

The orange prescription bottle drops into the sink, the top popping open. The pills fall into the ceramic, partially disintegrating from the leftover drops of water. I've just screwed up my chance to use them later.

"Damn it," I mutter as I scoop them up. This is exactly where my problem lies, isn't it? I shouldn't even be *looking* for Mrs. Richmond's pills right now. This should be over. *Blaze* needs to be reminded of our arrangement. We *both* do. We have a goal. It's the only way we can guarantee that we both get what we want. We can't lose sight of that.

At eleven, too antsy to do anything else, I head to Last Spring. Inside, a light trails from the crematory, and the thud of a body on metal echoes through the hallway.

I hold my breath. I know it's Blaze. Still, I never know what to expect with him.

I wait in the doorframe, watching him like he always watches me. He closes the metal door to the retort, the oven's lock clicking into place.

Is he burning a body?

Of course he's burning a body. What else would he be doing right now? I taught him how, and he's using that knowledge. It's part of our arrangement.

I need to stop forgetting who and what we are to each other.

He stares at the dials, then punches the control panel.

"You're supposed to preheat," I remind him.

He gives a slight roll of his shoulders. "We've got time."

The retort hums, vibrating through our silence. There's a

tangible nature to the white noise, like we both know we *should* be doing so many things, *except* being here with each other.

Neither of us moves.

Neither of us wants to.

"Is the body in the queue for tomorrow?" I ask. Immediately, I realize how dumb of a question that is. It's not a client's loved one. It's one of Blaze's kills.

He raises a brow at me, his only answer to my question, and I giggle to myself. Like an idiot. I should report him. It's what a *good* person would do, but why should I care? Humans have been killing each other since the beginning of time, and if Blaze is a killer who is willing to help me, then why should I judge him for that?

There are so many fucked-up things in the world. I'm one of them. Blaze is too. Maybe *everyone* is just as fucked up as we are. Maybe some people are better at hiding it.

With Blaze, I don't have to hide anymore.

My death. His murder. Sex is an afterthought. Teaching him to cremate bodies is a bonus. We can't lose sight of that.

"Blaze," I say quietly, focusing on my flats. Refusing to face him, knowing what it will do to me. "When we first started this, we agreed that—"

"I have something to give you," he says, cutting me off. "A present."

My nostrils flare. Was he anticipating what I was going to say next? Did he interrupt me on purpose? Is he avoiding it too?

But that would mean that whatever this is, this thing between us, *means* something to him. And that's not possible. I'm reading into him again. I'm his little corpse. His fourth victim. The one who came and died for him willingly.

I ignore my thoughts. I let him guide our conversation.

I tilt my head. "A present?"

He motions for me to follow him, then leads me to the embalming room. Everything is clean, metal, with crisp lines. A chemical scent wafts through the air, the faint sweetness of death at the back of it.

"Take off your clothes," Blaze orders.

I don't question him this time. I obey. Folding my clothes and putting them on the counter, I wrap my arms around myself, hiding my body. Blaze grabs my arms, forcing them down to my sides.

"Don't cover yourself," he snarls. He grabs my cunt, his fingers digging into my flesh. Pain shoots through me, and my eyes widen, relishing in it. "This body belongs to me, and you will *not* hide it from me."

I trace his eyes, seeing his absolute truth. He's serious.

I nod subtly. Trying not to disturb him more.

A smile stretches across his lips. "Good. Now, lie down on the table."

The coldness of the metal shocks me. I've laid on this table and masturbated before. This shouldn't be different. But Blaze's eyes are like a magnifying glass, peering into the layers beneath my skin. Seeing the muscle and bone and everything vulnerable underneath. I fight with myself to stay still, to expose myself to him. He *wants* to see me, no matter the situation.

My head spins. I lift my hips, resting my ass on my fingers. Keeping still for him.

"Have you ever had anal sex *before* me, love?" he asks. I subtly shake my head. "Some people say it's the most erotic activity there is. There are endless nerve endings down there, you know. Given the right set of tools, it can rip an orgasm right out of you." He chuckles. "We've done it before, haven't we? But not like this."

He opens the cupboard above the sink. Labelless water bottles filled with red liquid line the shelf. My ears throb, fear and anticipation clawing through my stomach.

"What is that?" I whisper.

He grabs the first bottle, then gives it a squeeze.

"You know what it is, my love. You don't need me to say it."

My love? When he calls me "love," that's all it is. A noun. Never a possessive. Never *his love.*

Am I hearing things? Am I—

He twists the cap, then pours the red liquid over his hands. The shiny crimson globs drip on the floor, the stark contrast of red blood on white tile glaring up at us.

"This is—" I sit up and shake my head. "This is unsanitary. We can't—"

He shoves me down, a giant red handprint in the middle of my breasts. His teeth bared, his expression full of warning, his jaw tighter than an oyster protecting a pearl.

"Question me again, little corpse, and see what happens," he growls. "I'm not fucking around anymore."

Our eyes lock, judging each other in a contest of dominance. This could be *it*.

I relax. Close my eyes. Force myself to trust whatever happens next. To trust *him*.

Liquid splashes over my stomach, the icy temperature rattling me.

"That's fucking cold!" I shriek.

Blaze chuckles, then massages the gloopy blood over my skin, hunger filling his eyes as he marvels at my red body. He nods at me, silently telling me to relax, and eventually I do. I don't think about the blood and whoever it belongs to, nor do I think about the fact that I'm letting a killer massage me with his victim's blood. I focus on Blaze. On his hunger for me. On the need in his eyes as he appraises me.

"Look at you," he murmurs, his voice as thick as the coagulated blood. He pinches my lips together, smashing me like a puppet, then he licks his lips, and those worries vanish. "You try to tell me that this is bad, that it's dirty, *unsafe*, but you don't try very hard, do you? You *like* this, love. You like knowing that I've drained a man's blood for you."

My heart beats rapidly, thudding against my rib cage like a fist banging on a door. I try to deny it. Try to shake my head. To move my lips. To scream internally and resist it all. To be a good person. To *not* give into the bad thing and enjoy sex covered in someone's blood.

The words don't come out.

Visible excitement bubbles up in Blaze, his chest expanding as he studies my inner battle. He tips the bottle again. The blood splashes his clothes, streaking him in blotchy patches of red, and my mouth drops open. His hands pool between my thighs, exploring me, conquering every valley and crevice I have in crimson.

The liquid is cold. His fingers are damp, slightly pruney from being soaked in liquid. He uses the blood to tease the ridges of my ass, his eyes locked on me, his mouth open, waiting for my reaction. A chill runs down my spine.

It's blood. He's using someone's blood as lubricant for ass play.

My cheeks flush at the reality of it all. *This is so messed up. What am I doing?*

"How does that feel?" he asks, his voice soft, yet commanding.

My mind is blank. I'm supposed to be disgusted. Revulsed. I should be repulsed by *everything* in this situation.

A thought reaches through me, coming out of the shadows, and those worries about what I should or shouldn't do melt away.

I don't care about who the blood belongs to. I'm supposed to.

But I don't.

Blaze's cock pulses against his pants, and my mouth waters.

He still wants me.

And I want more.

His fingers swirl around my ass, teasing the opening, the touch somewhere between tickling and massaging.

"It feels—" I start. I don't know how to describe it. I try concentrating on that ridge of muscle; my head floats. Tension releases from my body as I accept my own thoughts and come to terms with this moment.

Maybe we are bad people. Maybe none of us are good. Or maybe it's just Blaze and I that are the fucked-up ones.

Maybe I'm okay with that.

"It feels good," I whisper.

Blaze inserts an inch of a wide finger. I grimace. He moves the finger back and forth inside of me, slightly at first, then quicker as each second passes. I hold on to that sensation, onto me and him and everything that connects us to this place. Eventually, I exhale, and my body relaxes, sinking into the table. The metal is warm now, matching the heat of my body, and I realize that the blood is my temperature now too.

"It's different, isn't it?" He holds his finger still in my ass. My knees spread wider, my hips thrusting toward his hand, begging for him to do it again. "Do you like that, love?"

I bite my tongue. This is a feather of his brutality, but somehow, it doesn't disturb me. Not like a hug used to scare me from people who called themselves my friends. My family. How having sex with my fiancé took bottled lube and closed eyes just to get through it. Right now, I'm not disgusted with myself. Blaze wants to do so much more with me, and I know this is only the beginning.

He's not going to kill me. Not yet.

"Do you like it?" he asks again.

I honestly don't know if I do, but I know I want more of it.

I nod hesitantly.

"Say it," he growls.

"I like it," I whisper.

He removes his finger, and my hips twitch, the emptiness haunting me. I ache for his touch. He whips off his shirt. His belt buckle jiggles, his damp pants sloshing to the floor, and for the first time, I see Blaze completely naked. A dark pink scar marks his hip, as if it's healed over time and time again. His skin pale. Tiny red spots blotch against his naked chest, though they're obviously not natural. They're scars too.

His cock hangs down, full of blood. Rigid and ready for me.

Our eyes meet. Pale blue stillness full of arrogance and lust. His promise of unforgiving bliss.

I don't want to fight him anymore.

He steps forward. Grabbing my ankles, he slides my body against the metal, the extra blood gliding against my back until my ass rests on the edge, right against the embalming drain.

He fists his cock, edging it over to my dark hole, the tip massaging the ridges of my ass. I lick my lips and shift my hips closer to him. He quickly grabs another bottle, then unscrews the lid and pours more blood, drenching us in red.

"Is that wet enough?" he asks.

I nod as I thrust forward, silently begging him to take me.

"That's what I thought," he murmurs.

His cock breaks the barrier of my ass; I hold my breath. His fingers dig into my hips, locking in place. He sucks in a gasp, the sensation overwhelming him, and it gets to me too. I barely breathe. I'm full, and I'm tight, and I have to remind myself to breathe.

Breathe.

Blaze's fingertips rub my clit in agonizing circles, keeping his cock still, the purple head gloved by me.

"Look at the dirty, filthy toy laid out on the table for me," he says. "You like being fucked in the ass, little corpse?"

He pushes in another inch, deeper than I thought he could go, and my cheeks boil with shame and intense desire. I cover my face. It's too much.

He smacks my hands out of the way.

"Don't you dare hide from me," he growls. "I want to *see* you come. I want to see you lose yourself. See you forget everything you stand for. Being fucked in the ass. Drenched in blood. You're so fucking wet, aren't you, baby? It's not even the blood now. It's blood and *need.* Your depraved arousal. Because you're just a fucked up little whore who *needs* to be taken like this."

I nod. Bite my tongue. I don't know why I'm agreeing, but I don't stop myself. I can't. I want *more.* More of his madness. More of him. Blaze moves his hips, massaging my ass from the inside. The pain subsides, and the pleasure builds. Heat spreads across my chest. Every nerve ending in my body is electric, buzzing to life.

He pries a finger inside of my cunt, both of my holes filled with him. I groan like an animal and arch my back.

"Dirty little bitch," he laughs. "You're so fucking wet, you're sopping. A pool of arousal and blood. There's no shame when you know you love it. Don't you, slut? Tell me you don't love it. Lie to me."

"I don't," I whisper, my words hoarse. I shove my ass down onto his dick even deeper, grinding on his hooked finger in my pussy, and I cry out in pain. At the fullness. At the knowledge that *this* is what it's like to be complete.

"Beg me not to tear you apart," he yells as he pulls me closer. "Beg me not to rip your tight little ass open. Not to rip you to fucking shreds." His voice turns low, gravelly, full of primal rage: "Beg me not to kill you, Ren."

"Please, please, *please*," I cry. "Please don't kill me."

I rub my clit frantically, urging myself to go over that edge. He thrusts inside of my ass like he wants to scoop out my organs and bury himself inside of me. My thoughts—those worries about us forgetting who we are to each other—dissolve into something else. Something I need more than I need to die right then.

"There's no problem with natural lubrication," he says. He digs a second finger into my cunt, his dick still riding in my ass, against that thin wall of flesh. My mind flashes to my ex, and I glance at the hallway, toward the crematory. Is that who is burning right now? Is that the blood we're bathing in?

Does it matter?

Blaze grabs my chin, forcing me to look at him as he pumps inside of me, his cock taking my ass all the way to the hilt. The tears flood my face. It's not because I'm scared or in pain. I'm *overwhelmed*. Completely destroyed by the fact that Blaze wants me. *All of me*. Even in this fucked up, bloody mess. Even when I cry. Even when I beg to live and die and to do anything and everything he wants. He *still* wants me.

He grabs my neck and my body reacts, surrendering to the pleasure, convulsing like a demon. The orgasm slashes through me, and I have no control anymore. I have no say in who I am or what I want or how my body reacts. I simply exist. I'm nothing and I'm everything and I'm *his*.

Blaze.

The orgasm stops, but he keeps fingering my pussy as his cock tears my ass apart, and it's so fucking much, I'm close to coming all over again.

"Please," I beg. "I need this. I need *you*."

"Then fucking take me," he growls.

He takes his fingers away, and I howl in retaliation. Then he grabs the last bottle and empties the blood over our faces. We're painted in red, evil spirits from another world, and the blood washes away everything right and wrong between us until none of it *means* anything. His eyes hold me still, paralyzing me, and a thought pierces through me—

He told me to beg him *not* to kill me. He wanted me to beg for my life. If we bathe in anyone's blood, it should be mine.

But right now, all I want is Blaze.

"Please," I cry out. "Please. I'm begging you."

"Give it to me, you little cunt," he growls as he chokes me.

My vision goes blank. I forget about everything that led to this moment. About the fact that I was supposed to remind him. About the fact that I used to dream about dying more than I dreamed about the future. About the fact that I just begged to come and begged for my *life*. I let go, giving into pleasure, knowing that this is what I need. This is exactly how I want to spend the rest of my days, doing horrible things with someone who sees me. Who wants me. The real me. Someone who needs me too.

Blaze won't accept any less.

Chapter 24

Blaze

I whistle to myself, my fingers thrumming with vibrations, telling myself everything is fine. That this was a part of my plan: bleaching the tiles, soaking up the last bits of evidence from that fiendish blood bath, letting Ren sleep back in the safety of her grandmother's house.

But it's a lie.

I'm cleaning up after our mess. It's the exact opposite of what I wanted from her.

I need to get her out of my system. Right fucking *now*.

The day passes. Another shift. I ignore Ren, trying to convince myself that she doesn't exist. By the time evening comes, I have a new goal.

My fifth will be a random woman. A stranger like Ren was supposed to be. Killing and fucking this worthless stranger will cure me of my madness. I don't need *Ren*. I need a *hole*. Any corpse will do. I could fuck a man's skull for all I care. And if the bitch doesn't part her legs, then I'll rip them clean off.

So why is Ren still here?

I dismiss the thought and focus on my new purpose. I recline against a condo building across the street from the beach. A cigarette in my mouth, looking the part as I exhale into the night air. It's too early for the true Spring Break crowds, but there are a few college co-eds gathering in the area, hoping to score better deals on the vacation rentals.

On the ground level, an oyster shack with two-dollar well drinks sits directly across from the condo building, right on the beach, which makes this particular set of rentals appealing to the younger crowd. The partiers.

Women like my first.

A set of college co-eds who aren't old enough to be drinking stumble out of their rental. The brunette whistles at me, and I send a bashful smile back.

"You want to come with us?" the brunette asks. "We have a thirty-rack. You can—"

"Bitch, he looks like a murderer," her blond friend says. "Let's go."

Laughter erupts from them, and I force a placating, nervous smile. The friend is blond, like I *thought* my usual type would be. The brunette is closer to what I'm looking for tonight. Not close enough though.

Hours pass. I smoke to pass the time. Then, around two a.m., a young woman with black, shoulder-length hair staggers out of her condo. An ice bucket clutched in her hands, her steps swaggering like she's trying to be sexy. She passes me; coconut and hyacinth wafting in the air around her, her body spray too fragrant to truly entice me. She glances over her shoulder and bats her eyelashes at me, probably wondering if I can tell that she's drunk.

It's her. She's my fifth.

She leans down, then stumbles slightly before resting her hand on the ice machine and pressing the red button. The machine rumbles. Ice spills out, clanking into the bucket. She doesn't hear me coming.

I stab the needle into her neck. She crumbles into my arms like a rag doll. I scoop her up and adjust her head so that it's resting on my chest, like a protective boyfriend *ought* to carry his girlfriend.

In the parking lot, a security guard half my age points his flashlight toward me.

"Where are you two going?" he asks in a forced, gruff voice. "You two all right over there?"

"My girlfriend got real sick, sir," I say in my thickest southern drawl. "Gotta take her back to 'Bama, officer."

The guard nods, pleased to hear me call him "officer." A little flattery, and he's willing to look the other way. What a goddamn joke.

"Stay safe," he says. "You know how people get out here."

I bow my head, then head to my car. The funny thing is that I *do* stay safe. I look out for myself. That's how it's always been, and how it will *always* be. There's no use in getting attached when you know *nothing* is real. Not family. Not love. Not even a chaotic cunt who willingly agrees to be your next victim. Not a woman who you made beg for her life.

Ren wasn't my fourth, nor will she be my fifth.

But this bitch? Whoever she is—*she* will be my fifth.

Then I'll focus on making Ren my sixth.

I carry the drunk woman inside of my house. Gag her with a cloth. Then I dig out the syringe full of pure adrenaline. I stab it into her arm.

"Thanks so much for the adrenaline, big bro," I say sarcastically as I push the plunger down. "She *really* needs it."

The bitch gasps, wheezing around the cloth, and I grab her by the neck, bringing her to her toes. She trembles, fear boiling in her eyes. Her pupils are dilated.

She's tanner than what I was looking for but only slightly, so I give it a pass. The black hair is right though. They even have similar body shapes: average in every way. With my free hand, I squeeze my dick through my pants, readying myself to fuck this stranger.

But I'm soft. I strain my neck, irritation bubbling inside of me as she twitches in my grip. I've never had to get myself hard before killing. I don't have time to question it now. I play with my dick. Force it out of me. *Needing it.* Once this bitch is screaming, I'll be *hard*, and raping her will be worth the effort. I'll have my clarity back. Everything will make sense.

I choke the nameless cunt, conjuring up that future image of Ren's final breath.

Instead, my mind races to the past.

Stop fighting, my mother scolded as she grabbed my neck. *If you just listened to me, then we wouldn't have to do it like this. You're doing this to yourself.*

The memory of her fingers curl around my neck, and I strangle the stranger, matching the strength of my memory. My mother choked me until I stopped fighting. Until I took it like a good child should. Letting those men use me. Letting them fuck my ass and stab my side until they were finished.

Then another memory flashes forth: the scent of my resistance in the air; the rhythmic thrusting of my mother's boyfriend; the understanding that cunt or ass, woman or boy, it was all the same to him. My fists loosen around the stranger's neck, not because I care about her life, but because of that memory. That memory was the moment when I decided I had a choice: I could end my own suffering, or I could kill my mother.

And right now, I have the choice to kill this stranger.

Or I can kill Ren instead.

Air bursts through the woman's mouth, whistling against the gag now that she's finally able to breathe. I push down those visions of the past, and I try—try as hard as I can—to see Ren there. To find pleasure in this stranger's struggle. To see the truth emerge from her death. But none of this matters. Especially not this stranger's cunt.

She twitches in my arms like a worm. I try to laugh. To find amusement in it all. But this bitch is the same. Just like my second and my third. I can fuck her, but it won't give me what I want.

Besides, my dick is limp.

I can kill her. Whether or not she goes back to college doesn't matter to me. Her life? Her death? She's an animal, like we are all, and we all die.

But why torture her if I don't get anything out of it?

Why waste my time?

Her eyes bulge, frantically searching for a way out. I stare into those brown irises. Scrutinizing them. They're almost the color of honey.

They're too light.

She's wrong, isn't she? That's why this isn't working. She's all fucking *wrong*.

This bitch will never replace Ren.

Fucking her isn't going to change that.

A sob rakes through the stranger's body, and the frustration finally splits through the surface of my composure.

I take the gun from my holster and thrust it against her temple. The hammer clicks into place, the silencer numbing the bullet. The body falls limp, dropping onto my bed.

I grimace; this corpse has no place on my bed.

Using the tip of my boot, I shove the body off of the bed. It clunks down, thudding on the floor. A discarded piece of trash. Like Ren *should* have been.

The only corpse who belongs in my bed, living or dead, is Ren.

I crack my neck in an attempt to control the irritation. I could've made the woman's death a slow, excruciating process, much like I did with my first three kills, but it wasn't the appealing option. No matter how much this failed replacement screamed—no matter how much she fought or enjoyed what I took from her—this woman would never come close to what I want.

No matter how many women I kill. No matter how hard I search. Even if I find the perfect black-haired woman with dull brown eyes, who looks, smells, and acts like what I want, none of it will make a difference. Because it won't be *her*.

No one will ever compare to Ren, and that kills me.

Chapter 25

Ren

Blaze avoids me for three days.

I keep my eyes on the windows and doors of Last Spring, looking for a hint of his white-blond hair. It's stupid paranoia—why would he be avoiding me? I should be the one avoiding *him*—but the instinct that he's ghosting me follows me around like a shadow.

Last Spring carries on. Mourners. Clients. Corpses. During my lunch, for the third day in a row, I head to the embalming room. I'm not sure what I'm looking for. I know it's not going to be covered in blood; Blaze said he would clean it, and I've seen it since then. There's no trace of us. I'm not there for that, though. It's like I need proof of what we did.

Emily, our embalmer, inserts a needle into the corpse's vein. The part-timer bobs her head next to her. Emily twists around and messes with the machine.

"Yes?" she asks.

I bite my lip. I'm not supposed to be here. Emily is going to notice that I keep coming around here, and she's going to start asking questions.

I don't care.

"Have you seen Blaze?" I ask.

"Denise said he called in," she says. "Something about a stomach bug. Why?"

I mumble a lie—something about him giving me a ride home next week—then I shuffle back to the crematory.

My phone lies in my hands as I wait for the retort to finish its work. I want Blaze to call me. To text. To do anything to reach out to me.

My phone stays silent.

The shift ends. I clock out and drive. I don't realize where I'm going until I'm parked outside of his house.

I gaze at the steering wheel, hoping it'll steady me. Willing myself to go home. I shouldn't be here. He didn't invite me here. He doesn't want me.

This is insane. You don't mean anything to each other.

But I turn toward his house. The sun is set now, the sky dark blue. I can't make myself leave.

The front door opens. His house stays dark, and his shadow waits on the porch.

But *what* is he waiting for?

What am I doing here?

I don't dwell on those answers. I walk up to his front porch and meet him there. I tilt my head.

"Where have you been?" I ask.

"Working," he says.

"When?"

"At night."

I reason with myself. Emily would have mentioned that, right? He doesn't mean working at the mortuary; he means something else. Do I want to ask more questions? I shouldn't. I know what he probably means by working. With the amount of blood he poured on me the other night, I have no doubt that he's a killer now.

"Do you want to go get something to eat?" I ask.

The back of my neck tingles. I hold it, hiding my embarrassment. This is stupid. We're not friends. We're not lovers. We're definitely not *dating*. We're two people who agreed to a death contract so that someone random doesn't have to die. So that *I* can take their place. So that I give my life meaning.

You are nothing but a pleasure toy for me to fuck and kill, he had said. *That's all you'll be. That brings you comfort, doesn't it, love?*

His jaw ticks. "I don't go out to eat."

My chin drops, and he sighs deeply, aggravated by my reaction. And damn it, I am too. Why am I doing this to myself? To us? Thinking that we could "go out" together. That we're *those* kinds of people. We're not, and we never will be.

"I'm sorry," I mutter. I swivel around, heading back to the car. "I was being stupid. Sorry for bothering—"

His hand lands on my shoulder. Warmth flows inside of me.

I don't move.

"But we can order takeout," he says.

I look over my shoulder, and his pale blue eyes fixate on me.

"Stay," he orders.

I nod, then he pulls me inside. He leads me to his couch and slaps a stack of menu pamphlets on my lap. The overhead lights flicker on, and though I'm curious to explore his home, I focus on the takeout options. Blaze fixes himself a drink in the kitchen.

The shock swarms in my stomach, my eyes glazing over the words and pictures on the glossy paper. Blaze didn't have to invite me inside, but he *did*. Saying he doesn't go out to eat wasn't about rejecting me.

Why does that make me happy?

Blaze clears his throat, and I come back to my senses. I ask him for his order; he shakes his head, gulping down a drink as he motions to the phone, forcing me to decide. I call a pizza place. As messed up as it is, it's been on my mind since he told me about his past. Will it upset him, triggering an emotional response about his mother that he takes out on me? Am I playing with danger, *hoping* he'll hurt me?

I'm not sure.

I hang up, then glance at Blaze. His shoulders are loose, his stature intimidating even as he relaxes in his own home.

Pizza won't make him kill me.

The pizza is delivered with a complimentary bag of crispy chocolate chip cookies. We each take a slice of pepperoni and eat it on paper towels, and Blaze scoffs at the bonus treat.

"I hate those cookies," Blaze mutters. "The pizza shop back in Blountstown used to carry them too. They taste like nothing."

I snatch the bag off of the table. "Then I'll take them."

"Good. Keep them for the next time you forget to eat."

I stuff them in my purse. "I eat all the time."

"*Sure,*" he says as he gives me side-eyes. I furrow my brows, my stomach tingling. He's noticed that I forget to eat sometimes, hasn't he?

He pays attention to me.

I try not to think about it. I don't want to get my hopes up.

I reach for the glass of water between us. Blaze puts up a hand, stopping me.

"You afraid of germs?" I tease. "I think we've shared plenty."

"You can get your own drink."

I huff, pretending to be annoyed. It should be rude, and maybe it is, but it doesn't *feel* that way with Blaze. Blaze isn't the kind of person to be polite to a house guest, and I honestly never thought I'd be inside of his home in the first place. Fixing myself a glass of water in his kitchen, without his guidance, it's like I belong here. Like this isn't the first time I've been inside of his home.

Like he trusts me.

We eat. Neither of us tries to fill the quiet. We're comfortable like this, and it both comforts and unnerves me. I should be scared of him, but I'm just glad that we're enjoying a meal together. I try not to think about what it means that I'm here. That he told me to stay.

After we finish eating, I ask for the bathroom, and again, instead of leading the way, Blaze gestures down the hallway, expecting me to know where to go.

I wander deeper inside, exploring as I go. There are only necessary furniture pieces in his house—a couch, a dining table, a chest of drawers here or there—and the walls are blank. It's a livable place, not a home where someone has marked their presence, like Blaze knows he may leave at any moment.

Sorrow twists in my gut. It's a real possibility. I imagine serial killers can't stay in one place for long.

Maybe that's why I was searching for him for the past few days —because I was scared he'd disappeared.

Because I didn't want him to.

After I finish, I meander back to the living room. A gleam catches my eye from an open door. I push it open farther.

Handcuffs. Knives. Restraints. All sorts of intimidating metal instruments lie on the bed, waiting to be used. Like they're waiting for *me*. Each device is arranged carefully, as if he's displaying his wears proudly. Like he wants every onlooker to know how important they are to him.

He's used these weapons on his victims before. I can feel it.

He's used some of them on me too.

A pistol lies on top of the nightstand. It's different from the rest, cut off from the main display. There for convenience. Not for pleasure.

If he has killed women before, then he probably has a gun, I had told myself. That was the excuse I held on to, my backup plan in case I decided I didn't trust Blaze. I could still finish the job myself.

So many people—myself included—are all talk. We dream about our future deaths; we never actually go after it. Blaze could be just like me. Too afraid to end my life.

And maybe he is. I'm still alive, aren't I?

I should steal the gun. Keep it as backup. Insurance for the worst-case scenario.

I can finish this myself. I don't need him.

But that's not how this works.

I'm not going to end my life. Blaze will. That's what we agreed on. Still, if I had to do it myself, a gun would be the best option. Very few people survive a bullet wound to the head.

His voice echoes in my brain: *There's no art in a gunshot, love.*

And yet he still has a pistol ready to be used, like I anticipated.

I shudder, then tell myself I'll wait. It's not like Blaze can do anything worse than murder me.

I swing around, ready to get back to him. I knock into a towering form.

Blaze gleams down at me, a subtle smirk on his lips, like he knows what I was thinking. What I was *planning* to do. And from that single look, I can tell he knows exactly how he's going to punish me for those thoughts.

And that terrifies me.

Chapter 26

Ren

"Go on," Blaze says. He tilts his head. "Take it."

My stomach drops, my hands quivering at my sides, rattling like an umbrella trying to stay strong against the storm. But I'm fractured, being torn apart seam-by-seam.

Blaze narrows his eyes, a hint of contempt in his brow. I don't know if it's for me, or if there's something else I'm missing here.

I'm scared.

"This isn't what we agreed on," I whisper. I shake my head. *This can't be it.* "Please," I say, louder this time, finding the strength inside of me to resist. "Don't do this. You said you would kill me—"

"I never said I would pull the trigger," he says, that smug tone capturing his words. "I only said that I would help you."

He grabs the gun, forcing it into my palms. The weight pulls me down, my knees bending with it. My heart drums in my ears, my insides on fire as I try to process what's going on.

He put a noose around my neck. Lathered me in another person's blood. Choked me until I passed out. Why wouldn't he force me to shoot myself?

He takes his phone and casts the device to a television in the corner of the room. A video plays, static whirring through the speakers as he increases the volume. A few seconds pass before I realize what it is.

I want to die. I want you to kill me, the recording says.

My suicide note.

"Blaze," I say.

The tears pour out. What the hell am I doing here? Why did I come here?

Because I trust him.

Why do I trust him?

I shove the gun back toward him. "I don't want this."

"What do you want then?" he asks as he angles his chin toward me. He steps forward; I step back. We're two pieces in a puzzle, fitting into place, but this doesn't *feel* right. My back lines up against the wall, my hand clutching the gun to my side. Blaze cages me in, leaning on the wall, pinning me in place.

"Tell me, little corpse. You were always afraid to do it, but fuck," he says, rolling his head back. He snakes his hand into my pants, curving between my thighs, his fingers rough, pushing inside of my wet slit. "You want it, don't you? You want to die for me. Such a slut. Greedy until the fucking end."

The video recording is loud and on an endless loop.

I'm a burden, my voice echoes. *I'm useless—*

He yanks me back, and I scream. He rips my clothes off. Swipes the weapons and restraints off of the bed. Metal crashes to the floor. And I'm naked. Vulnerable. Exposed. He removes his cock, the bulging member swollen with blood, the purple crown causing my throat to swell.

He shoves me over the bed, and the gun falls to the mattress. I stare at it, the sobs crowding my throat as he licks my ass, his fat tongue darting in my hole, my arousal dripping between my thighs.

Abruptly, he shifts our bodies, changing us around and lifting me until I'm straddling his lap. We sit on the edge of the bed, me on top. He lowers my hips onto his cock, impaling my ass like a piece of meat on a rack. His cock cuts through me. Shreds me in two. My throat burns.

"It *hurts*," I beg.

"It's supposed to," he says, his voice elegant and menacing, every inch of me shivering with fear. Blood pumps in my ears, every nerve ending in my body like a million little fingers clawing for a way out. Frantic for it. My ass adjusts, expanding to his width, and his fingers trace my neck, tickling me, teasing me with desire. My nervous system becomes magnetic, every point of contact amplified, his penetration inside of me melting me down, molding me into what he wants. What I want, too. And it feels good. Better than last time. Because I'm scared, and I hate it, and I want him all the same.

"You're going to come for me before you die," he says in a low voice.

A tear rolls down my cheek, a shiver bursting through me. "Blaze, I—"

He reaches over. Finds the gun. His palm fits over my hand, and he uses my grip to hold the gun in place against my temple. My head pulses; each heartbeat races faster.

"Here's what's going to happen," he says. "When I say 'one,' you're going to shoot yourself."

"W-what?" I stutter. "Blaze, please! I—"

"Five."

My voice is on an endless track in the background: *No matter how hard I try, I'll never be good enough.*

"Four."

This isn't real. None of it is. My skin is clammy, and it's proof that this is a trick. A trap to manipulate me into some twisted game.

"Three."

He pulls back the hammer, then adjusts his grip on my hand so that my finger is on the trigger. His hips move, his cock massaging my ass back and forth, every sense in overdrive. Tendons strain my neck. I can't think.

Is this what I wanted?

"Two—"

Good enough for whom? the recording of Blaze says.

The video cuts to another clip. My voice is quiet, but the words are clear: *For myself.*

Every inch of me trembles, my ass gyrating on top of him. Blaze's cock twitches inside of my ass; his eyes stay focused on me. Only me.

This *is* what I wanted. What I promised I would do. Why I agreed to all of this. Why I trust Blaze.

And I do trust Blaze.

But I don't want to die like this.

"One—"

Suddenly he grabs my throat, the pressure violent, the will to fight oozing out of me, and my body reacts. Automatic. A system made for him. My pussy clenches, the muscles in my ass squeezing around him, and my finger tightens against the trigger—

Everything turns white. And I come, convulsing as the trigger clicks into place. The hammer falls to its position, and I twitch. My body flails. Blaze holds me in place. He fucks me harder, harder still, tearing apart my ass, and it hurts until the pleasure overrides it, forcing me to see the other side. Forcing me to breathe deep. Blaze growls, and my body tenses all over again, and his eyes roll to the back of his head as he comes inside of me.

Filling me.

Me.

His focus returns, and he holds my hips, standing as he turns around, lying me down on my back. The comforter is soft, softer than it should be with a man like him, and I blink.

I'm still here.

Every emotion, every pain that I've held on to for so long, comes rushing out, and I try to reason with myself. With the relief. With the fact that I feel good. That I did it. That I didn't want to shoot myself, but I did it anyway. I did it for him. And he made me come.

And I'm still here.

Blaze removes his cock slowly, his come dripping out of my gaping hole. A flicker of emotion washes over his eyes as he studies me. The corners of his face wrinkles in pride. Warmth. Is it joy?

He bends down, crawling on top of my exhausted body.

Then he presses his lips to mine.

The aching pressure of what could've happened surrounds us, filling the void with our erratic breathing as we swallow each other's air. I wail into his mouth, begging for an explanation, begging for the reasons why he kept the gun unloaded, why he taunted me that way. Why he forced me to endure that darkness. His hands dig behind my head, holding my skull like he's carrying a wounded animal. Metal clatters to the ground, and the gun is with the rest of the discarded restraints and weapons now.

I'm relieved. And I feel so stupid for that.

I'm wasting Blaze's time.

That's why he's doing this. To prove how stupid I am. That I don't know what I want. That I'm not good enough, even to kill. Why I can't—

"Look at me," Blaze growls, his voice so loud, his words vibrate in my chest. He pinches my lips shut, silencing those voices inside of my head. "I see what you're doing, Ren. I see it in your eyes." He slaps my face. "Don't you dare go there. Leaving this place like you don't belong to me. I took it from you, and you're not getting it back. So just fucking stop."

It.

The tears unleash. Whatever *it* is, my mind screams that he stole it from me, but my heart knows that it's not true. I *gave* it to him. I offered myself. I offered my *life*. I offered him everything I am, and for once, the emptiness inside of me is palatable. Like Blaze is filling it with himself. Like I can hold on to him.

Our foreheads press together. His cock enters my ass again, using me, giving me everything I didn't know I needed. This time, there's no pain, only sensation, and I stop questioning it. There is no chance to fail because there is no such thing as failure to Blaze. People are people. We are nothing. He isn't special. I'm not. And there's nothing in this world that matters beyond this moment.

And it's so freeing.

My cries catch in my throat, turning into moans, and Blaze's eyes bleed with desire. He pumps his cock inside of me, and my body clenches, so eager to be what he wants. To please him. His fingertips tickle my neck, teasing me. It's too much. Too much pleasure. Too much lack of control. Too much—

"Please," I cry. "Don't do this. You're going to make me come, and I can't right now—"

"I love seeing you cry," he interrupts. "You're such a wreck. A beautiful fucking mess." He pumps inside of me harder, his cock twitching, digging out my heart. I close my eyes, letting it overwhelm me. He slaps my face again, bringing my attention back to him. "You're *my* fucking mess. My bloody little corpse. You hear that, Ren? You're mine. Until the day you die. For the days after. Until both of us are worm food, and the world doesn't remember us anymore. You. Are. Mine."

His.

He squeezes my throat, and my vision goes black. In all of my ugliness, in all of my weakness, every time that I think I'm not good enough, Blaze still wants me. Sees me. *Needs* me. And I come, releasing all of that self-loathing, letting it go for once. Coming for him. Coming for myself too.

"You're going to make me come, little corpse," he groans, his hand finding my throat again, and I'm already there. Conditioned to respond exactly how he likes.

Those words split me apart.

Little corpse.

I've always been his little corpse.

"Then come," I cry, the pleasure taking over my mind and soul. "Come for me!"

And he does. We jump over that cliff together, our emotions taking control of our actions and our logic, destroying our reasons in the confusing wake of pleasure and pain, and we fall down, deeper, and deeper, until we're dissolved in the unknown, holding on to each other. Grasping for our last breaths.

Chapter 27

Blaze

Our breathing is thick, like fog over a pier swallowing up the end of the walkway. Needy. Desperate. And as the pleasure wears off, Ren cries harder, the realization of everything that's taken place finally becoming clear to her.

I forced her to face her fears. To acknowledge her mortality. To understand that it could still end right now.

And I had to face my own truth.

Neither of us wants that fight anymore.

I power off the television. She's a shell, an empty vessel of herself, alone at the bottom of the ocean. My shoulders strain, resisting the urge to comfort her.

But I choose to inhabit her.

I thrust my nose into her hair and sniff her natural, oily scent. I pull her closer to me, refusing to let go. Her sobs strengthen, filling the emptiness around us with relief.

Deep down, I'm relieved too.

The gun lies with the rest of the weapons on the floor. When I took out the bullets earlier today, I had no concrete plans to do this to Ren. I didn't expect her to come knocking on my door. But it was like my subconscious brain knew *exactly* what would happen. That I had to accept what's going on inside of me. To face my own fears too.

After a while, Ren's breathing relaxes. I force myself to match her, to surrender to the stillness, to use my own steady breathing as a way to bring her peace. She clears her throat, then snorts her stuffy nose. I turn toward her, my arm resting on her chest.

I've never had a woman in my bed before.

I fuck women. I rape them. I torture them. I *kill* them. I don't let them occupy a place where I rest.

Except her.

Ren's eyes are glossy, transfixed on the ceiling. She's not looking at it; she's thinking about us. I know that instinctively. Her cheeks are rosy, as if given an extra touch from an embalmer, and her skin glistens with sweat, shining like a plastic doll under fluorescent lights. Like a corpse in a casket, sullen and absent.

Her eyes grow lazy, exhaustion dominating her mind. Submitting to everything I forced her to endure. She'll fall asleep soon.

In my house.

In my bed.

I imagine her back at her grandmother's house. Staring at the ceiling like she did in my bedroom a few moments ago. Her blank eyes gazing up as she wonders how she'll die.

How I hope to the fucking ends of the earth that she thinks of me instead.

My jaw clenches, the pressure of our situation pushing down on my shoulders. She doesn't belong here. Not with me. Not in my bed.

I don't do anything.

I let her stay.

I rise from the bed, leaving her there. Her eyes sear into me, and those sniffles—those pathetic little whimpers—dig holes into me. I quicken my pace, hastily grabbing wet washcloths to wipe us, then the choke chain from the floor. I link the final o-ring to the metal leash.

Her eyes widen slightly as she realizes what I'm carrying; still, the little corpse doesn't move. Kneeling on the bed, I lift her head and slide the chain loop around her neck. I fix the links so that they lie perfectly between her breasts, balanced like a pendulum waiting for the first strike. I clean us, then I rest on my side next to her, a barrier keeping her away from the rest of the world. Keeping her to myself. I wrap the links around my palm, then rest my chained hand against her beating heart.

I don't pull the chain; she'll come for me if I want her to. This is different. This is about the power she thinks she's given me.

The power she still owns.

"Blaze," she whispers. It's a single word and it says so much. There are questions there, words she'll never say. Questions I'm wondering too.

What are we doing here?

"Shh," I murmur as I stroke the black, damp hair out of her eyes. She sighs, and that relaxation gets to me, warms me from the inside out. It's like my brain is cooking, and I'm happy, knowing that one day, my head will melt away with hers.

My stomach grows heavy.

This is wrong. It's against everything that I am.

But I don't want to kill her anymore.

A snore escapes her nostrils, and I glare down at her. Messy black hair. Sweaty sand-colored skin. Light pink lips. Small and pathetic. She's so fucking cute, it's annoying.

I soften too, because I'm not angry at her. I'm angry at *myself*. I'm the one who fucked up. Who went past our boundaries. Who didn't kill her when I could have. I'm the one who's pathetic.

Still, that anger isn't enough to stop me now.

I inch my palm up, curving it like a dome over the chain, then I press it flat against the leash and her chest. The metal links are warm now, heated by our skin.

My hand. The chain. Her chest. Her heart beating underneath.

I soak in her black hair, her yellow-tinged skin, in the dark circles under her eyes. Every part of her, even her death, is *mine*. And it shouldn't work. It won't work. *We* won't work. Two people like us, full of fucked-up memories and the hunger for violence? We aren't meant to be together. People like us only create more suffering.

And I know we already have.

Ren stirs, then nuzzles into me. I'm keeping her for myself.

Convincing myself that it's what she wants too. That this is *our* suffering.

I close my eyes, uneasiness urging me to resist that connection to her. I shove the questions down, letting relaxation fill me, as long as she's close. I slip off into unconsciousness, but I don't dream of her last heartbeat. I don't dream of her dying breath. I don't dream of her corpse and the power it will give me.

I dream of her screams.

I dream of her delight.

Chapter 28

Ren

Light streams in through the blinds; dust particles floating in the air, reflecting the light back. The acrid scent of roasting beans fills my nostrils.

I squint, piecing it together.

A nightstand. The bed. Blank walls. Most of the room is in shadows. And on the nightstand, a gun and a mug of steaming coffee.

Blaze's house.

I jerk up, pulling the comforter with me.

Blaze leans against the doorframe, his pale eyes on me. The side of his lips pull up in a smirk. A coffee mug in his hand.

There are two mugs. One in his hands. One on the nightstand.

He got a mug for me.

"I thought you were dead," he says dryly.

I lick my lips, my tongue skating over the dried, peeling skin. On the surface, his words are a simple joke about heavy sleeping, but it's more than that. Hesitation prickles in my arms, daring me to understand what he means. To acknowledge that we both know our arrangement is about to dissolve.

I stare at the black mug on the nightstand. When people get you things—whether it's a leftover teriyaki bowl or a simple cup of coffee—it's supposed to make you feel good. But the story goes that my mother bought me an expensive doll right before she died. After her death, my grandmother took it away from me. Told me my mother only bought it for me out of guilt, that I shouldn't want a present like that. Since then, kindness in the form of a gift, has symbolized danger to me. And while Blaze isn't taking his own life like my mother did, anything can change. You can't rely on anything, or anyone.

Everything can be destroyed.

"Not dead yet," I say quietly.

A chain hangs around my neck, looping through an o-ring and connecting to a similarly weighty leash. My neck is sore, and the chain brings me down, like a bucket full of seashells and sand. I don't remove the chain though; I keep it with me, attached like an umbilical cord.

"What time is it?" I ask.

"Almost noon."

I'm supposed to work today.

I flick the comforter off. "Shit—"

"Denise knows we're not coming in today."

My mind fixates on those words. I turn slowly toward him.

"We?" I ask.

"I assumed you wouldn't be up to burning bodies today," he says. "You seem rather exhausted."

Affection pinches his cheeks, smothering his condescension. An eerie tension floats between us, a strange mix of apprehension and comfort, both of us waiting for the next step.

Last night—eating pizza, the gun, the sex, and literally sleeping together—was strange, even for him. And now he's calling in to work for me?

"You called her for me," I say. "For *us?*"

"I told her to fire you. She wasn't having it."

My hand wraps around the chain hanging from my neck. The collar—or choke chain, whatever you want to call it—is loose. For a second, despite the heavy metal, I feel weightless. Like anything is possible. Like I'd float to the sky if I wasn't chained to the ground.

193

Blaze is keeping me here.

I'm still alive.

Blaze's eyes glimmer, pride expanding his chest. And it hits me. *This* is happiness, isn't it? Pure fucking happiness. That he cares about me. That he's looking after me. That he forced me to experience my final moments, but he didn't let me die.

It scares the shit out of me.

"Why are you being nice to me?" I whisper. A genuine smile spreads across his lips, and for once, his eyes soften.

"I care about my things," he says.

My shoulders tighten. Can a man like Blaze truly care about anything? It seems too good to be true. Blaze's expression changes, reading my apprehension. That arrogant side storms back in, saving it all.

"My body," he says, his greedy eyes washing over me from head to toe. "My choice."

Like he owns me.

Like I have no control.

The shadows close in, my vision darkening with powerlessness. Weakness invading my nervous system. It feels good *now*, but eventually it'll become hollow, and I won't be able to do anything about it. Any time something seems too good to be true, it *is*. It always is. And this? Blaze calling in to get me fired, when we both know he called in for me so that I could have a break? Getting me coffee? Acting like he's looking out for me? *This* is too good to be real.

I rub my forehead. It can't be real. I'm powerless.

And yet, Blaze showed me that I was capable of making those decisions for myself. I do have power. Just like my mother. Like my grandmother. Like Blaze.

"I have to go," I say. Blaze stiffens. I lift my shoulders. "I need to check on my grandmother."

"Last I saw, she was capable of taking care of herself."

I huff through my nostrils like I'm annoyed at Blaze; the truth is I'm more annoyed with myself. Mrs. Richmond *doesn't* need me. Just like my mother didn't need me either.

And I don't need Blaze.

"I just—" I fidget, trying to figure out how to say it without giving my fears away. "I need to go home. To think over everything that happened last night. Process it, you know? Is it wrong that I want to check on her? To make sure she's okay?"

The air conditioning buzzes at a low volume.

Outside, a car drives past.

Time ticks by.

Blaze sighs. "Then let me take you there."

I wrinkle my brow. "I drove my own car."

"Then I'll follow you."

He heads back to the kitchen, and that frustrates me. There's no space to deny him if he walks away.

But I'm not going to fall for this anymore.

I take off the choke chain and leash. The metal links clink together on his bed.

As Blaze paces in the kitchen, pretending to put away dishes, I get dressed, then examine the gun on the nightstand. I could take it *now*. Figure out which bullets it needs. I can choose the ending *I* want. I can take my power back.

I'm capable of ending things. Blaze showed me that. And I don't need to find out what happens when this situation with Blaze falls apart. I'd rather leave first.

"All right," Blaze says, startling me. He motions to the front of the house. "Let's go."

I leave the gun on the nightstand and follow Blaze out. A few minutes later, we arrive at Mrs. Richmond's house. Blaze walks me to the front door.

As our proximity closes in, the hairs on the back of my neck stand. Blaze is not a polite or chivalrous person. Why is he *escorting* me to my own door? It's like he's afraid. Like he's protecting me—

"Call me," Blaze orders, a hint of concern lingering in his voice. Like he knows what I'm thinking. That I still want to end it all. Like he wants to protect me from myself.

Why does he care? Why now?

Why me?

"What's up with you?" I ask, my lips pursing in annoyance. "You're acting weird."

"Don't forget what we agreed on." He tilts his head, his eyes narrowed in flirtation and the threat of danger. "I get to kill you. No one else."

Is he saying that to remind himself or to remind me?

None of it makes sense.

I spin around, facing the door. "My body, my choice," I snark.

He grabs me harshly, his fingers digging into my shoulders. Wrenches me toward him. My chest stings.

He glares down, his eyes like the sun, ready to incinerate me. Daring me to disobey. A chill sweeps through me.

"Don't," he warns. And in that moment, I know that if anyone could torture a dead person *past* their final breath, it would be Blaze.

He lets go, and I know he won't haunt me like that.

I unlock the front door and slip inside. I press against the front door's peephole. He drives, disappearing down the road.

I'm alone again.

I lie in bed on top of the comforter. There are a few pictures on the wall of my mother and me before she died. But the ceiling —the part of the room I look at most—is bare, like Blaze's house.

Why am I holding on to this place?

Should I go back to Blaze right now?

Any time I move my arms, body odor permeates the air. I reek of musk and sweat. I need a shower. Water would wash away Blaze's ghost soaking in my pores. My scent—sweat, fear, lust—all of it is mixed with him.

I don't move.

The doorbell rings. I turn toward the window, gauging the time of day from the angle of the sun. It's probably been hours.

My heart pangs. What if it's Blaze at the door?

Do I want that?

A man in a button-up shirt with yellow-blond hair stands on the porch. His skin is deeply tanned and leathery, as if he works outside. A sharp jaw, his cheekbones carved. He reminds me of Blaze. Maybe they're brothers.

But Blaze is as pale as an overcast sky. Could they truly be related?

"Are you Ren Kono?" the man asks, his voice formal, even scholarly. Like he's putting on a show of submission when it's obvious that he's the one in control.

I furrow my brow. "And you are?"

"Sorry," he says. He rubs his forehead, then offers his hand. "I'm Doctor Brody Barwick. You're looking for medical assistance in dying?"

My mind jumps back to the medical spa. The clinical white tiles. The paintings of ponds and flowers on the walls, every inch of the space generic and neat. This man could work there. He may even *own* the spa. And if that's true, then he *should* be trustworthy. Reliable. Doctors take an oath, don't they? They're supposed to help people.

His lips are smooth, like he's only interested in what's friendly and fair. Still, his eyes are blank, like he's hiding what's really there: judgment.

"I'm sorry; who are you?" I ask.

"Brody. Doctor Brody Barwick. Whatever you want to call me, really. Blaze said you're looking for an easy death. On *your* terms." He shrugs, then gazes to the side. "I get that. Trust me. You're not the first person I've met who wants that. Normally, I just get cheap prescription drugs for my patients. It's easier for everyone. That way, they can handle it themselves. Even so, I'm not opposed to physician-assisted suicide. If that's what *you* want, then it should be your final call. Not his."

His.

I swallow. My throat dry. He's talking about Blaze.

The memory of last night—the gun, Blaze's cock in my ass, the tears—flashes before my eyes.

Did I give Blaze the final call when he forced me to shoot that gun?

I study the doctor, analyzing the missing pieces. This man must be Blaze's contact—his dealer, or whatever he is to Blaze. Blaze would never let someone like him near me; he's too controlling for that. This entire meeting is suspicious. There must be animosity between the two of them.

"Blaze gets carried away," the doctor says, breaking the

silence. He pushes a hand through his blond hair, then glances around, like he's nervous that Blaze may be watching us from the shadows. "You have the right to decide what you do. It's your life. Not his."

There it is again: *His*.

The doctor pulls out two objects from his pocket; a plastic bag filled with items that look like oversized ear swabs, and an orange prescription bottle. The pharmaceuticals Blaze promised me for my birthday.

Wariness tingles in my hands and arms, pins and needles jabbing me. "I don't know how to use that," I say.

"You suck on this one, like a lollipop," he says. He holds up the plastic bag. "And this? It's a pill. You know how to take—"

I cut him off: "I want Blaze to do it."

The doctor's jaw drops, his entire posture stunned. After a while, he clears his throat.

"If that's what you want, then it's up to you." He shoves the bag and the bottle back into his pocket, his knuckles white with irritation, probably because I just wasted his time. "I'm in town for a few more days. If you change your mind, please reach out to me."

He places a business card in my hands. I stand on the porch, holding the card. Not reading it.

The doctor drives away. Both Blaze and the doctor parked in the same exact place. It's a coincidence, sure, but it's like it symbolizes something. A rivalry that I'm not aware of yet.

I stare at the empty space on the curb, trying to figure it out.

Chapter 29

Ren

I sit at the kitchen table for an hour and read the doctor's business card over and over again until its shapes and lines are meaningless.

Dr. Brody Barwick. Is he even a real doctor?

The front door bursts open. Mrs. Richmond smiles, but it's forced. She never smiles at me.

"I thought you had work today," she says.

Guilt settles in my chest. Missing work is like asking her to take care of me, a fully grown child. I'm an even bigger burden now.

If I had taken over the school like she asked me to, she'd be enjoying retirement right now, maybe even traveling. Instead, she's stuck here with me. Her feet sinking deeper into the sand.

"I called in," I say. Then I shake my head. "Blaze called in, actually."

For me.

"Blaze?" Mrs. Richmond asks, her voice practically a hiss, then she covers it up, adjusting herself. "Is that a work friend?"

She puts away her purse, and for the first time in years, it seems like she's genuinely curious. Like she wants to know who I've been staying with. Panic rises in my chest, filling my ears with throbbing pain.

Is this where it all comes crashing down?

199

When does it become my fault?

"Is that the work friend who picked—"

My phone buzzes on the table, jerking around with the vibrations. Mrs. Richmond rolls her eyes, her true self finally returning. She motions for me to take the call.

I close the bedroom door behind me. My heart leaps when I see his name.

"You didn't call me," Blaze says, his voice low and tenuous, like a song that's both sad and erotic.

He *is* worried about me, isn't he?

No. This is about what he wants from me. *My corpse.*

I'm just his little corpse. That's all I'm supposed to be. Even if he wants more, I can't—

"It's been a few hours. Not days," I mutter, cutting off my own thoughts, a subtle hint of annoyance in my voice. Blaze chuckles, and I wait for everything to break down. For the cracks to surface.

I should tell Blaze about the doctor. I should ask if he *sent* the doctor.

I tuck away those questions, not letting them out. I might not know the details, but I know they're not friends. If I tell Blaze about the doctor, it'll only create more problems, and right now, with the way things are? If I don't try to keep it together, it *will* blow up in my face. And I don't want that to happen yet.

I don't want to think. I just want it to be over. To end things while I still feel like I can.

"Is your grandmother fine?" Blaze asks sarcastically. "Come back. We need to use this day off to our advantage."

A minute passes, the phone line crackling. I was supposed to come home and process everything that had happened with Blaze. Last night with the gun feels like it was ages ago.

I run through every reason why I shouldn't go back to Blaze's house.

I remind myself of why I'll never be good enough. Not even for Blaze. That he'll be better off when I'm dead.

But it doesn't stop me.

"Okay," I say.

"Okay," he says.

It's one word, and yet there's an endless stream of complication behind it. You can show up on someone's doorstep and say that simple word, and it can sign away your death to a murderer. Or you can say that word, and you give yourself over to someone who cares for you, knowing that your love can still be ripped away in one breath. It doesn't matter who kills who. Who dies. Who lives.

It always ends.

I get in the car. The engine rumbles underneath me, my chest fluttering with anticipation.

I don't want this anymore. I don't need help in doing anything. I can do it by myself. I can end things, with or without Blaze.

Maybe I *want* to keep going. Even if it is fucked up and I have no control, maybe I like knowing that there's no way to tell what comes next.

Maybe it's my choice to stay.

Red lights fill the windshield. I slam on the brakes and my tires slide, squealing to a stop right before hitting a car.

I ran a red light.

Adrenaline pumps through my veins, shock hot on my skin. A car to the side of me honks, and I hold my chest briefly. I could've died right then.

Why haven't I died yet?

Quickly, I drive down the road, coming back down to earth.

Blaze is looking after me now, and it's like I've transformed from being Mrs. Richmond's burden into Blaze's burden. I don't want that. I'm his little corpse, and one day, he'll wake up and realize I'm better off dead.

And I can't leave that ending up to anyone else.

This is what's best for everyone. Including Blaze.

I exit the highway, then park in a strip mall. I dial the number on the doctor's business card and tear a sliver of chapped skin from my bottom lip.

"This is Doctor Barwick," a male voice says.

I pause. When Blaze finds out I'm calling the doctor, he'll be pissed. He'll never forgive me.

But I'll already be dead.

It's my choice.

"This is Ren Kono. We met today?" I pause. I'm not sure what I can or can't say over the phone line. "Your business card says you're near 30A. You still have that medicine?"

"Sure. Let's meet up. I'll text you an address."

As I punch in the location into my phone's GPS, the device vibrates: a call from Blaze. I silence it, then text him quickly: *Quick errand, see you soon.*

In Rosemary Beach, the tree branches frame the street, twisting with thin strings of lights, like a road winding through the woods of a storybook fantasy. I park at the outdoor mall, finding the ice cream shop the doctor mentioned.

Wealthy families in shirts more expensive than my car pass by me without a second glance, like I'm trash on the side of the road, not meant for this neighborhood. I always feel out of place here. I used to not care—my grandmother even bought me expensive clothes here sometimes—but once I was a teenager, she told me that she had backed out of an offer to buy property here, so that she could keep working at the school until I was ready to take over.

It was always my fault she couldn't have the life she wanted. And I won't let that happen with Blaze.

A man in salmon shorts and a white golf shirt strolls down the sidewalk. Our eyes meet, and he nods at me. His facial structure is jagged, so similar to Blaze's, and yet they have such opposite styles. Blaze wears plain black clothes. You'd never catch him in a golf shirt.

Just like me, Blaze would never belong in a place like this.

The doctor hands me a small paper bag with an ice cream parlor logo on the front. The contents shift as I take it. My phone vibrates again.

Don't keep me waiting, Blaze texts.

I stow my phone without replying, then open the bag. A plastic bag containing the lozenges. A pill bottle next to it.

I steel myself. Whatever *we* are—whatever Blaze has planned for *us* now—is *not* going to work. People like me bring others down, and there's nothing we can do to claw our way out of hell.

To make life better for anyone. We deserve nothing. We *are* nothing.

And Blaze has already given me way too much.

My eyes well up with tears as I stare at the bag's contents, sorrow squeezing my chest. I can't control it. Someday, I'll screw it up. I'll ruin things for Blaze, and I don't want to wait for that day to come. The only way I can be *right* for him is to be his next victim. The willing one. His practice run. The one that helps him find his rhythm here.

He doesn't need *me*. He needs a good victim. And to be a good victim, I have to die.

"When are you going to do it?" the doctor asks softly, breaking into my thoughts.

Before I meet Blaze, I think. I have to do it soon, or he'll stop me.

"I don't know," I say.

"Do you want me to be there?"

I shake my head. Logically, all humans want to be surrounded by their loved ones when life inevitably ends. This doctor isn't my loved one.

Blaze isn't either.

I strain, clearing my throat. The doctor raises his brows. I don't explain. Blaze never needed me for my corpse; he could have used anyone. And I never needed Blaze for his murdering skills—I just needed him to *push* me. To show me that I'm capable of making my own choice. Of taking my future into my own hands.

I have that power now.

"I'm fine," I say. "Thanks anyway."

The doctor nods. "Take care," he says.

I purse my lips together. It's an odd thing to say to someone when you've given them medication that will end their life. The doctor smiles sheepishly, understanding the awkwardness too, and we both return to our cars.

The drive back to Panama City Beach is slow, like a keel worm tunneling a path over a seashell. I open the windows. The exhaust mixes with the salty ocean breeze, and I blink back tears, the wind whipping my face. I hate this town—I always have—but there's something different inside of me now as I try to say goodbye to this city. Something inside of it that reminds me of *him*. This stupid town is where we met, where we began to see each other. And it's where we end too.

My throat closes up, the pain simmering in my neck.

Blaze. My killer, and my savior.

But I don't need him to save me anymore.

When I arrive at his house, the windows glow with light, and that, in and of itself, is an omen. Every time I've been here, it's like he *chose* to live in darkness. Now, he's preparing for my arrival. Anticipating my needs, even when he prefers the shadows.

You don't want this, Blaze, I think. *You don't want me. You don't need me here.*

I pull the plastic bag out and open the seal. The label blurs as I take out one of the lozenges.

Like a lollipop, the doctor had said.

I stick it in my cheek. It's bitter and synthetic, like fake cherry, and it reminds me of the doctor. The medical spa. The clinical kindness. Sweetness meant to cover up what's actually there.

Maybe I'll die tonight. Maybe I won't.

Either way, it'll be my choice.

I take out the lozenge, then leave it on the passenger seat next to me, partially dissolved. I wait, staring up at the house as black streams of smoke blur my vision. My head fills with fog, my limbs heavy and euphoric. It's working *fast.* Have I eaten today? Is it working faster because I haven't consumed anything besides coffee?

Do I really want to die?

Blaze opens the front door, his form silhouetted by the amber hue of the fluorescent lights. A devil rising up from hell, calling me down to his depths of depravity. But he's not the devil.

I'm the one dragging him down.

Somehow, I get out of the car. The world tilts. I keep focused. This is what I wanted all along, and now it's in my power to take back what's mine.

I can't let him forget who I'm supposed to be.

Chapter 30

Blaze

The late winter air clings to my skin as I wait for her. Ren steps closer, inching forward like a ghost crawling out of a well. I used to think she was the same as everyone else, nothing more than an animal. A skin bag full of meat. Like we all are.

But in this dim light, I see *her*. Ren doesn't give in to the emotional decay of society; she's numb to it, like I am. We understand each other.

I let her come to me. Her body ambles forward. Eager for it. Her walk is aimless, like she's not quite sure what to do or what to say. Wary.

I press my lips together. There's something different about her, and it's not the attraction that usually draws me to her.

It's almost like she's content.

Heat floods my chest. I ball my fists, resisting the emotions. *You think you're the reason she's happy?* I mock myself. And I hate it. Hate, hate, *hate* that I give a shit about anything, including her.

But I can't help it. I focus on her.

"You're ready, aren't you?" I ask.

A dreamy, sleepy smile perks her lips, then fades from her mouth. She steps forward again, her feet clumsy. I grab her wrist and lift her to her toes. She dangles like Spanish moss, resting her weight on me.

"Mhmm," she says.

She must think I'm asking if she's ready to die. What I have planned is so much more.

I pull the choke chain from my pocket, then slide it around her neck. The chain falls down her chest, and I quickly lock the leash to it. I yank the tether, and she falls to her knees with a thud. She crawls through the house, following me like a dog. Palms and knees. A fucking animal. My chest expands, and I don't question my response to her this time.

No one will ever compare to her. I know that now.

I drag her through the house. Down the hall. To the bed. She sprawls on the mattress like a corpse on display, ready for me to fuck and use. I hoist her legs onto my shoulders and gaze at her. Her eyes are lazy, barely open at all. She opens her mouth, whimpering as she takes each thrust. And I dig her out, taking everything she has, ripping her soul from the inside out. Then I tighten the chain, her cheeks reddening with blood, teasing her with that sweet ecstasy of relief. Of death. Lingering there. Giving her a taste. Her cunt pulses around me, grinding over that edge, falling down into the abyss, coming for me. She falls back, losing consciousness. She's at my complete mercy.

And it makes me come too.

Afterward, my dick softens, my come oozing out of her pussy. I loosen the chain, then slide onto the bed next to her. I let out a sigh, waiting for her to wake up. She stays still. Resting.

I rub her clit, itching for that little twitch she gives me when I touch her there. She doesn't move.

I prop myself on my elbow. Study her.

Her chest stays flat.

The little actress probably wants to excite me with the possibilities. It's a sweet gesture, but I'm impatient.

I tickle her neck, teasing her with another conditioned orgasm. Ren doesn't move.

I clench my jaw. A blue and purple bruise traces her neck, red streaks from where the chain strangled her. Everything about her is frozen in time.

I pry open her eyelids.

Pupils like black grains.

She took something.

No. That's impossible. She wouldn't take something without telling me.

Would she?

A million thoughts spiral out of control. I shake her shoulders.

"Don't fuck with me," I growl. I slap her face. "These games won't work. Cut the shit, Ren."

A red handprint appears on her cheek.

Ren doesn't move.

My ears throb with blood.

I can't take her to the hospital. They'll see the bruises on her neck and assume *I* did something. That I wanted her to die. That this is my fault.

My brother *can* help her. He's not much better than a hospital, but he can keep his mouth shut.

I can't leave her like this.

Chapter 31

Blaze

Brody resists coming at first, but after I threaten to expose our shared past, he rushes over. Gives her some sort of nasal spray. Ren's breathing immediately returns. She stirs, then goes back to sleep.

Her chest rises and falls. As long as that's happening, I can breathe too.

My knuckles are bleeding, blood drying in the bed of my nails. Brody pretends he doesn't notice the new hole in the wall. We both know it's there.

It's like waking up from a nightmare.

I stare at her sleeping form. I can't stand the way I feel, seeing her like that. A doctor within arm's reach. The fact that she's breathing.

She's okay.

"What did she take?" I ask.

"Could have been a number of things," Brody says. "We won't know unless we can take her to a hospital and test her."

I grit my teeth. The fucker probably *has* the tests; he just doesn't want to give them to me. He'd *like* taking her to a hospital so that he can get me under public scrutiny. So that someone else will see me and know my tendencies. So that if I go to jail, it's not on his hands.

"You can't find out here?" I ask. I get into his personal space, my breath hot and venomous. "There are over-the-counter drug tests. You can get sedatives, but not a test?"

"For a test like this, you need a lab," he says, his eyes darting away from me. His mouth twitches, holding something back. Fighting his natural responses. He doesn't want to give himself away.

And then I know exactly what happened.

He gave her the drugs.

I rush to the nightstand and check for the lozenges and the pills. Panic fills me when I see them there, because that means Brody has *more*. I run to the bathroom. Flush that shit down. It swirls like a bird's nest caught in a drain. It backs up, clogging the hole. With one quick pump of the plunger, it goes down the pipes. Once it's all gone, I rush outside. Ren's car is unlocked; she must've been too doped up to lock it, and that pisses me off even more.

A lozenge, partially corroded, lies on the passenger seat. A wet stain underneath it.

"Wait!" Brody shouts. He grabs my shoulder. "Listen—"

A roar erupts from my chest. I shove Brody back. He stumbles onto the grass. I find that brown bag with identical contents to what he gave me. I storm past him and go straight back to the toilet.

Brody deserves to die. Not Ren. Just him.

I watch the contents swirl again. This time, they flush easily. The partially used lozenge goes down last.

She didn't even consume all of it.

Why? So she could try it out? See what it was like?

Was she testing me?

How the fuck did it get this out of hand?

"This is bullshit, man," Brody shouts. "That cost—"

"*Me*," I growl, my voice vibrating through the walls. I point to my chest, pounding at it like a madman. "*I'm* the one who gives her the drugs. *I'm* the one who helps her end her life. *Not you.*"

"I didn't put it in her mouth!"

"You inserted yourself into her *life*," I say, my voice full of rage. "Her time of death was never *yours* to decide."

"Listen to yourself," Brody say. He shakes his head. "If you wanted to kill her, then you should've done it a long time ago. You didn't, did you? Because you didn't *want* to." He grits his teeth. "Me? I know better. I always have. And if she wants to die, then it should be *her* choice. Not your violent whims. Not some sexual fantasy." He hunches his shoulders, ready to tackle me. "She's not a dead girl that you can play with like a fucking doll. She's a person, Blaze. You can't control her."

Brody's anger is real. Palatable. This isn't only about Ren to him. It's about our mother. The fact that I killed her when he told me to wait.

He's right. I can't control Ren.

But it doesn't matter.

I punch him, my knuckles cracking against his skull in a loud pop. He crashes against the wall, the shock radiating through his shoulders.

Ren stirs, whimpering from the other room. I hold my breath, waiting to hear her next sound.

In, and out. Her calm breath.

Brody holds his jaw, bracing himself. I look down at him. Anger pierces through his expression, but mine is far stronger. I've never hit him before. When we were younger, I swore I would never do that to him, even though I was jealous of him. We had been through enough already. Even when we had our disagreements, we were in this shitty life together.

Now, I wonder why I waited so long.

The need to see Ren calls to me. I want to guard her sleeping form *more* than I want to kill Brody.

Ren is a person. Brody is right about that. But that's not his problem.

It's mine.

"Get the fuck out of here before I kill you," I warn.

Brody runs, scampering off like a cockroach. His car roars away. I stand outside of the bedroom in the doorway, watching

Ren sleep. My temples pound, sweat pouring off of my cheeks. I don't leave her side.

Everyone lives. Everyone dies. Nothing matters. These are the same lines I've told myself for years, justifying my actions. Forcing the world to make sense.

I can't stand it anymore.

Ren's death is *my* choice. I won't let anyone get in the way of that.

Not even her.

Chapter 32

Ren

My head pounds, the pain explosive, like a hammer pulverizing my skull. I turn my head, and the pain follows me. I blink.

A nasal spray lies on the nightstand. Wood-paneled walls surround me.

A throat clears. I shift my head, my temples pulsing. Blaze rests against the doorframe, his arms crossed. White hair disheveled. His face sunken, as if he hasn't slept or eaten in weeks.

I blink rapidly. Trying to understand. When did I get to Blaze's house?

"Took shit into your own hands, huh?" he says.

Then I remember.

Blaze surrounded by light. The chain. The lozenge.

"I overdosed," I whisper.

"Seems that way," Blaze mutters. "My brother came to rescue you, like the fucking savior that he is."

I gnaw on my bottom lip, the skin tender and raw.

Savior?

His brother saved me?

Did I want to die, or was I just seeing what it might be like?

It's hard to think straight.

"Who saved me?" I ask. "Blaze, I—"

Blaze kneels next to the bed, our eyes at the same level. Uneasiness creeps into my stomach, clawing for my heart. His gaze shifts back and forth across me, searching for the right words. He stays back. Almost like he's scared to touch me.

And that's not like Blaze.

"I had your drugs," he says. The spite comes through, even as he keeps his voice steady. "I had everything ready for you, and you thought you were better than me. Smarter than me. If you didn't need me, then you wouldn't have done any of this in the first place. But you do *need* me, Ren. Otherwise, you wouldn't be here right now."

His words echo inside of me.

I wouldn't be here right now. I'd be gone. A corpse.

He saved me.

Then my mind narrows on the first part—

I had your drugs.

He kept them from me. Played with me. Hid what he had promised.

He was supposed to give them to me.

I raise my voice: "You lied to me. You—"

"We made an agreement, and *you* fucking broke it," he says. He grips the bedsheets next to me, his eyes bloodshot, the veins in his neck engorged. "Do you know what happens when someone betrays my trust?"

I think of his mother. His second and his third. My destiny as his fourth.

I never truly needed him. He showed me that. He put my finger on the trigger, but I completed the shot.

He acts like he owns my *life*, and that's not what our arrangement is. All I promised him was my death.

"You don't own me," I hiss. "You never owned *any* of your victims. That's why you had to kill them, isn't it? They didn't do what you said. You couldn't control anyone. Not even your mother."

He leans in closer, daring me to speak. "Be careful of what you say now, my love."

"Or what?" I taunt. "Are you going to kill me? Going to live up to a threat for once?" Blaze's eyelids flicker. My stomach knots; I don't like hurting him, but I can't stop. I *want* him to hurt. To feel emotional pain. I want him to feel weak, like I do for once. I want him to understand how angry I am. That *he's* the one who showed me how to take back my power. That *he's* the one who taught me how to fight back too.

"No. You're just a scared little boy. Too stupid to actually do anything. To fight back!" I laugh, twisting the knife as hard as I can. He reddens, his chin held high, but his jaw tightens, and the pain seeps through. Cracks his hard shell.

Blaze doesn't need me. I have to force him to understand that.

I continue: "You're just a weak, insignificant, little—"

He reaches forward, aiming for my throat. I won't have that right now.

I block his shot.

I slap his face.

Blaze glares at me. My fingertips vibrate with the will to keep going. To see how far I can take him. To force him to finally finish it. To see that he doesn't need me. That I'll never be enough, no matter how hard I try.

Blaze cracks his neck, the rage dissolving. Dismissing me.

"We made an arrangement. And if you don't hold up your end of the bargain, then I will make sure you regret betraying me, even if that means forcing you to watch the people in your life suffer while you *live* through it all."

He's threatening me with *life?*

I slap him again, harder this time. His entire head swings from the impact, and for a few seconds, we stay like that. Frozen. My palm stings, but that's not what startles me.

Blaze simply turns back. Studies me. Contemplates what to do next.

As if he actually cares.

I pick myself up. The walls, the door, the nightstand—everything shifts off balance.

I need to go.

I face the hallway.

"Running away. How fitting," Blaze mutters.

"Fuck off."

I drop into the driver's seat of my car. A damp spot marks the passenger seat, but the paper bag is gone. The extra lozenges. The pills.

He stole those from me too.

I punch the steering wheel and I scream. My throat turns raw. Blaze storms down the driveway. Before he can reach me, I veer forward. Drive without any direction. I drive because I don't know what else to do. I drive because statistically speaking, I have a better chance of dying in a car wreck than I do with Blaze killing me.

I drive because I can't face disappointing him right now.

Eventually, I park outside of Last Spring. The sun beats down on the building, and an older man stands outside, right where Blaze and I first discussed our potential arrangement. The man runs a hand through his thin hair, and I think of Blaze, old and weathered like that. Tears well up in my eyes, blurring everything around me.

Am I supposed to apologize to Blaze?

Do I want to see him?

Would apologizing make a difference?

Do I have anything to be sorry for?

I shouldn't care. This is bullshit. He's mad at me for something he *knew* I wanted. We both had the medication. I didn't keep anything from him that he wasn't keeping from me.

He lied to me. And *that* fucking hurts. He's the one who betrayed our arrangement.

I call the doctor. He doesn't pick up. I call again, and again, and the line goes to voicemail. Frantic, I head to Rosemary Beach. I sit in that ice cream parlor, even buying a cone because the manager insisted that I had to be a paying customer to sit at a table. Rich families stream in and out, side-eyeing me, the poor woman who clearly hasn't taken a shower in a week and isn't here for a beach vacation.

I keep calling the doctor.

I ask the teens working at the shop for a cup of water. Hours pass.

Finally, the line crackles. I exit the shop and shield my phone as I step outside. My heart races.

"This is Doctor—"

"I need more," I say. "Blaze dumped everything. I can't—"

"Ren?" he asks. "I don't have any. Someone stole my inventory."

Weakness fills me. I lean against a column, trying not to fall. My vision fuzzes with white spots. A shopper dressed in pink passes by and sneers at me. She must think I'm drunk.

In a way, I feel intoxicated, like I have no control over anything. I'm back at the beginning where everything seemed hopeless.

Drug dealers must get their product stolen all the time. If Brody is a doctor, but he's still giving out medications like this, then he can still potentially lose his product like the others.

It feels personal though. Like it's an attack on me. I don't know the doctor, and he doesn't know me. But it hurts. My lips tremble.

"How?" I whisper.

"When was the last time you saw him?" he asks.

He doesn't even have to say his name. When I think about it, I realize it's only been hours.

"This morning," I say.

"So you haven't been with him since then?" he asks. "He must've stolen it—"

"Blaze?" My chest constricts, squeezing the last blood cells out of my heart. "Blaze stole your product?"

The phone line fills with emptiness. There's no verbal confirmation; still, the answer is there, strung up between us.

I groan, resting my head against the exterior of the shop. I just want to be done.

I want it to be my choice.

I want to prove to myself that I know what I'm doing. That I have the power to do what I want.

"Can you get more?" I ask quietly.

A beat passes. "If you can take it without him knowing, then yes," the doctor says. "But he can't find out."

It's what I should've done a long time ago.

"Done," I say.

After we make arrangements for a pickup tomorrow, I hang up, then block Blaze's number. It's a step.

Besides, I don't need to avoid him for much longer.

Chapter 33

Blaze

I don't know who I hate more at that moment.

The first option is my brother. My only *living* blood relative. The fucker who betrayed me because he claims he's a righteous hero, here to save a lost soul from her terrifying fate.

He's wrong. He's not righteous. We're the same. He sells prescription drugs under the table, even giving people ways to end their own lives. In the end, he's just searching for that high that makes him feel good about himself, and for him, that's the idea that he's doing something positive for the world.

Me? I kill people until it makes me feel something. I don't pretend to be anything else. I know who I am.

We're both desperate to make sense of our lives, and we use the hunt as an answer to it all. I'm just not arrogant enough to think I'm better than anyone else.

And then there's *Ren*.

Ren, the woman who was supposed to be my fourth. My little corpse. My dead girl. An unpredictable force of nature. She gets into her car, completely unaware that I've followed her to Rosemary Beach. That while she was out, sitting in front of Last Spring, I drove to my brother's condo. Stole his shit. Destroyed his perfect little home while I was at it. And while she was waiting for my brother to answer her calls, I fucked with her tires.

My throat is dry, sandpaper rubbing together each time I try to breathe. Ears pounding. Adrenaline rushes through my body. My knuckles are bleeding again, crusted over from the broken glass I left in Brody's place. If I wasn't sitting in my car, someone would be dead right now.

Instead, I'm caged in. Held back. Waiting for *her*.

Killing a stranger isn't as important as making her see my point of view. Forcing her to understand the way things are supposed to be.

She pulls out of the parking space. The car drives like normal. That will change.

I follow her out, pulling onto the main road. At the stoplight before the highway, I check my phone: two missed calls from my brother. I dismiss the notifications, then dial her, giving her the chance to pick up. To stop this whole fucking mess before it gets worse.

The call goes straight to voicemail.

My vision tunnels on her tail lights. Red floods everything. Blood courses through me like a tidal wave.

She thinks she can ignore me. Acting like I don't belong in her life.

I own her fucking life.

Dark woods and moonlit shores saddle each side of the highway, and her car swerves—her tire finally deflating enough to fuck with her ability to drive—and her car limps along.

She finds a safe pullout to the side of the road.

I park too.

My phone vibrates; Brody again. I ignore it.

I jump out of my car. Stride toward her. Cuffs in my pocket, a black canvas bag in my hand. She bends down, checking the tire. Her chin drops as she sees its wobbly shape—another damned hole in her plans. Plenty of people can see us. For all they know, I'm a civilian helping out some poor, stranded woman.

And it truly is like that. Ren was supposed to be my lost victim, an aspiring dead girl who found refuge in *me*. Who found her eternal resting place in *me*. Not Brody. Not herself. Not anyone, but fucking *me*.

And I refuse to give that to her now.

My boots crash on the ground. Ren spins, facing me.

"Blaze," she snaps. "What are you—"

I slam the bag over her head, obstructing her view, hooding her like one of those tortured prisoners she dreams of becoming. The fucking irony of it squeezes my chest with a death grip as she struggles against me, fighting me with fire. A mixed message. Her will to fight—to fight *me*—competing against her will to die.

I drop her in the trunk of my car. Use my strength to hold her down, locking the handcuffs over her wrists. She curses at me. Screams. Even sobs. As if that will stop me. As if that will make me question what I'm doing for a second. But I laugh. I laugh like a fucking maniac. Proving to her that I don't give a shit what she says or does to me. *She's still mine.*

Then she stills. I can't see her expression, but I know the look on her face by her languid body language.

She's smug. Too confident in her safety with me.

She thinks I'm doing this to protect her.

My scalp overheats. I'm *not* protecting her. I'm forcing her to understand that I own her.

I shut the trunk, my nostrils flaring as I concentrate on what I need to do. We drive. Ren doesn't make a sound, and that irritates me even more. Like she's taunting me.

My phone vibrates.

A text from Brody: *Where the fuck are you?*

I close the message. The rage boils over inside of me, bubbles over the edges. I can't think about anything but her. She thinks she's safe with me, and maybe she is. Maybe this is some bullshit excuse I'm telling to myself to make it seem okay. What the fuck am I trying to make her understand, anyway? It's like I'm in a competition where I don't know the rules, but I want my fucking prize. I want Ren.

Just Ren.

At my house, I scoop her up from the trunk, bringing her inside, not giving a shit if any of the neighbors see me carrying a hooded woman. I don't even lock the front door. Daring them to see us, to question what this is.

Because if someone finds out, I might go to prison, but Ren won't be able to escape. They'll keep her alive.

I tear through the hallway. Rip the canvas bag from her head and drag her across the hardwood floor by her hair. She screams, and those screams transform into mournful sobs, like the noises she made the first night I saw her in the crematory. I want to punch her for being so stupid and kiss her for the simple fact that she's *alive*. For the fact that she can scream. That she can cry. That there is still air in her lungs. That her pulse still races.

It races for me.

"You fucking pig!" she howls.

I throw her into the bathroom. Fling open the toilet. Scowling at myself for all of my stupid fucking choices. The toilet bowl is clean—all because I couldn't stand the thought of an ounce of that medication where I shit and piss. Because I didn't want to accept it. That possibility.

Ren's death.

"You are mine, little corpse," I whisper. She thrusts her elbows, but it's hard to do damage when your wrists are bound. I wrap an arm under her stomach, still fisting her hair. "It's time you understood exactly what that means."

I fall to my knees behind her and grip her tight. She twists her neck, spitting in my face, fury in her eyes. I bare my teeth, then push her head down into the bowl.

The water splashes. Her arms flail. She's handcuffed, bucking against me, and I hold her down. The liquid sloshes over the sides, and I keep her there. Submerged. Proving it to her. Proving that her breath is mine. Her body, her mind, her fucking soul—*I'm* the one who gets to decide when she lives and dies.

She jerks around, desperate for air, and I thrust my hips, my dick like a second knife threatening to cut her from behind. And I hold her there.

She loosens, her body trying to calm itself, and I give her a second of slack, barely enough time to pull my dick out. She coughs, water dripping down, drenching us both, and I pull down her pants, thrusting my dick inside of her. It doesn't take much; she's wet, but her body doesn't react to me. Not like it normally does. She's limp, like I've killed everything inside of her, like she's transporting her mind to another place. As if I'm just like her grandmother and her shitty ex.

And it fucking kills me.

I need this. I need this as much as I need her.

No. *I need her.*

My dick softens. I growl.

This is mine.

Her body is mine.

She is mine.

And if I can't have all of her, then what the fuck am I doing, letting her live?

But I know I'll never kill her.

"You see that?" I snarl. I thrust my hips, my dick barely engorged enough to get inside. I slap her face from behind. Fist her hair. Wrench her hair until her neck is taut, like a noose carrying a body. Somehow, she's still *limp*. A wet noodle. And it pisses me off even more.

"You *want* to live," I growl. "You want to live, Ren. You're a psycho bitch with a damned submissive side wider than the gulf, but you *want* to live, Ren. I gave that to you. I showed *you* what it meant to truly fucking live. And I'm *not* going to take that back."

"Fuck you!" she screams.

I hold her in a death grip; she doesn't fight, showing me she's given up. And fuck, my head spins, not wanting to acknowledge what that means. Refusing to. I pull us both forward until I'm leaning on her head, keeping her eyes and nose in the water. She sputters, and I count down. Waiting for her to fight me.

She doesn't fight. My head aches.

I can't stop. I *won't*.

I own her death. I own her life.

But my little corpse stays still.

My heart sinks.

Fucking her like this isn't going to prove anything.

I pick her up, then swing her down the hallway. She coughs, lazy in my arms. I force her down to my bed. Even when I unlock her handcuffs and transfer her to a new set, each shackled wrist bound to the bedposts, Ren *lets* me. Resigned to her fate.

As I'm fumbling with the chain to get her ankles strapped to the bottom posts, she punches me in the nose, the chains clinking behind her.

Blood gushes from my nostrils, and I beam.

She's fighting. Still resisting. The fire still burns inside of her, even while it's slowly dying.

I killed that fire, didn't I?

No. She's still here. Still alive.

Sorrow and joy radiate inside of me. Pushing against my shell. Threatening to break me.

I keep it locked inside. I have to.

"You want to play that game?" I ask.

"Fuck yo—"

I punch her in the solar plexus. She coughs, the wind knocked out of her, and I use that time to finish chaining her to the bed. Her wet hair soaks the sheets, her mouth panting. Last time, I put her in a choke chain that she could take off at her own will. This time, she's wearing special cuffs that require a key. She'll stay on that bed until *I* let her go. She's not in a shipping container, but she's still trapped. She'll die like them. *My way.*

And yet, I know that's not what's going to happen.

"The fuck is wrong with you?" she hisses. "You think you can keep me here? Like a pet? I'm not one of your victims, Blaze. Fuck—"

The words drown out, her eyes red. Angry tears stream down her face with more force than a hurricane.

Everything inside of me breaks. Crushes me. I no longer have air to breathe.

Her mouth moves. I can't hear her words.

I hurt her.

I'm as bad as them.

For a second, I wonder if I should let her go. If what I'm doing is wrong.

Her eyes widen, focusing on something behind me. A shadow looms over my shoulder, a presence erasing those thoughts.

My hearing tunnels. My vision sharp. I grab the gun from the nightstand, dropping the keys to Ren's restraints in the process. My only focus is the intruder. Whoever it is that threatening our moment here.

I jerk forward, facing him.

My brother.

His mouth contorts, exploding with expletives. I shove him, his body smashing into the wall. Denting it.

He gasps, startled by my force. I open the nightstand. Find the bullets. Load them into the chamber.

Ren's voice sears into me, but I can't understand the words. I only know what I have to do next.

I won't let anyone fuck with Ren ever again. Even him.

Brody stumbles to his feet. Reaches the bedroom. Pulls my arm. Tries to grab the gun. I slice through the air with my fist, the full impact on his jaw. He trips. Falls to the floor. I stomp a boot on his chest, pinning him to the floor.

Brody looks up at me, his executioner. And fuck, if I don't feel *righteous* right now.

There's no art in a gunshot, but Ren is right. It's definite.

I shoot him in the forehead.

He collapses on the hardwood floor. Blood drips down the sides of his face, each stream slow, like the last drops of rain drying on a window.

I turn to Ren, and my chest heaves. Not because my last blood relative is gone. Not because I killed him.

Because of Ren.

Fear wavers in her pupils, threatening to boil over. Those vibrant brown eyes focus on me. Afraid of me. Emotion taking over her body, and not because I forced her to endure my cruelty. Not because I forced her to watch me kill my brother.

Because I forced her to live.

My shoulders drop, heaviness controlling every part of me.

I'm just like them, aren't I?

We're all the same.

"You," she stammers. Her voice stabs into me. I stare at the corpse on the floor, unable to face her. "You killed *him*, but you can't kill me?"

She's not shocked that I killed someone in front of her. She's jealous.

And that *hurts*.

I can't make her want to stay. That's her will. Her decision. No matter how much I do or force her to take, she'll always have control over that.

"I told you," I say as I grasp for those last bits of power that I have left. Clinging onto the denial that I've failed her. "I'll kill you—"

"When?" she cries. She gestures around us. "*When?* When you feel like it? When I'm not good enough for you anymore?" Her body shakes, the tears reaching the surface again. "You think it's funny to keep me in limbo, don't you? So that you can destroy me. So that you can play with me like—"

"You're nothing to me," I say, the words dry on my tongue. They're not real. Seeing her like this, I try to remember what we agreed on. The promise I refuse to follow through on now. Desperate to make her feel okay, like I'll give her the death she wants, even if it's just a lie. To comfort so that she trusts me again. At least until I can figure this shit out. Until I can convince her to stay. "You're a future corpse," I say. "You're nothing."

I'm nothing.

We're nothing.

There is no "we."

"You want to know why you're pissed off at me?" she snaps. "Because you can't kill me. Because you can't control your feelings for me. Because you damn well know that you don't *want* to kill me anymore. You caught feelings for your next victim, and it's fucking pathetic. You thought you could *save* me, like you're some kind of hero. Well, congratulations." She jerks her chest forward, the chains jingling beside her. "I still want to die. Are you happy now?"

A throbbing pain begins in the back of my neck, stretching up to my temples.

"This isn't about me," she snarls. "It's about you, and your weak—"

"Everything is about you, Ren," I say, raising my voice. "Don't you get it?"

We stare at each other. My body heats, and I realize I'm holding my breath. Afraid to let it out. To understand what this means to both of us.

The truth is out there now, and it's like I'm handing my life to her.

She's right. I *am* weak. Weak for her. Weak like a little boy. Weak like a fucking idiot who thinks a woman like her could see something in a piece of shit like me.

No matter what I do, I can't kill her.

Her fists ball at her sides, rage building in her chest like a bomb ready to explode. I blink at her, imagining a future where I keep her here. Chained to my bed. Brainwashing her into thinking that this is a life worth living.

Then she wouldn't be Ren anymore.

Strength empties my body. It takes everything I have to step around the corpse. To go to the other bedroom. I sit on the trunk full of my victim's hair, and I clutch the gun in my lap, refusing to let her have access to it, even now. The medications are gone now; Brody never gave her the final order of it. He might've been on his way to deliver it to her now. Maybe he thought she'd be here with me. He probably knew I was going to do something stupid.

I've fucked everything up.

I open the wooden trunk. The shades of blond hairs mix together like sun bleached shells in white sand. Her ex's short hair is mixed in there too, along with a few black strands from the random college girl I killed. Those shells are new, not yet damaged by the sun.

Ren's hair is still locked inside of the top compartment.

I take out her hair. Let it drop on the floor. The long strands spread across the hardwood, like the legs of a spider too proud to crawl to safety, even when it sees a human's crushing fist.

Ren pants in the other room. Scared.

I'm scared too.

Fuck.

The chain links clink together. The cuffs thud on the mattress. The bed springs creak.

Footsteps fill the hallway.

Even if I forced her to stay, locking her in this house with me, she's already gone.

The front door opens.

Stay, I think. *Please stay.*

The door slams behind her, her choice loud and clear.

It's her choice.

I don't stop her.

Chapter 34

Ren

Day after day, it's a slump, rolling over from one day to the next. The tears form; they don't fall. My mind is a groggy mess full of thoughts that never finish. It's like I'm looking over the edge, waiting for that moment when I know it's time to take that final step.

My stomach growls, and sometimes, I satiate its incessant cries with coffee, and sometimes, I ignore it. Sometimes, I don't even shower before I start my shift. All the energy I have goes into work.

Take the body from the refrigeration unit.
Turn on the machine.
Place the body on the conveyor belt.
Burn the body.

Every day, I stare. My eyes focus on everything above me, like I'm another corpse lying in the ground. Staring up at the sky. Sprawled on the conveyor belt, inching into the retort.

Everything bleeds into the next, and I can't keep anything straight.

"I understand that you're going through a tough time," Mrs. Richmond says, her voice muffled through the bedroom door. "Really, I do. But you need to get on with it. You have a job, Ren. You're lucky your boss and I are on good terms; otherwise, you'd be fired, and you already can't handle the late fees on your loan payments." She scoffs. "I can't keep doing this for you."

All of those promises that things would be different, now that I stood up to her, vanish.

Life goes on.

Every once in a while, my stare shifts in front of me. The empty doorway. The cemetery. As if I'm searching for someone. Waiting for Blaze.

Do I really care, though?

At the end of the eighth day, a new person—a small woman with a pixie cut—smiles at me as she heads to the back exit. I barely nod at her. A few minutes later, the excavator rumbles outside, like a beast emerging from a cave. My temperature elevates like I'm the one cooking inside the retort.

The loss settles inside of me. An empty husk.

Blaze has been replaced.

I watch my new coworker through the break room window, a coffee mug cold in my hands. The new hire works efficiently, and it's what I thought I wanted: another female coworker.

I swing open the cupboards until I find Blaze's artisan coffee beans, and I throw them in the trash. I don't *need* Blaze. He showed me that I have the power to make my own choice. I can throw away his coffee beans, just like I can end this stupid life if I want to. I don't need his help for anything.

I go through my shift.

After the last bones are granulated and stored, I clock out a few minutes early, mumbling an excuse about a headache. Then I sit at the kitchen table with an empty mug in front of me.

Mrs. Richmond opens the door, a flash of surprise brightening her features.

"You're home early," she says with suspicion in her eyes. She tilts her head. "Are you feeling alright?"

It's an afterthought. She doesn't care if I'm okay; I'm just throwing her off.

I shrug.

"Happy birthday," she says, then gives me an uncharacteristic squeeze on the shoulder. She slips an expensive greeting card into my lap. A jeweled cupcake decorates the front. I open it, and my eyes fixate on the only thing written besides her name: *I hope this year is better for you.*

My heart sinks like dead weight drifting to the bottom of the ocean. I keep my head down. It's not supposed to be like this. She's not supposed to notice that I'm off, or that I've been having a hard time. I'm already a big enough burden.

It's just a card. Logically, it's not a big deal. At the same time, it means something to me. She took the time to get the card for me. To write a note. She sees me, in a way, even when she despises me.

Why is she being kind to me?

"After what *happened*," she says as she eyes the front door, referencing the conversation between me, her, and Blaze. "I realized that you need more support right now. That's fine; I can help you. You can use your time off to get a better job. You can even go back to school. Become a lawyer, perhaps. Or finish your doctorate at another university. The funeral home is a reliable job, but it's not enough, Ren." She purses her lips. "It won't take you anywhere. This year, you can fix all of that."

Fix all of that.

I wait for those tears to boil over the edge, at the realization that my grandmother still doesn't see *me;* she sees that I'm not enough. And I know I will *never* be enough.

But those tears don't come.

Maybe I don't care anymore.

"Anyway, I ordered you a cake. Want to pick it up with me? It's over the bridge," she says.

She hasn't gotten me a cake since I was still in high school, and it's like she's infantilizing me all over again. I'm twenty-six years old today, and for the first time since my mother died, my grandmother actually wants to celebrate my birthday.

Still, I don't cry.

I'm alive.

I shake my head. "Thanks though," I mutter.

"I'll be back in a bit."

The front door closes, and I'm alone again. The same question lingers in my mind, each answer floating away from me like the cattail seeds in the wind, drifting off toward the sea.

I was supposed to die today. Blaze said that if he didn't kill me before I turned twenty-six, he'd give me those drugs on my birthday. We agreed on that.

And it still is *my* choice.

I'm still here.

After a half-eaten slice of cake, I go to bed. I stare at the ceiling, not really seeing it. It's the same every night.

Eventually, I find myself in the empty, dark hallways of Last Spring. I'm alone—there's no sign of anyone else in the building —but Blaze's ghost is everywhere. In the empty champagne bottle in the break room cupboard. The dirt clumps near the back exit. His icy white eyes reflected in the corpses.

I move the gurney to the crematory. I lie on the cold metal, imagining my own death. I go through each scenario: Blaze asphyxiating me while I drug myself. Blaze holding my hand as I shoot myself with a loaded gun. Blaze killing me while we're fucking, exactly like he had promised.

Would I have wanted any of it?

Those visions mix until all I see are Blaze's promising eyes.

You. Are. Mine, he had said. *My little corpse.*

The entrance door creaks like someone is about to enter. My heart pounds. I sit up, not bothering to hide my presence.

I just want to see him.

The wind whirrs against the windows, the closed doors sighing in protest.

It's a breeze. Not him.

I turn on my side, the gurney squeaking with my weight, and I let it go. Toes curling. Shivering with each breath. My corded neck straining as the tears rush down, pooling on the metal surface, shining with my dark reflection.

I don't know why I'm crying. I'm the one who walked out. I'm the one who pushed him away.

Why did I do this to myself?

Because you don't deserve him, my inner voice says. *You don't deserve anything.*

Blaze's voice interrupts: *You're such a wreck. A beautiful fucking mess. You hear that, Ren? Until the day you die. For the days after. Until both of us are worm food and the world doesn't remember us anymore. You. Are. Mine.*

Anger tears into my soul. I howl into the darkness, screaming into the solitude. Blaze *should've* killed me. It's torture that he didn't. At the same time, if he had killed me, I would've missed so much *more* of him.

Instead, Blaze exposed me to his fullness, taught me what it felt like to ache for someone. Where everything is nothing and nothing is everything. Where I'm worth it. A place where I might not be a high-achieving granddaughter or a respectable fiancé, but a place where I still *deserve* joy. Where he sees me, even when I fail. Even when I push him away. Even when I still want to die.

What am I supposed to do now?

No matter how loud I scream, the tears don't stop. I fall asleep in the mortuary, and when the morning comes, the crematory door is closed. As if Denise didn't want to acknowledge my presence. As if I'm just another body, waiting to be burned in the retort.

Chapter 35

Blaze

Every night, I wait outside of Ren's bedroom window while she sleeps. I don't enter. Once she's dreaming, I slip inside and gaze down at her body.

She made her choice. All I can do is watch over her.

On her birthday, she goes to the mortuary. Though I jiggle the handle, ready to interrupt her old ritual, I think better of it.

She doesn't need me.

I used to think she was my unlucky fourth victim. My fourth was her ex. That should've been my clue that I was losing control, but I ignored it. Then the fifth was some random girl. The sixth? My brother.

Ren won't be the seventh, eighth, ninth, or tenth.

Eventually, light starts to surface, and I enter the mortuary. Ren left it unlocked, like she was waiting for someone to find her.

That's stupid; she's not waiting for me. I scowl at myself, for the stupid wishful thinking I've wrapped myself into yet again.

I find her asleep on the conveyor belt. Too tired to care about the consequences.

I close the door. Return to the window facing the parking lot. I bang on the window once, loud enough to wake her. Then I wait across the street, to the side of the margarita shack, out of sight.

A few minutes later, she stumbles out of the building, her eyes groggy with sleep.

That day—the same day I help her escape possible termination from her job at the funeral home—is the day that I take out my frustrations on my house. I don't understand the anger, but my knuckles pound into the walls until they're caked with blood. My temples pound endlessly. I can't get rid of it.

That night, once Ren is asleep in her bed, I drive to Blountstown. I wait outside of the gas station, the one right next to the pizza shop. It used to make me sick being here, memories surfacing of my mother leaving me in the closet, forcing me to take whatever those men wanted. Now, I rub my dick through my pants, watching the store clerk clock out and walk to her car. Forcing *myself* to see the truth in this.

I need to get Ren out of my system. Once I do that, everything will fall into place. I'll move on.

After that, Ren won't mean shit to me.

The clerk jerks around, alarmed by my footsteps. I knock her in the head with a crowbar. Bind her in rope. Throw her in the trunk of my car. My mother's house comes into view, surrounded by towering trees, and I leave the bitch in the trunk for a minute, consumed by my own thoughts.

I stand over the open grave. While the random college girl is buried in the woods like my second and third, this grave—this hole I dug near my mother's grave, the cavern I built for *Ren*—is open, my brother decaying inside of it. Burying my brother so close to my mother is a bad idea, but it seemed right at the time. Like they belong together. A mass grave full of people who wronged me.

People who wronged *her* too.

I curse under my breath, infuriated with myself. I'm done with this shit. This pity. This self-indulgent guilt. Sulking won't bring Ren back, neither will stalking her. She *made* her choice, and no matter how tightly I bind Ren in my chains, I'll never be able to control her like I want. I don't have that kind of power, and even if I did, it wouldn't be *her*.

And maybe that's for the best.

The clerk's garbled screams rattle from inside of the trunk. Finally, I retrieve her. Drag her by the hair to the open grave. The foul stench of decay and turned earth permeates the air, and the clerk's sweat—ripe with the scent of fear—trickles over it, overpowering everything else. I toss her in the grave, and she screams as her eyes widen, taking in the dead body. I look at the clerk, but I see Ren. I see the fear in Ren's eyes when she saw me kill my brother. How she forced me to see myself. How I couldn't be what she wanted.

The stranger twists, her hair mixing with the dirt, and for the first time, I realize the clerk is blond. I didn't plan for that; I simply found myself outside of that pizza shop.

Life is life. Death is death. Killing a random blond woman won't make a difference.

Ren makes a difference, my mind argues. *She's changed you.*

I pull out my dick, ignoring those words, focusing on the primal display of survival in front of me. Even though the woman is bound in so much rope that she can barely move, she still inches across the dirt, trying to crawl out of the grave. As if she'll escape somehow. As if she'll actually live.

It *should* be intoxicating, this pitiful act of survival. But my dick stays soft.

I bite my tongue, tasting copper. Using my sadism on *myself.* Anything to stir that need inside of me. I squeeze my balls through my pants and urge myself to get hard, and though my body reacts, my dick doesn't get full enough. Not enough to fuck this stranger.

It should be the lack of blood, I tell myself. *Once I see her bleeding, I'll get hard. I always do. Even with Ren's ex.*

The stranger whimpers, gurgling into the rope. I open my switchblade, my mind wandering to the first time I saw Ren laid out on the conveyor belt. Spread out before me. How I held the knife inches from her neck.

The images consume me. Ren covered in dirt. A bag over her head. Lying still, pretending to be a corpse so that I didn't notice her. The scent of her fear.

Fear, because there was hope for once. Longing for something more.

Longing that I destroyed.

The clerk wails. Irritation and disgust floods me.

My brother was right. Ren *deserves* a choice. She's always had that inner-strength to choose her future, and now, she's finally embraced it. It's why I'm attracted to her. Why I envy her.

It's why I love her.

Fucking this woman isn't going to bring Ren back, neither will killing her. None of us are any better than insects in the ground, and one day, when we're worm food, at least we'll have a purpose.

I'd rather be worm food with Ren than pretend like she doesn't matter.

She matters to me.

I slit the woman's throat. The blood rushes over my fingers, the warmth soothing me. Not because of the violence, but because of the choice ahead of me.

I know what I need to do now.

I don't care what happens anymore. I don't care about anything. I don't care if I live or die. I *want* Ren, and I can't make her choose anything. I know that now.

But I can decide my own ending.

I wipe the knife on my shirt, then check my gun in the holster. It's loaded. I make a plan to find heroin in the parking lot behind Pier Park. There's always someone selling there. I'll use my brother's money and buy enough to kill an elephant.

Ren will have her choices. I can't change what she decides.

But I'm choosing her.

Chapter 36

Ren

I sit at the edge of the Last Spring, behind the newest row of gravestones. My phone is open to the block list. All it would take is one click, and Blaze would be able to call me again.

Has he thought of me at all since I left his house?

The fury builds inside of me, a heat that tightens my jaw, pain gathering in my shoulders. It's pathetic—being your own worst enemy, ruining every good thing that happens in your life. I told myself I'd go to the medical spa and end things for good this time. I haven't yet, and despite the rage building inside me, I know I won't.

I don't let myself admit why. I'm not ready to accept those beliefs with my entire being yet.

But they're there, and I can't ignore them anymore.

Denise opens the back exit and waves at me from the patio.

"You staying late?" she asks.

It takes me a second, but I nod. "Best view of the sunset," I explain, though it has little to do with the view and everything to do with the peace I get here. Being with decomposing corpses is a hell of a lot better than facing people you can disappoint. And there's a comfort in knowing that Blaze and I sat here together once. That I shared myself, and he listened. That he was mad *for* me. That even though I argued that life didn't mean anything, he showed me *why* he wanted to live every single time.

Maybe that's when I started to question my death too, if I really wanted to die.

"Trina and I are heading to Sharky's," Denise says. "You want to come? It's happy hour."

I pause on that name: Trina. Right. The new hire who took Blaze's place. Going to Sharky's would fill my time. It would be something other than sitting on the edge of the cemetery with the symphony of the crashing waves and honking tourists to keep me company. I'm sure Trina is normal.

Hanging out with normal people isn't what I want, though.

I shake my head. "I'm going to stay here for now. Thanks," I say.

Denise's eyes sparkle like she can read the deeper meaning behind my words. She winks. "Whatever floats your boat. Have a good night, Ren."

A few minutes later, their cars drive off, disappearing onto Front Beach Road with the endless stream of tourists. The sun sets, and as I stare at it, my stomach pangs. I don't have any coffee.

I pull a pack of cookies from my purse, the same small bag I took from Blaze's house. The plastic crinkles as I rip it apart. I lift a jagged half-circle into the air, the chocolate splotches dotting the crust. I raise it higher, cheersing the pink and orange sky.

"Thanks for looking out," I say, as if Blaze can hear me.

I chew methodically, tasting every crumb. Blaze is right; even though there's chocolate, these particular cookies are bland. I swallow it down though, savoring the memories of that night together. The rush of asking Blaze to dinner. The fact that he told me to stay.

A dark figure stretches across the grass. I clutch the bag in my hand, afraid to see an empty space.

Eventually, I look.

Blaze, dressed from head to toe in black, takes me in with his pale blue eyes.

"I brought you options," he says. Annoyance flares in his

movements, jagged like broken glass. He lifts his hands, exposing the dangling items: a small bag of white powder, a rope, a knife, and a gun. "You want to overdose again? Hang yourself? Stab yourself? No—you want a gun. You always preferred that option, right? It's the one with a guarantee."

I furrow my brows, my chest cramped with tension. "Excuse me?"

"You know what I'm talking about," he scoffs. "You're capable. But you need to decide if it's what you *really* want." I huddle my shoulders, caving into myself. His jaw clenches. "You need to decide if dying is what you want with all your fucking mind. Not this numb shit you've convinced yourself of. Not what society wants you to do. Not your grandmother. Not your ex. Not me. Just *you*, Ren." His nostrils flare, and he tilts his head to the side. "So, what do you want?"

I study him. His posture strained. His white knuckles wrapped around the weapons and drugs.

"You know what I wanted," I say, even though it hurts. "I wanted you to kill me while you fucked me. It didn't matter how it happened; I just wanted to feel *something* before I died."

"The deal is off," he growls. "I'll fuck you. But I'm not killing you."

My world slows, like water caught in a tide pool, seeping out through the cracks.

Blaze's eyes stay fixated on me.

"I don't give a fuck what we agreed on," he says. "The rules have changed. And I choose you, and if it's not the same for you, then you're going to have to—"

"Choose me for what?"

"I choose *you*, Ren. Your life," he growls under his breath. He steps closer and kneels down beside me, putting the weapons and drugs on the ground within my reach. He takes my hand and places it on his chest. Even through the shirt, his heart races, drumming against my fingers with panic. With fear. With promise too. "You feel that, Ren? Until that stops, you're not going anywhere." His eyes search mine. His voice softens. "I choose whatever fucked-up life we have left."

239

Our surroundings blur. My pulse matches his.

I take a breath, but it's hard.

"You don't mean that," I whisper. "You deserve better than me."

"I love you," he says, his voice full of anger and pain, everything inside of him melting. His eyes water. He presses my hand tighter to his chest. "So if you want to die, then you're going to have to kill me first. Because I'm not going to let you do this to yourself. Not while I'm alive."

Not while I'm alive.

"*I* get to kill you," he murmurs, his voice shaking. "No one else. And I refuse. I fucking refuse with everything in my life. None of it is worth killing you. So if you leave this world, you're going to have to kill me first."

My eyes burn, the overwhelming emotions swirling inside of me. The powerlessness that's always been there. The force that grew when my mother died. When my grandmother threw out my stuff, replacing it with hers. When I was forced to drop out of the doctorate program. The hopelessness. Like there was nothing I could do. Like I had no choice.

I take a deep breath, and Blaze clutches both of my hands, keeping them against his body. The ocean beats against the shoreline. A pack of tourists shout from a neighboring restaurant. The faint hum of a guitar drifts over to us.

Blaze's eyes focus on me. *Only me.*

He sees so much more in me than my mother did when I was little. Than my grandmother does now. More than I see in myself. And for once, the potential of it all—the possibilities—they don't seem so unnerving anymore. I'm not strong because Blaze gave me strength. I'm strong because that ability to choose has always been inside of me; I just didn't see it before.

I look at the weapons on the ground. The loose rope. The powder scattered in the bag like snow. The metal of the knife shining with dull glimmers of the fading sun. The gun digging into the dirt.

I meet Blaze's eyes, my spine tingling as his pupils wash over me. I've dreamed of dying with a killer's cock inside of me for as long as I can remember, and maybe I'll still meet that bittersweet end someday. Maybe each time Blaze and I have come together, he's killed the hopelessness inside of me a little more. Put something new in place of that emptiness.

Maybe I'm grateful for that.

"Ren," he begs. And it's like he can't say anything else or it'll break him apart. I know what he's truly asking.

What do I want?

My entire mind fills with the need to feel his arms around me. I do want to die in his arms. I want to feel his comfort as life leaves my body.

But I don't want to die. Not yet. Not right now. Not for a long time.

"I want to live," I say.

He cups my face in his hands, a tenderness in his touch that seems unreal, like he knows how fragile I am, that I still might break. And he kisses me. Kisses me like he doesn't want to crush the petals of my lips. Kisses me like we mean something. Like our lives mean more than life, death, and existence. Like *we* matter.

"I want to live," I say, through those murky tears. "I want to live."

"I want you to live," he says, gripping my face now like he's afraid I'll float away. Like he knows what might happen if I leave him now. "I want you to scream, Ren. I want you to cry for me. I want to make you scream and cry for the rest of our lives."

Our lives.

He wraps his arms around me, holding me close, his arms like bandages keeping me together, our hearts matching each other's beat. And I let it go. I cry. I don't hold back. And Blaze holds me, letting me release all of that tension, letting it wash into the dirt underneath us. He holds me, letting me know that he's still here. That he still sees me. And when the tears finally dissipate, I accept the fact that I don't know what's coming tomorrow.

It's not so bleak anymore.

I can't bring my mother back from the dead. I can't make my grandmother accept me for who I am. I can't make my ex want to marry me. I can't change how a client feels about the way his post-mortem wife looks. And I definitely can't control Blaze.

But I can embrace the ugliness inside of me and see every part of me for what it is. I can choose myself.

Just like Blaze chooses me.

The darkness devours the sea, the barest hint of stars skirting across the water. I rest my head against Blaze's chest as the night surrounds us too. He kisses the top of my head, sucking in a long breath, inhaling my scent. His pulse beats against my ear, each thump keeping time with the roll of the ocean waves.

And I let it be.

Epilogue

Ren

one year later

"He looks like a clown," she snaps.

I stare down at the body. There's a shine to the corpse, too perfect to be natural, and the rose-tint in his cheeks is a tad heavy; I can admit that. But there's only so much you can do to make a deceased seventy-year-old man look like a picture from his thirties. It's not perfect; nothing ever is. At least this time, I've had practice on a few more corpses. In fact, I'd say this corpse was my best embalming work yet.

The client probably won't appreciate a comment like that though.

"Well?" she asks, putting a hand on her hip. "Are you going to fix him?"

There are so many things I could do right then. Apologize. Beg for forgiveness. Ask Denise to give her a discount on her funeral package. The truth is that no matter what I do to "fix" her husband, his corpse won't look like he did when he was alive. Nothing I say or do can change that.

"I'll get the director," I say.

She swats my arm.

"No—" she shouts. Embarrassment flushes across her as she

realizes that she's accidentally hit me. She slumps into the folding chair next to the table. "You did great." Her head falls into her palms, her voice muffled now. "I miss him. The real him, you know? He'll never come back. I know that."

I stand there awkwardly, a pole without a sail. She whimpers, and uneasiness drips down my back. This mourning is private, something I'm sure this woman doesn't want to share with me, but I've been around death for so long that I know what to expect.

Some people are afraid of death. They're scared of the unknown, of that vast emptiness, when they don't even realize how numb they are to their everyday lives. Others are shocked by death. And still, others refuse to acknowledge mortality until it's too late.

And then there are those who seek it out, who think that death will give them relief.

I was like that once.

I put a hand on the client's shoulder. She squeezes my hand, a sob leaking out of her chest. Snot trickles between our fingers, and even though it's gross, I stand there with her. It's the only thing I can do right now.

Eventually, Denise finds us, and I head back to the crematory and finish up my orders for the day. After that, I drive to Blountstown. It's a commute to get to Last Spring now, but I'm more at peace there, in Blaze's childhood home. It took us a while, but eventually, we dug up his mother, brother, and the others buried in his backyard, and we took them to the funeral home after hours to dispose of them properly.

We're making the house our own now. A true home.

One day, we're going to dig up my mother and bury her here instead. I can't change the way she died, but I can move her body, putting it in a place where I can honor the life she had, and that seems better than pretending she never existed, like Mrs. Richmond wanted. It's a memorial I can look forward to.

Blaze's car pulls into the dirt driveway shortly after mine. His job working security at the university in Tallahassee is a commute too, and it comes with benefits for both of us. Marriage is that way, after all. We're tied together, even if we don't wear rings to symbolize our love.

Blaze pulls me into his arms, his teeth cutting into my shoulder. I yelp with laughter, and he growls into me, his jaw growing tighter. His teeth break the skin slightly, and he sucks at the wound, my head swirling in the clouds.

No, we don't need rings. We wear our love in different ways.

He breaks the kiss, then smacks my ass, heading to the backyard to check the shipping containers, bringing a thermos of water—just enough for his victim to survive. He returns, meeting me in the kitchen. He laughs with a sigh.

"You ought to choose someone with more vigor next time," he teases.

He doesn't mention Mrs. Richmond in the other shipping container; we don't talk about her anymore. There's nothing to say. She has enough food and water to live, and she stopped trying to talk me out of her captivity after the sixth month. Blaze says I should just kill her, that it would be more satisfying than what I'm doing to her now. But to me, her death would be too easy on her. I don't want to kill her. I want her to live a life where she's alone. Dismissed. Not good enough. Like she made me feel.

How my mother probably felt too.

"I figured I'd give you a break after the last one," I say with a smirk. He laughs.

These days, I help find people who remind Blaze of his mother. Men. Women. It doesn't matter, as long as they embody the neglect of others. When I can't give him that high through sexual sadomasochism, killing those victims satisfies his need. He doesn't fuck them though; he kills them, *then* fucks me. Sometimes at the same time.

I like to choose people from the funerals. The death of a loved one tends to bring out the best and worst in us, and though I don't judge, I know what Blaze is looking for.

Blaze will never change. Being a killer is who he *chooses* to be, and though I used to think that I would choose to leave this world, like my mother, I choose the other option now.

After all, death is just like life. In death, you give up control to the natural world, letting the earth rot your corpse. You can't control which kind of bugs decide to decompose your remains, nor can you decide whether or not your loved ones—or a serial killer—cremates your body or gives you a natural burial. We're all bags of rotting meat, and in the end, not even a final will and testament can change that.

But in life, we have the power to surrender to the chaos of the world, to the imperfections, to the ugliness, to the loss of power. We can accept that there is beauty in what we cannot contain.

Blaze grabs my hair, twisting his fist until I whimper in pain, his tongue searching my mouth, making me promise that this is enough for me. And it *is*. Blaze is enough. And I am enough. Together, whether it's good or bad or straight up fucking miserable, in our little screwed up piece of paradise, this *life* is enough.

Blaze carries me to our bed, biting into my fresh wound again. He fucks me relentlessly until the bleeding stops. Then he takes a wet washcloth and wipes it across my skin with tenderness, stroking my hair with his free hand. A slow heat builds in my stomach. I'm cherished. Loved. And he's helped me love myself too.

Right before we fall asleep, he puts the choke chain around my neck and attaches it to the leash. I lock the other end of the leash around his choke chain too.

It's funny; both of us could take the choke chains off any time we want, and to be honest, wearing chains like that while we sleep —it's not safe; we could accidentally choke each other to death in our sleep. But when one of us pulls, the other wakes up, and we crawl back into each other's arms, finding safety in that proximity.

It's not safe. It's not sane.

But we aren't either.

The chain clinks around us, and Blaze kisses my forehead. I smile up at him, then glance at the nightstand. On top, there are two mugs of cold coffee and a gun full of blanks. Sometimes, we use it for the thrill; I still like knowing that death is around the corner any time I come. And these days, Blaze trusts me to handle the bullets—to put in blanks, leave it empty, or even actually load the gun—and he always tests the first bullet on himself.

I don't need the gun, or the rope, or the knife, or even pills like that anymore. Sometimes, life isn't what you expect, and it's shitty waking up. Day after day, you feel like no matter what you do, you're a burden to the world and everyone in it. That your breath isn't worth the wasted air. That you have no power, no control. That your life is meaningless.

And maybe life *is* meaningless. Maybe there's no concrete, meaningful reason for Blaze to love me, or for me to love Blaze. But I do. I love him, I love us, I love myself, and I love our life together. And he showed me how everything is possible.

Killing Blaze, just so that I can end my own life, won't happen.

I snuggle into his neck, grazing the scar on his side with my fingertips. We'll probably die in some boring way, like old age, or perhaps a disease associated with it. And I know us; when that time comes, we'll laugh at the pointlessness of it all.

And I'm okay with that.

THE END

Also By Audrey Rush

Dark Romance

Stalker

Standalone
Crawl
Dead Love
Hitch

Assassin

The Feldman Brothers Duet
His Brutal Game
His Twisted Game

Mafia

The Adler Brothers Series
Dangerous Deviance
Dangerous Silence
Dangerous Command

Secret Society

The Marked Blooms Syndicate Series
Broken Surrender
Broken Discipline
Broken Queen

Secret Club

The Dahlia District Series
Ruined
Shattered
Crushed
Ravaged
Devoured

The Afterglow Series
His Toy
His Pet
His Pain

Billionaire

Standalone
Dreams of Glass

———

EROTIC HORROR

Body Horror

Standalone
Skin

Acknowledgments

A special thanks to my author friend, Ashley Michele. You probably have no idea how much you helped me get through my writer's block, but seriously, you did! And on top of that, you helped me figure out Blaze and Ren's story. Your brain constantly inspires me. Thank you so much for your friendship.

Thank you to my editor, Jackie Moore Kranz at PR Publishing Group, for beta reading and copy editing this book baby! It was my first time working with an editor, and you made the process so easy. I can tell the final story is the best version it can be! I will be recommending your skills to all of my author friends, and I can't wait to work with you in the future.

Thank you to my husband, Kai, for making the most brilliant covers, going over all of the ideas with me, and putting up with my social media shenanigans. Your love means the world to me.

Thank you to my amazing beta readers: Andrea, Becky, Brandy, Jenni, Johanna, and Lesli. You are all so freaking brilliant, and I honestly don't know where this story would be without you.

Thank you to my ARC readers for your honest reviews; you have no idea how much you help a book launch. (And a special thanks to Abby Adams, Aulia, Breeann Waller, Kelani, Kristal, Lauren, Meagan, Randi, Reunna Wolff, Sara Flavo, Tammy, Teresa Eads, and Tiffanie Emans for catching typos!)

And thank you to my daughter, Emma, for being such a good kid at preschool.

But most of all, thank you to my readers. You are the reason I love to turn my daydreams and nightmares into books. I'm endlessly grateful for your support.

About the Author

Audrey Rush writes kinky dark romance and erotic horror. She currently lives in Florida with her husband and daughter. She writes during school.
TikTok: @audreyrushbooks
Instagram: audreyrushbooks
Reader Group: bit.ly/rushreaders
Threads: @audreyrushbooks
Reader Newsletter: bit.ly/audreysletters
Amazon: amazon.com/author/audreyrush
Website: audreyrush.com
Facebook: fb.me/audreyrushbooks
Goodreads: author/show/AudreyRush
Email: audreyrushbooks@gmail.com